MOONLIGHT AND PROMISES

MICHELE BROUDER

This is a work of fiction. Names, characters, places and incidents are either a product of the author's imagination or are used fictitiously, and any resemblance to actual persons, living or dead, events, or locales is entirely coincidental.

Editing by Jessica Peirce

Book Cover Design by Rebecca Ruger

Moonlight and Promises

Copyright © 2022 Michele Brouder

All Rights Reserved. No part of this book may be reproduced or transmitted in any form or by any means, electronic or mechanical, including photocopying, recording, or by any information storage and retrieval system, without permission in writing from the author.

All rights reserved.

No portion of this book may be reproduced in any form without written permission from the publisher or author, except as permitted by U.S. copyright law.

Chapter One

Isabelle

The heat was relentless in New Smyrna, a small town on the Atlantic coast of Florida, north of Canaveral National Seashore. Isabelle Monroe had been drawn to the city by the fact that New Smyrna Beach was known as the shark-attack capital of the world. She'd made it the focus of her next writing assignment, in fact, and was happy to spend a few weeks in the sun, investigating the veracity of the claim.

She'd arrived via Gainesville, where she spent an interesting morning with an effusive and knowledgeable research associate at the Florida Museum of Natural History, where the International Shark Attack File was housed. From there, she headed southeast on the I-75 and crossed through Ocala National Forest, unable to resist the urge to check out Juniper Springs, where she rented a canoe and took notes and photos of the clear turquoise water and the grand trees heavy with Spanish moss as she paddled her way across the calm surface.

Swirling in the back of her mind was a potential article about the state's natural springs, Florida's best-kept secret. Like any good travel writer, Isabelle stopped and investigated anything that roused her curiosity, wanting to see things for herself and experience them in person so she could write about them effectively. She might never use the information, but it was always good to have.

So it wasn't until late afternoon that she finally set foot on the long, narrow beach at New Smyrna, so different from the shores of Lake Erie in Hideaway Bay, New York, where she'd grown up and where she'd developed her lifelong love of the beach and the water. But she'd no sooner dipped her toes in the white sand than she was hit with debilitating pain encircling her chest.

She took in a deep breath and tried to calm herself, concentrating on the view in front of her—the navy ocean and the endless hazy blue horizon—rather than the vice-like pain running along the band of her bra. Counting to ten, she drew in a long breath and held it, watching her abdomen expand before exhaling slowly. This was the second time she'd had an acute attack of pain since she'd arrived in Florida the previous week. The first had lasted less than fifteen minutes. A fine sheen of perspiration broke out on her forehead that had nothing to do with the heat and humidity. Her mouth was parched, and her stomach roiled.

Soldiering through it, she sat on the beach and took some notes on her surroundings, trying to distract herself from her discomfort. She checked her watch; this episode had been going on now for twenty minutes. Briefly, she contemplated going for a soothing swim but when there was no letup, she decided it was best to seek medical attention. Sighing, she stood up after another few minutes. She held her breath and clutched her side, unable to discount the fear that she might be having a heart attack. She was on the cusp of forty and, aside from her love of wine, took pretty good care of herself. She didn't smoke, and she swam regularly and did yoga. But Gram had died of a heart attack almost a year ago, and that event was now part of her family medical history.

Slowly, she made her way back to her rental car, the sun beating down on her back. When she unlocked the vehicle, she didn't sit down in the driver's seat right away as she knew it would be almost a hundred degrees inside. She started the car and waited a few minutes, standing outside the open driver's-side door, leaning forward with her hands on her knees to see if another position would bring relief. But it did not.

When she was assured the car was cooled down, she sat inside and closed the door. Using her phone, she looked up the nearest urgent care center and discovered there was one on the other side of the Indian River. As she made her way there, driving carefully, mindful of the unrelenting pain, she prayed it wasn't anything serious.

Later, when Isabelle emerged from the medical center, the sky was a cerulean blue with a thin white glow where the sun had just dipped below the horizon. It was a beautiful evening.

The long and short of it was that after multiple tests to rule out a myocardial infarction, or in layman's terms, a heart attack, they'd sent her over to the hospital emergency room, where an ultrasound was performed and it was determined her issue was gallstones. She was advised to contact her primary doctor. When she informed them that she didn't have one—she'd almost never been sick, and she traveled too often to put down roots—they gave her the name of someone local and advised she might have to have her gallbladder removed. By the time she made it to her car in the hospital parking lot, the pain had subsided considerably. On one hand, she was relieved it hadn't been a cardiac event and on the other, she was annoyed that she'd have to pursue this: deal with it and possibly have surgery.

It meant that she might have to stay longer in one place than was normal. Although she had a career she loved, she had no permanent address. She had a PO box she used in Hideaway Bay and had her mail forwarded to her. She did have health insurance from a company near her hometown, but until now she'd never needed to be under the care of a doctor.

Even though it was late, she headed back to the beach. She stared out at the ever-darkening night sky, the ocean long since disappeared, only a vague, murky, indistinct dark shape in front of her. But the sound of the surf rolling in, that constant rhythmic crash and receding and then building up again, began to lull her. She leaned against the hood of her car, head lowered, worrying the space between her eyebrows with her thumb and index finger. She took in some deep breaths and explored her options.

There weren't many. Actually, only two. She could take the card for the primary care center and make an appointment to have the surgery done right here in Florida. Or she could go home to Hideaway Bay, back to the place she still thought of as Gram's house, where both her younger sisters, Lily and Alice, had returned after Gram's death almost a year ago.

For most of her adult life, Isabelle had had little to no contact with her younger sisters. They'd all grown up and left the beach town of Hideaway Bay. Lily had gone to California, and Alice had settled in Chicago. They'd rarely kept in touch over the years, only recently coming together for the funerals of Lily's husband, Jamie, and then Gram a few months later. The reunion, despite some tense moments, had not been unpleasant and had gone better than Isabelle had anticipated.

When she left Hideaway Bay all those years ago, she thought she'd never return. But now she might have no choice.

Chapter Two

1956

Barb

Barb Walsh was on her stomach on the pink needlepoint rug in her room with her legs bent at the knee and her feet up in the air. Her chin rested on her cupped hand as she finished her homework. Her record player spun in the corner, playing the newest hit single from Elvis Presley, "Heartbreak Hotel." The volume was turned down because it would annoy her mother if she heard it downstairs while she was trying to listen to her own albums. The music was loud enough for Barb to hear it but not so loud that it would interfere with her completing her homework.

In her other hand, she twirled her pencil, contemplating the essay before her.

There was a soft knock at her door and quickly, she leaned forward, lifting the arm off the record.

"Come in," she called over her shoulder, knowing it was her mother.

Mrs. Walsh appeared in the doorway. She was the mature version of Barb, and had been considered a great beauty in her youth. Barb's father had pointed out on more than one occasion that all Barb had to do was look at her mother and she'd know what she'd look like when she was in her forties. But Barb didn't think she'd wear pearls or twist her blond hair up in a tight chignon at any age. And forget about peach-colored lipstick, though she'd love to try pink. But her mother had said no lipstick until she was fifteen.

"Are you still doing homework?" Mrs. Walsh asked. She stood in the doorway, her back ramrod straight, her arms folded demurely beneath her small bosom.

"I'm almost finished." That was a small lie. Barb was nowhere near being finished, but she didn't want her mother to know she'd wasted time after school reading her newest library book.

"Do you want to go the show?"

"Now? On a school night?" Barb asked, her eyebrows furrowing.

"Sure, why not? Tomorrow's Friday, and we won't be out late. You'll be in bed in good time."

"What do you want to see?"

"*Carousel*?"

Barb didn't say anything.

"I know we've already seen it, but I'd love to see that again," her mother gushed. "And next month we'll have to go out to Hideaway Bay to get the cottage ready for the summer, and we won't have a lot of time to go to the show."

"Where's Father?"

"He was called in to the hospital." There was a hint of exasperation in Mrs. Walsh's voice. She liked the fact that her husband was a doctor; she didn't like the fact that sometimes he had to practice after hours.

"Okay, I'll be down in ten minutes," Barb said, dropping the pencil and closing her English book. She jumped up from the floor and set her book and pencil down on the French provincial desk in the corner.

"All right, see you downstairs," her mother said, closing the door softly behind her.

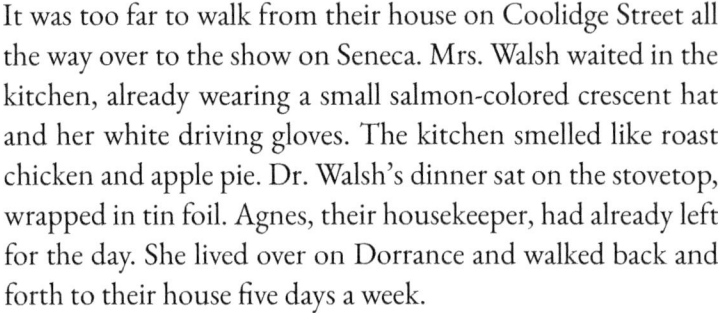

It was too far to walk from their house on Coolidge Street all the way over to the show on Seneca. Mrs. Walsh waited in the kitchen, already wearing a small salmon-colored crescent hat and her white driving gloves. The kitchen smelled like roast chicken and apple pie. Dr. Walsh's dinner sat on the stovetop, wrapped in tin foil. Agnes, their housekeeper, had already left for the day. She lived over on Dorrance and walked back and forth to their house five days a week.

Mrs. Walsh frowned at Barb. "Is that what you're wearing? Why don't you put on that blue skirt with the blouse we bought on Saturday?"

"Mother, it's a school night. Does it matter?" Barb did not treasure the thought of having to put on a skirt. She'd pulled on a pair of denim pants, thinking it was easier. Usually at this time, she'd be getting into her pyjamas.

Her mother scrunched up her nose and said tightly, "You know how I feel about dungarees. If you were a farmhand or worked at the steel plant, Barbara, I could understand it, but you are the daughter of a doctor and should dress accordingly."

She paused, pressing her lips together before rolling them inward. "I think hanging around Thelma Kempf might not be in your best interest."

She's not going to start this, now, is she? Barb's shoulders sagged. She glanced at the clock and wondered if they had enough time to argue. Finally, deciding it wasn't worth it, she huffed, "All right, Mother!" and dashed up the stairs and hurriedly discarded her dungarees and shirt, replacing them with the skirt and blouse her mother had suggested—which Agnes had laundered and ironed at some point—all the time muttering to herself.

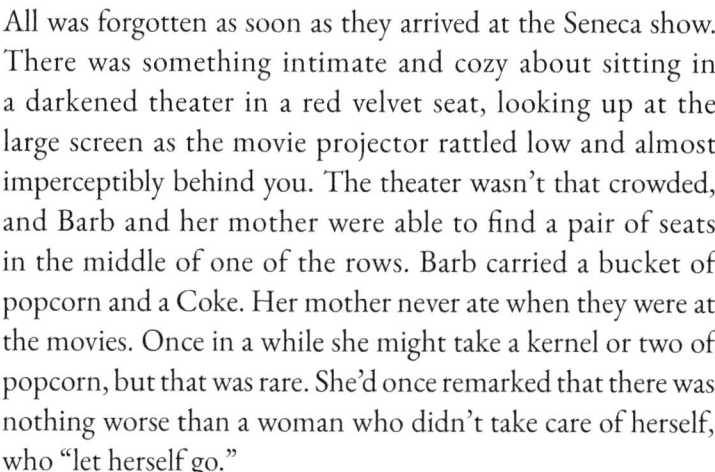

All was forgotten as soon as they arrived at the Seneca show. There was something intimate and cozy about sitting in a darkened theater in a red velvet seat, looking up at the large screen as the movie projector rattled low and almost imperceptibly behind you. The theater wasn't that crowded, and Barb and her mother were able to find a pair of seats in the middle of one of the rows. Barb carried a bucket of popcorn and a Coke. Her mother never ate when they were at the movies. Once in a while she might take a kernel or two of popcorn, but that was rare. She'd once remarked that there was nothing worse than a woman who didn't take care of herself, who "let herself go."

Even though Barb had seen *Carousel* before, she loved the experience of the cinema and although she would never admit it, like her mother, she loved musicals. All that singing and dancing. After they'd seen *Carousel* the first time, her mother had purchased the album, and it played a lot in the Walsh household. Barb knew the songs by heart.

It was a thrilling two hours, and Barb thought she much preferred going to the movies over doing homework. At the end of the film, a tear formed in her eye, and she sighed audibly. In the darkened theater, her face illuminated by the movie on the screen in front of them, Mrs. Walsh turned to her daughter and smiled.

"That was better the second time," Mrs. Walsh said as they drove home.

"It was."

"There's a movie coming out at the end of June called *The King and I*. Maybe it will be showing at the cinema down in Hideaway Bay."

Barb made a face of disgust. "I hate that place. It's so small, the chairs are uncomfortable, and it stinks."

"Barbara, please don't use the word 'hate.' Or 'stink.' It's unbecoming," her mother said, her gloved hands at the ten-and-two position on the big steering wheel.

Barb slouched in her seat. She loved their cottage at Hideaway Bay, but she didn't want to spend the whole summer down there. She'd miss her friend Junie and even to some degree, Thelma.

"Are we staying all summer in Hideaway?" Barb asked, even though she already knew the answer.

Her mother looked over at her. "Don't we always? We'll leave right before the Fourth of July and be back after Labor Day, in time for you to get ready for school."

"I don't know if I want to spend the whole summer down there."

"What do you mean? You love Hideaway Bay."

"I know I do, but I'd like to stay in the city for a bit too," Barb pushed.

"Why? The city's unbearable in the summer. At least down in Hideaway Bay, the lake cools everything down."

"I know, but I'll miss my friends too much," Barb whined.

"Junie and Thelma?" Mrs. Walsh asked, pursing her lips. Her hands tightened on the steering wheel.

"Who else, Mother?"

"When you get older and go away to college, you'll make proper friends."

"But Junie and Thelma *are* proper friends, Mother." Barb wasn't so ignorant that she was unaware of the differences in their upbringing and the homes they lived in, but she'd been friends with them since they all started first grade together.

"I know you think so, but people grow up and tend to stray away from each other," her mother said simply. "Look at my friends."

"Helen and Eleanor?" Barb quizzed. They were her mother's sorority sisters from college with whom she remained in regular contact. Barb had met them and thought they were clones of her mother: women with nice clothes and hair, who didn't work, had help, and liked cocktails at six in the evening. Thinking about it, she realized her mother had never mentioned friends from her childhood. Not once.

"Helen and Eleanor and I formed strong bonds," her mother explained. "You'll see for yourself when you go off to college. You'll have the time of your life and make some nice friends."

Mrs. Walsh pulled the car into the driveway of their house on Coolidge Street. She pulled it around back and parked it next to Dr. Walsh's car.

"Oh good, your father's home," she said with a smile.

As they got out of the car, Barb asked, "Can Junie and Thelma come out to Hideaway Bay for a bit this summer?"

"We'll see," Mrs. Walsh said.

Barb huffed, slamming her door. That was code for "no."

The following afternoon as the record player in the living room cranked out the sounds of "You'll Never Walk Alone" from the *Carousel* soundtrack, Mrs. Walsh was curled up on the sofa with her book, and Barb had her homework spread out on the coffee table when Agnes stuck her head in the doorway.

"Everything's all set, Mrs. Walsh," she said. Agnes was about five foot one and had iron-gray hair that she wore in short curls. She wore the same fitted navy housedress all the time, but it didn't seem to bother her. "The dinner's all wrapped on the stove and ready to eat."

"Thank you, Agnes. As soon as Dr. Walsh comes home, we'll sit down to eat it," Mrs. Walsh said.

"The meat will have gone dry by then."

Mrs. Walsh eyed the housekeeper over the top of her book. "Thank you, Agnes, but we'll wait for Dr. Walsh. We'll see you tomorrow."

Agnes nodded toward the record player and said, "What's he squawking about? I walk home alone every evening." And before Mrs. Walsh could parry a reply, Agnes ducked out and disappeared.

Barb suppressed a grin and chewed on the end of her pencil.

Chapter Three

Isabelle

As Isabelle neared Hideaway Bay, she noticed the sky had darkened, and the lake appeared murky with choppy waves. Out to the east, a low-hanging shelf cloud stretched as far as the eye could see. It was ominous for its size alone. She'd no sooner spotted it than there was a boom of thunder followed by a crack of lightning. Within minutes, the rain came down, heavy and insistent.

She slowed, not wanting to get into an accident on the rain-soaked highway. The rain, thunder, and lightning continued all the way into Hideaway Bay and although she kept her windshield wipers on high speed, they couldn't seem to keep up with the deluge and she was unable to see anything of her old hometown. The only sounds were the insistent drumbeat of rain against the windshield and the constant, rhythmic squeak of the wipers.

When she pulled up in front of Gram's house on Star Shine Drive, she was surprised to see her two sisters sitting out on the covered porch. Granddad used to say *you don't know enough to get out of the rain.* They appeared to be watching the springtime storm. She hesitated for a minute, looking around. The house looked the same: an imposing three-story structure with faded green shutters. Wicker furniture and potted plants on the large front porch. The front lawn and flower beds needed some work, but they were as she remembered them. She hadn't been home since Gram's funeral almost a year ago. How would her reception be? Her younger sisters, Lily and Alice, had been living together for months, had forged bonds she didn't have with them. When she spoke to them on the phone from time to time, it appeared they were getting along fine. Would she, Isabelle, be an unwelcome interloper? Would she upset their newly formed but tenuous connection?

As her sisters stared at the car, probably wondering who had just parked in the short driveway, Isabelle opened the door, deciding she couldn't wait for the rain to stop; she'd have to make a run for it. As soon as she stepped out of the car, she heard one of them squeal excitedly, "It's Isabelle!"

Despite the rain, her sisters rushed off the porch with tentative smiles. They met her in the driveway, Alice stepping forward first to wrap her in a hug. When she stepped back, Lily pulled Isabelle into her embrace. The rain fell around them, and Lily and Alice spoke all at once.

"What are you doing here?"

"We didn't know you were coming. Why didn't you call us?"

Isabelle laughed. "I wanted to surprise you. Come on, let's get out of the rain."

She followed them up the porch steps, shaking the rain off her light jacket. One of the steps creaked suspiciously beneath her.

Over her shoulder, Alice asked, "Do you have a suitcase?"

"I do, but I can get it later when the rain stops."

The three of them stood in a semicircle on the porch. Lily and Alice wore expectant expressions on their faces, probably looking for an explanation as to Isabelle's unannounced arrival.

"What brings you to Hideaway Bay?" Lily asked as if Isabelle were a casual acquaintance.

"It's a long story, but I was hoping to stay a bit, if that's all right," Isabelle said.

Her sisters exchanged a glance and looked back at her. Alice shrugged, her red curls falling over her shoulders. "Don't be silly, of course you can stay. It's your house too. It'll be nice to spend some time together."

Lily headed to the wicker chair she'd been occupying when Isabelle pulled up. With a wave of her hand, she said, "Come on, sit down and tell us what's new."

So far, so good.

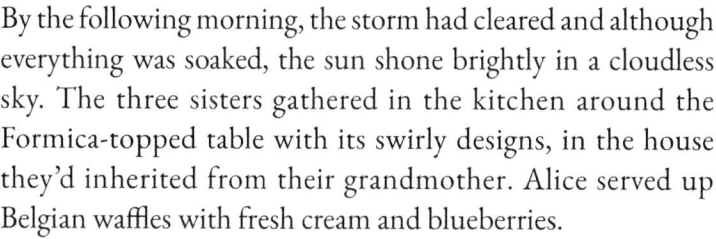

By the following morning, the storm had cleared and although everything was soaked, the sun shone brightly in a cloudless sky. The three sisters gathered in the kitchen around the Formica-topped table with its swirly designs, in the house they'd inherited from their grandmother. Alice served up Belgian waffles with fresh cream and blueberries.

Isabelle refrained from a second serving. She probably shouldn't have had the first, in deference to her twitchy gallbladder. It had settled down from that day in New Smyrna Beach, allowing her to spend another week in Florida to research her article and write some short posts for her travel blog. Only her anxiety over getting her medical issue sorted had made her leave the Sunshine State. She held a mug of coffee—no cream, no sugar—between her two hands and sipped at it.

Her sisters looked better than when she'd last seen them. Lily appeared to be recovering from the loss of her husband and their grandmother in a short space of time. She no longer looked so pale and had put on a bit of weight, which suited her, filling her out and making her appear curvier. Her blond hair had been recently highlighted, bringing out the blue in her eyes. She'd made a nice life for herself here in Hideaway Bay, working for the writer Simon Bishop and starting up her little cottage industry of beach-glass crafts, which were sold in the shops and boutiques in town.

Alice seemed happier too. She'd left her corporate job in Chicago, moved back home, and was currently working as an attorney at a small firm off the main highway outside Hideaway Bay. Her mane of curls, similar to Isabelle's dark hair but red in color, was as wild as ever.

As Isabelle sipped her coffee, she looked around the kitchen. So many memories. The ghosts of Gram, Granddad, and even their late mother lingered.

The kitchen had a sunny feel with its yellow cabinets, white Formica countertops, and white eyelet curtains at the windows. A pink, lavender, and blue wallpaper border depicting various herbs like basil, oregano, and mint ran along the top of the walls near the ceiling. A whimsical old tea set that had once belonged to their great-grandmother sat in one corner of the counter. Isabelle had always been intrigued by the set as a child: the faces on the front of the coffeepot and the creamer and sugar bowl with white hair, big eyes and on the top, kernels of corn. It was heartwarming to see it still there.

The breakfast was leisurely with no one seeming to be in a rush. Lily and Alice didn't have to leave for work for another hour.

"Is Clumsy going to work with you today?" Isabelle asked, referring to Lily's merle Great Dane, Charlie. She leaned forward, elbows on the table. Beneath the table, she crossed one leg over the other and swung her foot.

Lily nodded, finishing her second helping. "He goes to work with me every day." She looked fondly at the dog, who was on the floor, leaning against the wall, trying to get at the peanut butter inside his Kong. "He's a great work partner."

"If you want, you can leave him with me," Isabelle offered. She liked dogs, especially this one, despite his complete lack of grace and his penchant for knocking people off their feet and breaking things with his wagging tail.

Lily hesitated and Isabelle said quickly, "I mean, if you ever want to leave him with me, feel free."

Lily nodded. "Maybe tomorrow? I thought you might want to relax and get settled in today."

"Good. If it's nice tomorrow" —she glanced out the window at the vast blue sky— "I can take him for a walk on the beach." She didn't think it would be wise to walk him along Main Street, as he was too big and as mentioned, clumsy. And despite his gentle nature, his size could be intimidating. No, they'd stick close to the beach; it wouldn't be too crowded as kids were still in school for a few more weeks.

"More coffee, Isabelle?" Alice asked, standing near the counter and holding up the pot.

Isabelle looked at it longingly. There was nothing she wanted more than another cup. Her sisters were tea drinkers but to her, coffee was one of life's best pleasures. She shook her head.

Lily arched an eyebrow. "'No' to coffee? Are you ill or something?"

Isabelle folded her arms on the table. "I don't know. My gallbladder has been acting up."

Alice set the coffeepot down and returned to the table.

Lily made a wince of sympathy. "Ouch."

"Yeah, ouch is right," Isabelle said. "It's a pain that resembles having a heart attack." Or at least, she imagined it did.

"What do you do for that?" Alice asked.

"The pamphlet said to avoid fried and fatty foods," Isabelle explained. "But I'm afraid to eat anything. I've been limiting my coffee and I love your Belgian waffles, Alice, but one serving will have to be enough."

She explained what had happened in Florida and how, if she had to have her gallbladder removed, she'd prefer to have it done in Hideaway Bay.

"You can stay here while you recuperate," Alice said enthusiastically.

Isabelle gave her a grateful smile. It was so like Alice to always want them to be together. Although she had no idea how long she'd stay after the surgery if she had to have it.

"Do you have health insurance?" Lily asked.

Isabelle pressed her lips together and regarded her sister. Why did people automatically assume that because she didn't have a traditional job or own a home or a car, she wasn't responsible? She reminded herself to relax. How would her sister know about her life when they'd barely kept in touch over the last decade or so. "Of course I have health insurance. I even have a bank account and a couple of credit cards." She raised her eyebrows and smiled at Lily.

Lily put her hands up. "Sorry."

Isabelle crossed her arms over her chest. "Anyway, is there a doctor in town I can make an appointment with? I'd like to get this over with right away."

"There's that new doctor, Sam Morrison. He took over after Dr. Tylock retired. He's running the practice now," Lily informed her. "He's nice."

"So you've met him?" Isabelle asked.

"Sure. Once I decided to stay, I established myself as a patient," Lily replied.

"Who's your primary doctor?" Alice asked.

"I don't have one," Isabelle said.

Her sisters exchanged a glance and then turned their attention back to Isabelle.

"How can you not have a doctor?"

"I don't know, I've never been sick. I've never needed to go to the doctor before now," she said.

Alice sat up straight and blinked. "But what about female stuff?"

Isabelle waved her hand away. "Of course I've kept up with that. There's clinics all over the place for that."

"I have Dr. Morrison's number. I'll text it to you," Lily said, lifting her phone off the table.

"Thanks, I appreciate it," Isabelle said.

"While we're at work, you call the doctor and make an appointment," Alice said.

Isabelle laughed. "Okay, boss."

Chapter Four

1958

Barb

Thelma prattled on about something that happened over at the baseball diamond in the park. She let out a bark of laughter and shook her head. Barb smiled politely as she was only half paying attention. The night air was chilly for late April. The buds on the trees were a mossy green, and the air was redolent with the scent of damp earth. It looked as if finally, winter was behind them.

Barb was preoccupied, thinking about the movie *South Pacific*. Of all the musicals, this one was by far her favorite, even more than *The King and I*. She'd seen it five times since March and knew the soundtrack by heart. Last night, she'd lied to her mother and father and told them she was going over to Junie's, and instead walked from her house off a side street of McKinley Parkway all the way over to the show on Seneca Street. Her mother would have a stroke if she ever found out. The only place Barb ever walked alone was to the library or to the drugstore to pick up her mother's prescription or to Junie's or Thelma's houses. Her frame of reference was small, but she figured she was fifteen now and it was time to be a little more independent. Last night, the sheer thrill of doing something by herself was as exciting as the anticipatory pleasure of seeing the movie again.

"Um, hello, earth to Barb, earth to Barb," Junie said, swaying toward her and nudging her with her elbow.

Ahead of them, Thelma paused and swung around, her arms draped over a baseball bat behind her head.

"Oh boy, she's got that dreamy look on her face again," Thelma said with a grin. "Who is it this time? Elvis? Johnny Mathis? Kirk Douglas?"

Ignoring them and needing an answer to a pressing question, she asked, "Do you believe in love at first sight?"

Thelma snorted. Junie hesitated. Of course, Barb knew of Junie's long-standing crush, and that begged the question: had Junie fallen in love at first sight or had it been a gradual thing? Junie claimed she no longer carried a torch for Paul Reynolds, especially after that incident with the dime, but Barb wondered. He'd yet to be replaced—although Junie never mentioned him by name anymore, she didn't mention anyone else either.

Junie avoided answering by asking a question of her own. "What brought this on?"

"You know the song 'Some Enchanted Evening' from *South Pacific*?" She ignored Thelma's pronounced eye roll.

"Yes," Junie said.

"You're still going on about that movie? Would you get over yourself?" Thelma said, turning around and walking on.

"I love that movie," Barb said softly.

"We *know*," Thelma grumbled.

Ignoring Thelma, Barb turned to Junie, who walked beside her. "Can that happen? Can you spot someone across the room and just know?"

"Know what?" Thelma said ahead of them.

It was Barb's turn to roll her eyes. Thelma could be so obtuse sometimes. Half the time, Barb wondered if she did it on purpose.

"I don't know about love at first sight," Junie started. "But I bet you could meet someone and there'd be a connection, you know?"

Barb nodded. Although she didn't know that firsthand, it was what she believed.

Barb lowered her voice to a whisper. "Do you believe there's someone out there, just for you? Someone that was put on the earth only for you?"

Junie opened her mouth and then closed it and conceded, "I suppose."

"No, listen, Junie. I mean like, there's a person out there, the love of your life."

"I hope so, but I'm not sure," Junie said. "I hate to think Bill Jenner is the love of my sister's life."

The three of them went quiet and continued walking, the looming spectre of Junie's older sister and her abusive marriage settling in around them and weighing them down. Barb looked up to see where they were, and her heart sank. They were headed in the direction of the park; no wonder Thelma was up front leading the way. She probably wanted to see if anyone was playing baseball.

"I'm never getting married and I'm never having children," Thelma announced. "I'm going to get a job right out of high school, and I'm going to get my own place. I'm going to live alone for the rest of my life."

"You can't mean that," Barb cried. "You don't want to be alone."

Thelma swung around and leaned against her bat. "Oh yes, I do," she said vehemently. "I've had my fill of men and boys. I want to be alone." In the glow of the streetlight, Thelma's eyes were dark and glittery.

Barb knew Thelma's life wasn't ideal, not with all those brothers and a father who worked her like a rented mule. Barb had an older brother, but he always seemed to be doing his own thing. He planned to follow in their father's footsteps and go to med school. Barb knew she'd be going to the same college her mother had gone to; it had already been decided.

"Even though my experience is limited, I like to think you could have one love, a love of your life," Junie said evenly. She tripped on the dip in the sidewalk and teetered, bumping into Barb. "Sorry."

Barb chewed her bottom lip thoughtfully. Oh, how she wanted to believe that there was someone just for her, out there somewhere in the world, waiting for her. She mused as to how they'd meet. And at the same time, she was anxious for it to happen, as she wanted to live it. She didn't want to just daydream about things, she wanted to experience them. It seemed to her that when you were a teenager, you were always waiting around for something to happen. For your life to begin.

"Hey, Thelma, game going on at the park—wanna play?" Stanley Schumacher called from the darkened shadows.

"Yeah, be right there," Thelma called back. She looked over her shoulder at her friends. "I'll catch up with you tomorrow." And she took off, running, the baseball bat swinging wildly at her side.

"Are we going to the show this weekend?" Barb asked.

Junie nodded. "I think Thelma wants to see *Dracula*."

Barb winced. "Oh no, not that. I thought we could go see *South Pacific*."

"Again?" Junie questioned.

Barb's cheeks reddened.

"It's Thelma's turn to pick the movie," Junie pointed out.

Barb gave her friend a quick smile. "That's fine." But in her mind, she envisioned her mental calendar, trying to decide when she could sneak off to the show again to see her favorite movie.

CHAPTER FIVE

Isabelle

Within two weeks, Isabelle had seen the town's new doctor and had been referred to a gastroenterologist, which was timely as the gallbladder attacks were happening with alarming frequency.

With Lily and Alice at work all day, Isabelle found herself at a loose end. She kept busy, walking the beach and waiting for the weather to warm up so she could go swimming. But she could feel herself getting restless already, itching to leave as her wanderlust began to gnaw at her.

"Isn't there an article you could write about Hideaway Bay?" Lily asked one evening as they sat around the living room watching old black-and-white movies on Gram's ancient TV, fed by the likewise ancient VCR.

Isabelle knitted her brows together and sighed. She'd had a restless night due to another gallbladder attack, and she didn't need a lecture from her younger sister.

"And what would I write about?" Isabelle scowled. She needed to hang on for two more days until the laparoscopic surgery, then the pain would be gone and she could move on with her life.

"I can think of a million things," Lily said.

"Name one," Isabelle challenged.

"You could write about Lily's beach-glass art," Alice piped in.

Isabelle nodded, tilting her head to one side. She'd been tripping over beach glass all her life. There might be something there, she admitted reluctantly.

"I can think of a few things: What about Mr. Lime's five-and-dime? I bet there aren't too many of them around. And what about Hideaway Bay being like a slice of small-town Americana?" Lily suggested, warming up to the subject.

Isabelle made a face of disinterest. She took a sip of her ice water, the glass sweating in her hands.

"And back to the beach glass, that could be an interesting article. Aren't people collecting it all the time? There's been a lot of things found here on the beach," Lily said.

"Remember when Granddad found the cannonball from the War of 1812?" Alice said.

"I'll think about it," Isabelle said.

"But you're not leaving right away, right after your surgery, are you?" Alice asked. "We were going to remember Gram on her anniversary next week."

"I'll be here for that," Isabelle said. She certainly wouldn't miss the one-year anniversary of Gram's passing.

"And we have to decide what to do with the house," Alice pushed.

Isabelle put up her hand. "One thing at a time." That was Alice, easily excitable, full of ideas, wanting everything discussed and figured out at once. Isabelle didn't operate like that. "Let me get through my surgery. Let's remember Gram, and we'll take it from there."

Alice and Lily exchanged a glance, but Isabelle remained silent. She wasn't in the mood to bicker with her sisters. She felt like she was spinning her wheels, waiting for her surgery, and it was a feeling she was unfamiliar with and didn't like.

Gram had built a condition into her will: that the three of them had to wait one year before they sold the house. And the end of that year was coming up soon. While Isabelle had been traveling and working for the past year, at the back of her mind had skated the reality that she would have to make a decision regarding her share of the house. That her sisters had returned to Hideaway Bay, settled in, and apparently were getting along was nothing short of miraculous. All she remembered growing up was the constant fighting with Lily, and Alice crying in the background.

Truthfully, Isabelle wasn't sure what she wanted to do with her share of the house. She'd never owned property before, and she wasn't sure she wanted to be tied down. She liked to be able to pick up and leave on a moment's notice.

The laparoscopic surgery was performed on an outpatient basis, so Isabelle wouldn't have to stay overnight. Alice waited with her. Lily had wanted to stay home from work, but Isabelle had told her no. What use would that be? She wouldn't be home until later in the day, and she had Alice to help her if needed. There was no sense in the two of them being there, hovering over her. Reluctantly, Lily had agreed and gone off to work, saying she might try to leave early if she wasn't too busy.

Normally an easygoing person, the thought of having any kind of surgical procedure made Isabelle a little nervous. All along, she'd taken her great health for granted. She wasn't even forty yet and they were starting to remove organs.

But everything went according to plan and by the end of the day, Isabelle was heading for the house on Star Shine Drive.

"How do you feel?" Alice asked as she helped her into the car.

"Fine. I just have some shoulder pain and nausea," Isabelle told her.

"Shoulder pain?" Alice repeated.

Isabelle nodded. "To be expected." She'd been given a sheet of discharge instructions when she left the outpatient clinic and had only stumbled once when she scanned them. It would be three to four weeks before she could resume her normal activities. She'd blinked, read it again, pursed her lips, and let out a long breath. Three to four weeks in Hideaway Bay? Doing nothing? That thought alone resulted in a fine line of perspiration breaking out on her brow. What would she do for a month in Hideaway Bay? Pushing it as far as possible out of her mind, she decided she didn't have to think about it for that day. She only needed to concentrate on feeling better.

CHAPTER SIX

1960

Barb

Barb teetered around her bedroom. This would be her first time wearing heels out of the house. And although she loved the way they looked and how they slenderized her leg—as her mother was apt to say—walking in them was a whole other thing. She'd been practicing all week, ever since her mother had agreed it was time for a pair. She'd paired the shoes with a fitted skirt and matching blouse.

A magazine lay cast aside on her bed, open to an article about the presidential candidate's wife, Jackie Kennedy. Barb hoped they would win if only to have someone stylish and beautiful in the White House. Better than that dowdy Mamie Eisenhower and her penchant for frills and bangs.

She gripped the banister as she made her way down the staircase. The faint scent of lemon Pledge hung in the air. Agnes must have dusted and vacuumed earlier in the day. There were fresh flowers—orange and yellow roses—in a tall crystal vase on the console table in the foyer.

Her parents looked up when she entered the living room. All her life, she would always think of them like this: relaxing together in the evening with books and cocktails and music playing in the background. The record player in the corner crooned out the sounds of Cole Porter's "Begin the Beguine." Her father looked tired. Her mother always made him a rusty nail cocktail. It sounded god-awful, but her father drank two every evening.

Mrs. Walsh's face creased into a smile. "You look lovely, Barbara."

"There's my girl, all grown up into a beautiful young lady," Dr. Walsh said with pride. His pipe hung from his mouth, and a medical journal lay open on his lap.

"Are you ready?" Mrs. Walsh stood, setting down her book on the coffee table.

"Yes, Mother."

Usually, Barb and Junie and Thelma met up on McKinley Parkway and walked over to the high school for the dances but because she was wearing heels, she didn't treasure that prospect at all, and her mother had offered to drive them. Thelma had scowled and said she didn't need a ride and would meet them in the gymnasium. Right before they were to pick Junie up, she'd called saying her sister Margaret had stopped over and she'd meet them at the school.

"Good night, Dad," Barb said, leaning over the back of the sofa to kiss her father on the cheek.

"Enjoy yourself. Remember, you're only young once." Smiling, he reached up and patted her hand.

As they pulled up in front of the high school, Mrs. Walsh said, "Remember your posture, Barbara."

"Yes, Mother," Barb said, pulling the door handle and carefully stepping out of the car. Not for the first time, she wondered how women didn't break their necks wearing these kinds of shoes.

She waited for her mother to pull away, then stood on the sidewalk, looking at the front doors of the high school, thrown wide open like a gaping mouth. Music and light blared from the open doors. With determination, she straightened her spine, lifted her chin, and began her trek to the entrance, trying not to wobble. As she passed groups of students, some she knew, some she didn't, she was aware of their eyes on her. At first, she thought there was something wrong, that she looked funny walking in high-heeled shoes, but when she passed a group of leather jacket–clad toughs and they whistled and catcalled after her, she clamped her lips together to stifle a grin. She lifted her head a bit higher and picked up her pace, the front doors in sight.

As she approached the two-story redbrick building, she thought how her days there were winding down, as the three of them would graduate in June. Junie's older sister, Margaret, had told her that high school was the best time of her life. But maybe that's because she ran away and got married at seventeen. Barb didn't agree with her. There'd been no great moments where she would define it as the best time of her life. She hoped that wasn't it, at any rate. Because if high school was anything to judge her life by, she'd be sorely disappointed.

Thelma was outside, waiting for Barb and Junie. She sat on the balustrade of the landing at the top of the steps, swinging her legs. She let out a low whistle and said, "Would you look at you! All dressed up and with somewhere to go!"

"Hey, Thelma, how are you?"

"Can't complain," Thelma said, brushing her chin along her shoulder.

Barb nodded and parked herself next to Thelma, leaning against the stone balustrade. "Is Junie here?"

Thelma shook her head. "Nah. Not yet."

They waited, quiet. Sometimes there wasn't a lot to say to Thelma. She was so unpredictable that Barb often thought the best practice was to remain quiet. It was different without Junie there, who often acted as a buffer. No matter what she said or what topic of conversation she brought up, Barb was never sure how Thelma would react. She might agree, but more often than not, she scoffed. Trying to predict which reaction she might encounter often left Barb on uneven, constantly shifting ground, and she hated that feeling.

After a few minutes of silence during which Barb wondered if Thelma felt the same way about her, Thelma said, "There's Junie now. I don't know why she's rushing. It's only a dance. Now if it was a baseball game, I could see the hurry."

Junie walked briskly up the sidewalk and dashed up the stone steps. She was breathless when she reached them. "Sorry I'm late, but Margaret stopped over, and you know there's always some kind of drama going on with her."

Barb nodded. She didn't know how Junie's sister handled a marriage like a verbal minefield. She herself would find it exhausting.

Junie smiled and then took in the sight of Barb. "Oh wow, you got them. Let me see!"

Barb, laughing now, bent her knee and turned to one side, lifting her heel and pointing her toe on the landing.

"Oh, they're gorgeous! I'd love a pair, but Daddy says not until I'm eighteen." Junie made a face of displeasure. She eyed Barb's shoes longingly.

"Let's go to the ladies' room and you can try them on," Barb said.

"Come on you two, let's get this over with," Thelma said, hopping off the balustrade and leading them into the school.

"Thelma, if you behave yourself, I might let you try on my shoes, too," Barb said, elbowing Junie beside her, who giggled.

Thelma guffawed ahead of them. Barb had a picture in her mind of Thelma tottering on heels, and she laughed silently to herself.

Barb had given up on the idea of meeting the "love of her life" at these high school dances. She'd been going to them since freshman year and as this was her senior year and it hadn't happened yet, she doubted it would. And that was fine. Maybe she'd meet someone next year. A nice college boy, as her mother would say.

Junie nudged her and pushed her into the ladies' room.

"What about Thelma?" Barb asked.

"She probably hasn't even noticed we're missing," Junie said with a laugh. "Now come on, get those shoes off and let me try them on."

Barb slipped off one shoe and then the other, handing the pair to her friend.

Junie took them both, set them down, and stepped into them. She teetered and reached an arm out, which Barb took hold of to steady her.

"Oh jeez! I feel taller already," Junie said. She walked forward, her knees knocking together, and then one ankle bending outward until she was almost standing on the side of her foot. Barb winced at the sight of it.

Junie slipped the heels off and handed them back to Barb. "How do you walk in them and not fall over?"

"I practiced all week," Barb told her. "Look, I'll bring them in Monday morning, and you can take them home for the week. Practice walking around in them in your room."

"Oh, really? You don't mind?" Junie asked, her face lighting up.

Barb shook her head. "No, not at all."

"Thanks," Junie said. "Come on, let's go before Thelma has a conniption, wondering where we are."

Barb glanced quickly in the mirror that ran the length of the wall above the row of sinks. She leaned against the edge of the sink, not realizing there was a small pool of water, and it left a dark spot on the front of her skirt. She groaned, looking around to see if there was something she could blot it with, but there was nothing. On the wall at the end of the bank of sinks was a cloth roller, but she didn't have to touch it to know it was already damp.

Instead, she pulled a tube of pink lipstick from her purse and dabbed it on. Then she wiped a smudge of mascara from beneath her right eye and patted her hair with both hands before turning to Junie and smiling.

"Come on, you look beautiful as always," Junie said.

The lights in the gym had been dimmed, and a band played on the stage. The crowd had broken into couples, who swayed slowly around the dance floor.

They found Thelma on the other side of the gym, standing there with her leg bent at the knee, her arms across her chest.

Barb scanned the gymnasium to see who was there and more importantly, if there was anyone different, anyone that would interest her. A quick perusal of the crowd showed it was just about everyone she knew in South Buffalo. She slouched slightly, and then she heard her mother's voice whispering in her head about her posture. Immediately, she straightened up.

The band went into another slow song and Thelma shouted, "Boo! Boo! We want to twist!" To emphasize her point, she put her arms out, planted her feet, and swiveled her hips.

"Here comes Stanley," Junie said.

"I hope he doesn't ask me to dance," Thelma said.

"It's a dance, Thelma, not a marriage proposal," Barb said.

"But with Stanley, any interaction is viewed as a marriage proposal," Thelma joked.

"It takes a lot of courage for a guy to walk across the dance floor and ask a girl to dance," Barb said, parroting what her mother had told her.

Thelma snorted. "I don't care."

"Besides, if you say no, other guys might not approach you," Barb pointed out.

"Oh jeez, he is coming over here," Thelma said. "I gotta go." And she pushed her way through the crowd and disappeared.

"I don't know why she has to be so mean to him all the time," Barb said.

"You know how she is," Junie said.

Stanley approached them, hands in his pockets, and stood before them, rocking on his heels.

"Junie, Barb, how are you?"

"Good, Stanley," Junie answered.

"I thought I saw Thelma standing here," he said. "I wanted to ask her to dance."

"She had to go to the bathroom, couldn't hold it any longer," Barb said.

Junie shot her a withering glare, but Barb didn't care. Sometimes, she didn't like how mean Thelma was to Stanley.

His only fault was that he adored Thelma. And that got on Thelma's nerves.

"Come on, Stanley, I'll dance with you," Junie said, leading him out to the dance floor before he could reply.

"Gee, that's great, Junie," he said, following close behind her.

Barb stood there by herself, humming along to the music and tapping her foot. She found that the longer she stood in one spot, the more the balls of her feet ached, so she shifted from foot to foot from time to time and watched the crowd. It didn't bother her that no one asked her to dance. There was no one she wanted to dance with. She knew just about everyone there or at the very least, recognized them by sight. How was anyone going to sweep her off her feet if she already knew them?

Teachers, acting as chaperones, circled the dance floor and wove through the crowd, making sure boys and girls were maintaining a respectful distance. Barb was able to spot Junie with Stanley. Stanley danced properly, one hand on Junie's waist, the other holding Junie's hand. But looking at them, watching them, Barb laughed to herself. Junie and Stanley talked non-stop. It was truly a platonic dance. She couldn't understand why Thelma wouldn't give Stanley a chance. He absolutely adored her! Oh, to have that kind of power over a man, to be in receipt of that kind of devotion. She fingered the locket around her neck, bringing it up to her mouth to run it against her teeth, a bad habit her mother frowned upon. In her mind, she could hear her mother's voice: *Jewelry is to be worn, not eaten.*

Bored, her mind drifted, thinking romantic thoughts about meeting a handsome man beneath a row of blossoming cherry trees. She could practically feel the warmth of the weak spring sun on her face as she strolled hand in hand with the love of her life.

Her reverie was interrupted by the return of Junie and Stanley.

"Could you put in a good word for me with Thelma?" Stanley asked.

"Thelma doesn't listen to me, Stanley," Junie told him.

"What about you, Barb?" he asked.

Barb gave him a sympathetic look and said, "If Thelma doesn't listen to Junie, she certainly isn't going to listen to me."

He pushed his glasses up on his nose and turned back to Junie. "Come on, be a pal and talk me up in front of Thelma."

"Okay, okay, I will," Junie finally said.

"Gee, that's swell, thanks," he said and bounced off, buoyed by hope.

"What is it you think he sees in Thelma?" Barb asked.

"I don't know. But he's got it bad," Junie said as they watched him disappear.

"Maybe love is blind and deaf."

Chapter Seven

Isabelle

Thelma Schumacher stepped up onto the porch and took a seat, her back to the lake across the street. "How's the patient?"

Thelma had been one of Gram's best friends. Creeping up on eighty, she looked well. The carrot-red hair she'd been born with and that Isabelle vaguely remembered from childhood had morphed into a steel gray, accentuated with unruly curls.

"I'm fine," Isabelle told her. "The first day was a little rough with pain and gas but from then on, it was fine. I'll have to watch my diet."

It had been almost a week since Isabelle had her gallbladder removed, and she felt better. Having never had surgery before, she'd been unsure what to expect, but it had been pretty straightforward. She would have liked to leave, but she still had to go to her post-op follow-up visit with the surgeon.

She had been working since she was sixteen, and it was nice to put her feet up for a change. But she didn't totally waste her time; she thought about where she might want to go next in the world and what article might interest her to research and write. Sitting around and doing nothing was alien to her. Slowly, she was becoming accustomed to living with her sisters again. It wasn't like she and Lily were teenagers and fighting all the time with a much younger Alice whining in the background. Maybe people mellowed with age.

Her sisters both worked, so she was home alone most of the day. She found old photo albums in the bottom cabinet of the bookshelves, and she went through them one day. It was hard to imagine Gram, Granddad, and even her mother as being young. More than once, her eyes filled with tears and her throat constricted. There were even some old photos of her father. Maybe it hadn't all been bad.

"Are Lily and Alice at work?" Thelma asked, crossing one leg over the other.

Isabelle could not remember a time when Thelma hadn't been a part of their lives. She wondered if it ever bothered the other woman that she was the only one left. But she felt it would be rude to ask.

"Yes," she said. She'd discovered her sisters had a nice routine here: they went to work at jobs they loved, one cooked while the other did the cleanup, and they had nice hobbies—baking for Alice and crafting with beach glass for Lily. Although she didn't envy them, she was glad they had found their new lives in their old hometown. Still, it wasn't for her.

"Thelma, would you like some coffee?" She knew by now that the elderly woman only drank instant.

Thelma shook her head. "No thank you. I had some before I left the house."

"Can I ask you a question?"

"Shoot!"

Isabelle smiled, amused by the other woman's plain speak. "What do you know about my father?"

Thelma looked startled but recovered quickly. "Dave? Dave Monroe? Not too much, to be honest."

Isabelle lifted her eyebrows and sighed. Her father had been on her mind since returning home. She thought of him often but seemed to focus more on him any time she was in Hideaway Bay. Maybe because that's where her memories of him were.

Thelma looked at her hands in her lap and did not meet Isabelle's gaze. "It's hard growing up without a parent. It always leaves you wondering."

Isabelle agreed. She knew that Thelma had lost her own mother when she was a young girl.

"Your grandfather never warmed up to Dave," Thelma said.

Isabelle had gathered that growing up, especially after her father left.

"He always wanted better for Nancy. Paul and Dave were two very different people."

"What about Gram?"

"Junie was always of the mind to keep the peace no matter what."

The older woman was on a roll, and Isabelle peppered her with questions.

"But what about Dad? What was he like?"

Thelma shrugged. "He was all right. I never had a problem with Dave, but then he hadn't gotten my teenage daughter pregnant."

Isabelle wanted to point out that her mother was responsible for that too and her father shouldn't be the one to bear the brunt of the blame. It took two to tango as the saying went.

"Dave was always polite to me. Friendly," Thelma said.

"Did you ever hear any news as to where he went?"

Thelma shook her head. "No. Not so much as a whisper on the wind."

"What about Miriam?" Isabelle inquired, referring to her father's sister.

"No, pretty tight-lipped all these years. But then she's never seen around town, kind of a recluse," Thelma said.

"I heard that too," Isabelle said. "But she still lives here in Hideaway Bay, doesn't she?"

Thelma eyed her. "Did you ever hear the expression *let sleeping dogs lie*?"

Isabelle blew out a frustrated breath. "I'd like to find him."

"Is that a good idea? After all this time?"

"I won't know the answer to that until I find him," Isabelle replied.

"*If* you find him. God knows where he is," Thelma pointed out. "How long ago did he leave?"

"Almost thirty years ago," Isabelle said. "I was eleven. Lily was nine and Alice was three."

Thelma lowered her voice. "It's a long time for someone to be gone."

Silence stretched out between them.

They were momentarily distracted by three kids, one of whom was pulling an old red Radio Flyer wagon behind him. In it was a much younger child who couldn't have been more than four or five. The older two, in front of the wagon, were about eight or nine years old and talked amongst themselves.

Isabelle watched them as they looked both ways and crossed the street, heading toward the boardwalk that led to the beach.

"I understand, more than most, your desire to find your dad," Thelma said. "Have you thought about the possibility that he might be dead?"

"I have," Isabelle said, rocking gently in the chair.

"Do your sisters know you're going to try and find your father?"

"No, I haven't told them yet," Isabelle said.

"For what it's worth, Isabelle, I'd advise you to steer clear of Miriam or Dave. If Dave wanted to be found, your mother would have found him all those years ago."

Isabelle's head snapped up. "What do you mean Mom would have found him? She looked?"

Thelma scowled. "Of course she did. A year after he left, Paul hired a private detective to see if *he* could find him. He did not."

"Why did Mom want to find him?"

Thelma looked at Isabelle as if it was obvious. "Because she still loved him."

Isabelle did a slow nod as she considered things. Their mother never remarried after she divorced their father. And she'd dragged her heels on divorcing him. It wasn't until he was gone ten years that she filed for divorce.

Thelma pushed herself up from the chair. "Well, I gotta shove. Glad to see you're on the mend."

"Good to see you, Thelma, you know you're always welcome," Isabelle said.

"I know, and I appreciate it," Thelma said. "If you need anything during the day while Lily and Alice are at work, give me a call."

"I will, thanks."

CHAPTER EIGHT

1960

Barb

B arb, Junie, and Thelma were gathered around the dining room table in the Walsh house on Coolidge Street, wrapping their Christmas presents. From her seat at the head of the table, Barb had a direct view of the large Christmas tree in the front window of the living room. It was the largest tree they'd ever had, both wide and tall, and it had given her mother an excuse to go out and buy four more boxes of glass ornaments. The sounds of the Ray Conniff Singers from the *Christmas with Conniff* album drifted out from the record player in the corner. She had it on low so it wouldn't disturb her mother, who was upstairs taking a nap.

She eyed what the other girls had gotten their families. Alarmed wasn't the word for what she felt as she watched

Thelma pull out plain white T-shirt after T-shirt and underwear from a brown paper bag at her feet. Junie had gifts for Margaret's little boy, a box of handkerchiefs for her mother, and socks for her father. Barb's pile had a lovely scarf and perfume for her mother and a new pipe and his favorite tobacco for her father. For her older brother, Mark, she'd chosen a stylish tie.

Agnes stepped in and set down a platter of Christmas cookies. There was a variety as Agnes had been baking all week: snickerdoodles, meringue kisses dyed red and green, and cutouts with a lemony icing.

"I thought you might need some refreshment," Agnes said in her nasal voice, picking a cookie off the platter for herself and biting into it. Her gaze swept over the piles of gifts to be wrapped.

Barb had gotten Agnes a box of chocolate-covered maraschino cherries as she knew they were a favorite of hers. But she'd already wrapped that gift, and it was hidden in the closet upstairs along with her presents for Junie and Thelma.

Agnes took another bite of her cookie and nodded toward Thelma's pile. "Now those are sensible gifts. Men always need T-shirts and underwear."

"Especially in my house," Thelma said with a grin. Thelma had on brown-and-red plaid pants with a yellow blouse with a Peter Pan collar. Sometimes, Barb wished she could take Thelma shopping and redo her wardrobe. But she knew her friend would never go for that. If Barb suggested shopping for a baseball bat or a new glove, Thelma would jump up and down.

Agnes snorted. With one more final glance around the room, she said, "I better get back to work."

Once Agnes was out of earshot, Thelma asked, "Why don't you let Agnes wrap your gifts?"

Barb frowned. "What fun would that be?"

"You think this is fun?" Thelma said, screwing up her face in displeasure.

"How do you get your corners to fit so nicely?" Junie asked Barb.

Thelma glanced at Barb's neatly wrapped pile, and her eyes widened. She held up one of her own wrapped gifts. The paper was all bunched together at the ends, and it appeared as if she had used about twenty pieces of tape to close it up.

"Here, I'll show you," Barb said, standing up. She reached for the box that contained the scarf for her mother. She unrolled a bit of wrapping paper, laid the box on the inside of it, marked the area with a pencil, and cut the paper on a straight line.

Deftly, she folded the paper around the box, and when she came to the ends, she used her finger to create a sharp crease in the corner. Junie and Thelma watched her intently.

"Fold your paper like this at the end of your box," Barb said, demonstrating.

Junie tried it Barb's way and after a few tries, she had the hang of it.

"That looks much better!" Junie said, satisfied.

Thelma tried but soon gave up in frustration, letting out a sharp breath that lifted the bangs off her forehead. "Forget it. Do you think my brothers are going to notice how the gifts are wrapped? Not on your life!"

Barb did not comment, agreeing with Thelma's assessment of her brothers. She took spools of ribbon and wrapped the ends around a pencil to curl them.

"Show me how to do that," Junie said, leaning toward Barb to watch.

Once they had enough red and green ribbons, they affixed them to their wrapped gifts, except for Thelma, who said it would be a waste.

They were almost finished, and Barb thought the wrapped presents looked merry all stacked up on the dining room table. She leaned back and helped herself to a snickerdoodle.

Her thoughts drifted toward the nebulous future. She imagined herself wrapping gifts for her husband and children while a Christmas album played in the background and the kitchen was filled with the scent of vanilla and sugar. She would spend days shopping in department stores, her arms laden with gifts for her family. Then on Christmas Eve, she'd make her grandmother's recipe for eggnog, add a bit of brandy, and get comfortable with her husband while they placed presents from Santa Claus under the tree for the children. A smile formed on her face.

"Oh boy, we've lost Barb," Thelma said. She stood, leaned over, and waved her hand in front of Barb's face. "Where'd you go, Barb?"

Barb blinked and realized her best friends were staring at her. Thelma smirked while Junie looked at her with concern.

"I've never met anyone who could daydream like you," Thelma said, wrestling with wrapping paper and another round of T-shirts and underwear.

Barb reddened. "You should try it. It's so pleasant."

Thelma snorted. "When would I have time to daydream? I barely have time to wind my watch." She smiled to herself as a thought occurred to her. "Is there music in your daydreams?" she asked Barb.

Barb frowned, confused. "What do you mean?"

"I wonder if your daydreams are like the musicals you love so much." Thelma said with a grin. Thelma herself preferred action movies, westerns, or horror. Barb supposed it had to do with growing up in a house full of men.

Barb felt the heat creep up her neck. "Not always."

"I can just picture you and your future boyfriend dancing around with each other under the streetlamps on McKinley Parkway, singing some song about falling in love," Thelma teased.

Junie chortled. "Like *Singin' in the Rain*!"

"Except without the rain," Thelma said with a laugh.

"Oh, don't make fun. Someday we'll all have boyfriends. Won't that be wonderful?" Barb could picture the three of them, triple-dating she supposed, although she had a hard time getting an imaginary boyfriend into focus for Thelma. She couldn't imagine who Thelma would end up with.

"This sounds like a classic case of as soon as you get a boyfriend, you dump your friends," Thelma grumbled.

"Not at all," Barb rushed to assure her.

"Don't we all want boyfriends?" Junie asked. "I mean, I don't know about you, but I want to find someone and get married and settle down."

Thelma scowled. "That's the last thing I want. Sometimes I think it would have been easier to be a man."

"But it's lovelier to be a woman," Barb said.

Thelma turned her head. "Sometimes I wonder what planet you're living on, Barb Walsh."

With that, the three of them burst out laughing.

Chapter Nine

Isabelle

By the end of the third week, Isabelle was bored out of her mind and frustrated with Hideaway Bay. There were so many memories everywhere she looked; she'd turn a corner and slam into the past head-on. At Lime's Five-and-Dime, she'd gone in and felt as though she were being transported back in time, back to her childhood when Granddad used to get her and her sisters their own bag of saltwater taffy. She left with a bag of candy and a lump in her throat. Stan Schumacher's Red Top restaurant on the beach at the end of Main Street was boarded up, the paint peeling, having been closed since Stanley's death thirty years ago. But that didn't stop Isabelle from remembering how her father used to take her there by herself as a child for a foot-long hot dog and a chocolate milkshake. Funny how back then, she hadn't realized she was happy. She supposed she'd been too young to know any better.

MOONLIGHT AND PROMISES

Only after it was gone, after it was over, did you realize the meaning something held for you.

They'd had a small gathering at the house to commemorate Gram's death. It was a subdued affair with the usual suspects: Thelma and her granddaughters, their old babysitter Sue Ann Marchek, and other neighbors and friends filled the house until it was packed. There'd been tea and coffee and of course, baked goods courtesy of Alice. Simon Bishop stopped by with Colonel Jack Stirling, and Isabelle couldn't help but notice the attraction between Jack and Alice. She'd even bet there was something stirring between Lily and her boss, though Lily would be loathe to admit it. As long as Isabelle's sisters were happy, she was happy.

Preceding the gathering at Gram's house, the three of them had driven over to the cemetery on the other side of town to stand at the grave and say a few prayers. They were silent, each one of them lost in their own thoughts. Staring at the common headstone for their mother, Gram, and Granddad, Isabelle couldn't help but feel like an orphan. Granted it had not been easy when Mom or Granddad had died, but Gram had always been there holding things together, and now that she was gone, it felt as if the three of them were adrift on an ocean, scrabbling to get purchase and to keep their heads above water.

The day had been overcast and chilly for early May, unlike last May when Gram had died unexpectedly and the weather had been unseasonably hot. They laid a large bouquet of mixed flowers on the grave and were quiet on the walk back to the car.

In the early evening after all their guests had left, the three of them went outside, followed by Charlie. They had planned a private moment to plant a cherry tree in Gram's memory. Alice and Lily carried the sapling they'd purchased from the nursery from the backyard to the front. They'd paid one of the nursery workers some cash to dig a hole to the left of the porch. Lily and Alice gently set the little tree into its new space. Isabelle held the trunk as Lily and Alice shoveled dirt onto the roots to cover it up and secure it, then tamped down the topsoil around the tree with their shovels.

"It will be nice to sit on the porch when the blossoms come," Isabelle mused.

The three of them stood there looking at the tree for a few minutes, satisfied, and then Lily announced, "We should go inside and clean up."

Isabelle started with the dining room, stacking cups and saucers that had been left on the table.

"Um, hey, no lifting, remember," Lily said, reaching over and taking the dishes from Isabelle.

"I don't consider teacups heavy lifting," Isabelle protested.

"Sit down and relax, Izzy," Lily said. "Alice and I will do the cleanup. There's not much here anyway." And she left the room, her hands full of tableware.

Isabelle sighed in frustration. She wasn't an invalid. She'd spoken to the surgeon, and everything had gone smoothly. Once Lily was out of sight, Isabelle removed the linen tablecloth, took it outside, and shook it out over the porch railing.

The sky remained a dull gray with no break in the cloud cover. The lake appeared churlish and lapped roughly against the shore. She couldn't wait for the weather to warm up as she was anxious to start swimming. She missed it. Swimming was such an important part of her daily routine that she was at a little bit of a loss without it. Another week and she'd brave the lake; she didn't care how cold it was.

She carried the tablecloth back inside, folded it up, and laid it on a chair by the front door. Alice had mentioned there was a dry-cleaning place in the strip mall where she worked, and she planned on dropping it off in the morning. There was a nasty red wine stain on it; hopefully, they'd be able to get it out.

Alice and Lily were back in the kitchen, chatting. They appeared to be getting along fabulously and sometimes, Isabelle couldn't help but feel like a third wheel. Alice stood at the dishwasher, loading it up while Lily scraped dirty plates over the garbage bin.

"Sit down, Izzy, and take a load off," Alice said with a smile.

Isabelle blew out a breath. She didn't want to sit down. It was the last thing she wanted to do. She wanted to *do* something, anything, other than sit around. But she obediently sat at the kitchen table, playing with the spoon in the sugar bowl.

Alice shut the door of the dishwasher and turned it on, its low hum background noise. She and Lily joined Isabelle at the table.

"Are you all right?" Alice asked.

Isabelle shrugged. "Bored, I guess. I'm not used to sitting around and doing nothing."

"Sitting around post-op is not doing nothing," Lily said.

"I know what we can do," Alice said, seated across from Isabelle with her hands folded on the table.

Isabelle looked at her suspiciously, unable to imagine what she had in mind and dreading it at the same time.

"While the three of us are together, we should talk about what we want to do with Gram's house," Alice said.

That question was always at the back of Isabelle's mind. Her inclination over the past year had been to sell it. With its location and beach view, it would command a good price, and even splitting it three ways would give her a hefty chunk of money. Not that she was in need of it, but it would allow her to venture further. Long trips to either China or India were in her sights, and the money would allow her to explore those regions. But it was becoming increasingly clear that the decision to sell wasn't as simple as that.

When she didn't answer immediately, Alice said, "Look, Isabelle, we understand you might want to sell, but Lily and I talked about it, and we don't want to."

Two things about that irritated Isabelle. One, that Lily and Alice had already discussed the future of Gram's home without her and two, that they assumed she'd want to sell it. They weren't wrong, but she hated being predictable.

Before Isabelle could say anything, Alice added, "I'd like to buy out your share. Of course, we'll get a realtor in to get an appraisal of fair market value so you get what's coming to you but as I've said, Lily and I discussed it, and this is the way forward for us."

Acutely aware that her bored restlessness and Alice's presumptions were putting her in a foul humor, Isabelle chose and weighed her words carefully.

"I'm not sure what my plans are in regard to the house," she said. She looked at Lily, who appeared tentative and thoughtful, and then to Alice, who could not hide her eagerness, and said, "I'm thinking of hanging out a bit in Hideaway Bay."

Alice's response was the more enthusiastic of the two. She clapped her hands and said, "Oh, that would be wonderful. The three of us, finally together again—"

Isabelle held up her hand, aware that Lily remained silent, regarding her. Alice wore her heart on her sleeve and Lily kept hers well-guarded. But she didn't want Alice to get any ideas about it being a happy family reunion. Of course she hoped she'd get on with her sisters and it might be nice to spend some time with them, but there was a reason she'd decided to stay on in Hideaway Bay. And she supposed now was as good a time as any to tell them.

"I can write my travel blog from anywhere in the world," she said. Besides, from all her travels, she had enough material to write magazine articles until kingdom come. "But there's another reason I'm staying."

Both her sisters looked at her, their expressions curious and expectant.

"I'm going to start looking for Dad and find out why he left us," she said.

Chapter Ten

Fall 1961

Barb

Her mother had been gone all of ten minutes when Barb felt the first wave of nausea. She stood in the middle of her new dorm room at the women's college in Vermont, trying to get used to the unfamiliarity of it.

It was a decent-sized room with two twin beds and two desks. She'd never shared a room in her life, so she was curious about how that would play out. She'd met her new roommate, Bunny Alder, a freshman like herself who was studying French and art history. Barb didn't have the nerve to ask her if that was her real name or a nickname.

Barb had spent the weekend with her mother decorating her side of the room. She'd brought her record player and some books and had them stacked in the corner next to her bed.

MOONLIGHT AND PROMISES

Above her desk was a corkboard, and she'd tacked a "Kennedy" banner right in the middle of it. Her mother scrunched up her nose and said, "Really, Barbara, politics are a private affair." Barb ignored her and tacked up pictures of the stylish first lady along with an eight by ten glossy of Paul Newman and another of Rock Hudson. On the other side of the room, Bunny had a framed black-and-white eight by ten photograph of a young man, who was at a sideways angle and looked as if he might fall out of the frame at any minute. Barb supposed her photos of movie stars appeared childish, but she didn't care.

Bunny flitted into the room. She was petite with short blond hair. Barb admired her hair but knew that she wouldn't be cutting her own any time soon. It was her unfounded belief that men preferred long hair on women.

Bunny jumped on her bed and sat cross-legged on top of it. "Has your mother left?"

Barb nodded. "Yes, she left half an hour ago."

"Thank God. I won't see my mother until Thanksgiving and even then, it will be too soon," Bunny declared.

Barb felt the opposite but kept it to herself. She already missed her mother and wished she didn't have to go to school out of state. She'd asked if she could go to college in Buffalo, but her mother had said absolutely not, that she was expected to go to the Vermont college just like she had. But now, looking around at her strange new environment with a roommate to boot, she knew without a doubt she would have preferred to stay home. In her own room, with her own things. Another wave of nausea swept over her, and her hands felt clammy.

She straightened up and decided to write some letters. The distraction would be good. She was stuck here whether she liked it or not. She pulled out the chair from her desk and sat, rooting through the drawer for pen and paper and envelopes.

"Did you want to go to the student lounge?" Bunny asked.

"Not yet," Barb said. She wasn't ready to venture out onto the campus yet. Her mind was set on letter writing. There was a large ink stain in the top drawer and when Barb touched it and pulled her finger away, the pad of her fingertip was blue.

She closed the drawer and laid her stationery on a slant on the desk blotter. She wrote the date in the top right-hand corner.

"Who are you writing a letter to?" Bunny asked from her bed. She yawned and picked up a magazine off her nightstand.

"My friends," Barb said, although she didn't expect Thelma to start writing letters. Still, she would keep in touch.

Bunny stared at her expectantly, and Barb surmised she was supposed to ask her a question. She nodded toward the framed photo behind Bunny. "Is that your boyfriend?"

Bunny beamed. "It is. Henry Lee Mendelson the fourth."

Barb giggled. "That's a mouthful. How long have you been together?"

"What, like dating?" Bunny asked. When Barb nodded, she said, "A couple of years. He was two years ahead of me in prep school."

Prep school? Barb held up some sheets of loose paper from her stationery box. "Did you want some paper to write Henry?"

Bunny burst out laughing. "No thanks. I don't write letters. Thank-you notes and cards, yes, but not letters. Besides, he might drive down for the weekend to see me." She pulled out a compact and a gold tube of lipstick from her purse. After she powdered her nose, she applied the lipstick to her lips. It was a lovely shade of pink.

"Doesn't he have school himself?" Barb asked.

"Yeah, he does, but sometimes he skips classes." Sounding bored, Bunny flipped through the pages of her magazine.

Barb looked at her, wide-eyed. She wondered what kind of people these were that they could skip classes and "drive down" to see their girlfriends. As hard as she tried, she couldn't picture herself leaving the dorm room much less the campus.

"I'll wait for you. Write your letter and we'll go to the student lounge."

"I was going to write to my two best friends, Junie and Thelma."

Bunny rolled her eyes. "God, that is so boring. What is this, *Little Women*?"

Barb felt the heat crawl up her neck and cheeks.

"Where are they? What college?" Bunny asked.

"They're not at college. They're back home."

Bunny looked up from her magazine. "They didn't go to college? What happened? Did they get married or something?"

"No, they went out to work after high school graduation."

"Oh, that sounds cruel," Bunny said with a grimace.

Barb decided she would not disclose the fact that Junie worked at a drugstore and Thelma did shift work at a cardboard box factory. Somehow, she knew it wouldn't pass muster. "They've been my best friends for a long time," she said more to herself than anyone else.

"You're at college now, Barb, and you'll outgrow them and make new friends here," Bunny said with a sweet smile. "And you and I will be best friends because we share a room."

Not wanting to subject Junie and Thelma to any more scrutiny, Barb folded her sheet of paper in half, having gotten no further than "Dear Junie," and slipped it into the top drawer, saying, "Come on, let's go to the student lounge."

CHAPTER ELEVEN

Isabelle

Once Lily and Alice recovered from their shock over Isabelle's bombshell announcement, they both spoke at once.

From Alice, "Why? What brought this on?" A frown burrowed between her arched eyebrows.

"That's not a good idea," Lily said next to her. She folded her arms over her chest.

"I'm going to be here for a few weeks, so I thought I might as well do something," Isabelle explained.

"By all means, do something. Do yoga, volunteer work, get the garden beds ready. But why do you want to look for the man that abandoned us?" Lily asked. Her face bore a distressed expression.

Although Isabelle was sympathetic to Lily's point of view, this was something she had to do for herself. "Why? I want to know why he abandoned Mom and us and why he never came back," she explained. That one pivotal event in her childhood had shaped her as an adult, and not necessarily for the better.

"Who knows why? Who cares? I said it before and I'll say it again, that's on him, not us," Lily said, her voice rising slightly.

"Alice, you're pretty quiet, what do you think?"

"To be honest, I'm not sure," she said. "Do we want to stir all that up? After all this time? And where would you even look? He's definitely not in Hideaway Bay anymore. Someone would have said something."

"No, but his sister Miriam is still here in town," Isabelle said.

"That's another thing. She's our aunt and she's been here all these years, and yet she never bothered with us," Lily pointed out.

"I'm going to see her," Isabelle said firmly.

Lily groaned. "Don't do this to yourself, Izzy. You'll open a whole can of worms."

"I have to," Isabelle said.

"What are you going to do? Show up at Miriam's and wave your hands around and say, 'Hey, Auntie Miriam, remember me? Your long-lost niece?'"

Isabelle winced. Her opening line—the one she'd crafted in her head—was similar to that. Now that Lily had said it out loud, it did sound a little trite.

"Don't do anything rash. Think about it," Alice said, clasping her hands in front of her on the table.

"Says the one who quit her corporate job in a heartbeat and moved back to Hideaway Bay," Isabelle snapped.

Alice slouched in her chair.

"That's not nice," Lily said.

Isabelle exhaled a jagged breath. She did not want to fight with her sisters. She ran her hand along her forehead. "I'm sorry, Alice, that was uncalled for. But each of you had to do what was best for you, and that included returning to Hideaway Bay. Looking for Dad is what's best for me. And although I don't expect you to agree with it, a little support might be nice."

Neither sister looked at her.

"You're right," Lily said softly, unfolding her arms, putting her hands in her lap, and staring at them.

Alice stood to turn the kitchen light on as evening was falling and the sunless day was darkening.

An awkward silence ensued until finally, Isabelle said, "Look, if it makes you feel better, I won't tell you anything I find out about him. I'll leave you in the dark."

Lily tilted her head to one side and narrowed her eyes. "I'm not totally devoid of curiosity. Obviously, if you find something out or find *him*, I'll want to know. But I don't think I'd want to meet him at this point."

"I can respect that," Isabelle said. She cast a glance at their younger sister. "Alice, what about you?"

"Almost the same. I do want to hear about what you find out, but I'm not sure I want to meet him."

Isabelle nodded. "Honestly, realistically, he's probably dead. I find it odd that there's never been any mention of him in all these years."

"How would we know?" Lily asked. "We haven't lived here in years."

"But don't you think Mom or Gram would have said something to us? Or Thelma?"

Alice shook her head. "Not necessarily. They might have wanted to protect us."

"When I spoke to Thelma, she didn't seem to know anything about him," Isabelle said.

"You spoke to Thelma about this already?" Lily asked.

Isabelle couldn't determine if Lily was upset by that, but she decided not to create an issue where there was none. "I did. She said there wasn't so much as a whisper on the wind."

"If Thelma has never heard anything, then no one has heard anything," Alice said. "She knows everything that goes on in this town."

"That's for sure," Isabelle said.

"When do you plan on visiting 'Aunt' Miriam?" Lily asked. Isabelle did not miss the sarcasm in her voice.

Their father's abandonment had affected each one of them differently. Whereas Isabelle had trust issues, Lily seemed bitter. Alice seemed ambivalent about it but then she'd been little, only three, when their father took off.

Isabelle shrugged. "Maybe tomorrow. Or the day after."

When neither of her sisters said anything, she asked, "Did either one of you want to come with me?" It wasn't that she was afraid to go by herself—hell, she'd been doing things by herself since she left Hideaway Bay fresh out of college—but some backup would be nice.

Lily was shaking her head before Isabelle had the whole sentence out of her mouth. Alice hesitated and made a face of displeasure before she spoke. "As interesting as it sounds, I'll give it a pass."

They were quick to refuse, didn't even have to think about it, and it made Isabelle wonder why they weren't interested in finding out what happened to their father.

She'd be flying solo with this one. Again.

Chapter Twelve

Thanksgiving 1961

Barb

Barb walked up the long driveway and around to the back door of her home. The house was lit up, and a quick glance at her wristwatch told her that she was on time, with minutes to spare. There were only three—her parents and herself—for a dinner of Thanksgiving leftovers. She'd spent the afternoon with Junie and Thelma over at Junie's house. They hung out and even as she sat with them, she realized how much she missed them—even Thelma. It made her homesick.

The day had started out with fog and mist and gradually as the morning passed, the fog lifted but the sky remained overcast. The air was damp, and Barb was glad she'd worn her heavy winter coat.

As she pushed through the door into the back hall, she was assailed with the smell of roast turkey. She'd always loved Thanksgiving, gathering around a table of abundance with no worry over gifts, just a day to be grateful. When she entered the kitchen, she found Agnes busy at the stove, stirring a pot of gravy and then lifting a lid on the pot of boiling potatoes and piercing one with a fork. The windows in the kitchen were clouded with condensation. On the counter were the leftover pies from the previous day.

"Hi, Agnes," Barb said, removing her coat and gloves and laying them, along with her purse, on the kitchen chair. She looked at the empty table.

"Aren't we eating here?"

Without turning around, Agnes shrugged. "No, your mother said the dining room, and you know your mother: she wants what she wants."

Barb agreed with a laugh. "Truer words were never spoken. Can I do anything to help?"

"If you'd like, you can carry in the cranberry sauce and the tray of olives," Agnes said over her shoulder.

"Sure," Barb said. She picked up the crystal platter of green and black olives and small stalks of celery and the serving dish of cranberry sauce and carried them into the dining room.

Mrs. Walsh, dressed in a slim skirt, blouse, and high-heeled shoes, was setting linen napkins to the left of each place and looked up, smiling, when Barb entered. "There you are. Just in time too."

Of all the rooms in their two-story house, the dining room was the most elegant, or at least that's what Barb had always thought. It was the room her mother used most when she entertained, and she had guests over regularly, from other doctors and their wives to the junior league and many of the charity organizations she volunteered at. On the top half of the walls was a heavy silk wallpaper resplendent with peacocks in shades of teal, green, hot pink, and yellow. The bottom half and the wainscoting were painted a dark cream. A pale pink fringed Oriental rug lay on the floor. The furniture, including a china cabinet and sideboard, was all of cherry hardwood. Heavy teal damask drapes lined the windows. The table was set for three with Mrs. Walsh's new service, Royal Doulton Melrose, with its gold flowers and scrolls over a turquoise trim.

Mrs. Walsh walked to the kitchen and asked, "Agnes, are we almost ready to serve?"

"As soon as I mash these potatoes," Agnes said and then muttered, "because they can't mash themselves."

Mrs. Walsh rolled her eyes and said to Barb, "Will you call your father and tell him that dinner will be on the table in five minutes?"

Barb nodded and headed toward the front of the house, where her father's study was located. She rapped softly on the door, opened it, and popped her head in. Her father sat behind his desk, pipe in hand, a smoky blue halo around his head. The air was redolent with his cherry-scented tobacco. The lighting was soft; the only lights were the lamp in the front window, which cast a warm amber glow, and the desk light with the green shade on her father's desk. In the background, classical music played.

"Dinner in five minutes, Dad," she said.

"How are you, Barbara?" he asked, setting aside his newspaper.

"I'm great," she said with a smile. "Happy to be home."

"Good, we're glad you're home too. The house isn't the same without you," he said.

She wondered what her parents did now that it was only the two of them. She couldn't imagine.

"And how are Junie and Thelma?" he asked.

Barb nodded. "They're well. I miss them."

"Thelma still at the box factory and Junie at the drugstore?" he asked, leaning back in his oxblood leather chair and clasping his hands over his abdomen. That was one of the things she loved about her father: Even though he was a doctor, he didn't put on airs. He always asked after her best friends, and unlike her mother, he seemed to understand how important they were to her.

"Yes," Barb said.

"Good, I'm glad to hear it. Working at the factory can't be easy, but it's honest work."

"It is."

He nodded and said sagely, "Not everyone gets the opportunity to go to college—"

"Dinner is on the table, what are you doing?" Mrs. Walsh asked, coming up beside Barb and peering into the study. "Come on, we can talk at the table, the food is getting cold." And as quickly as she appeared, she disappeared.

Dr. Walsh stood and smiled. "The food is getting cold; we better get to it." He followed Barb into the dining room, and they took their seats around the table.

Mrs. Walsh and Agnes carried in the dinner in various dishes. It was a rehash of yesterday's meal: hot turkey sandwiches covered with gravy, and mashed potatoes and yams prepared with butter and brown sugar. There were side dishes of corn, green beans, and mashed turnip. The last tray Agnes brought in held warm bread rolls.

"I think this is everything, Mrs. Walsh," she said, her eyes scanning the table.

"Thank you, Agnes, we'll let you know when we're ready for coffee and pie." Mrs. Walsh reached for the bowl of mashed potatoes and placed a small scoop on her plate.

Barb exchanged a glance with her father. This was always the awkward moment at dinner. Agnes would eat her meal in the kitchen. Somehow it didn't feel right. One time her father had suggested Agnes join them at the table, and Mrs. Walsh had had a conniption. As soon as Agnes was out of earshot, she had hissed, "We don't mingle with the help."

"Agnes is practically part of the family," Dr. Walsh had protested.

Mrs. Walsh had blanched at that remark. Nothing more was said, and the subject had never been broached again and Agnes had never been invited to join them.

Halfway through their current meal, Barb summoned her courage and said, "I was thinking of transferring to one of the local colleges here after Christmas."

Her father simply looked up from his plate and appeared stunned. Her mother's response was slightly more dramatic. She dropped her fork, and it clattered against her half-empty plate.

"What?" she finally asked.

"I said"—Barb paused and cleared her throat—"I'd like to transfer to a local college after Christmas."

Her mother's expression was grim. "I know that part, but I don't understand the what and why of it."

"Are you not happy there, Barbara?" her father asked.

Barb looked to her father and lowered her head. "No, I hate it." And that was the truth. She'd tried to get over her homesickness, but it hadn't abated.

Her mother scowled. "Hate it? How is that even possible? You'd be hard-pressed to find a better women's college. Do you know how many girls would kill for your opportunity?"

Barb didn't say anything. She stared down at her half-eaten hot turkey sandwich, the gravy congealing. Her appetite abandoned her. Finally, she lifted her head and said to her mother, "I don't like it. It's not for me, and I'd like to come home and finish college here."

Mrs. Walsh threw down her napkin. "That's just wonderful. What brought this on?"

Dr. Walsh put up his hand and said, "Take it easy, Evelyn."

"Are the two of you conspiring against me behind my back?" Mrs. Walsh asked, looking from her husband to her daughter.

"No!" Barb said.

"Of course not," Dr. Walsh said reassuringly. "But I think we should listen to what Barbara has to say."

Barb looked at her father and gave him a small smile.

Her mother stood from the table and Barb thought she was going to leave, she was that angry. It certainly wasn't going as well as Barb had hoped.

But her mother stood in the doorway of the kitchen and said, "Agnes, please bring in the pie and the coffee. We're finished with dinner."

"That soon?" Agnes said from the kitchen. Barb knew the housekeeper had heard every word.

"*Please*," Mrs. Walsh said. She returned to her seat and pushed her plate away.

Dr. Walsh continued to pick away at what was left of his dinner.

"I don't like it. I miss home and I miss my friends," Barb said.

"Junie and Thelma?" her mother said. "And what, would you like to join Thelma at the cardboard box factory? Because that's a job that's going places."

Barb felt the heat creep up her neck and spread into her face. She didn't like it when her mother found her best friends lacking. And sarcasm was a tone that never suited her mother.

"It seems so superficial," Barb said. "The trying to be better than the next person and speculating who has a trust fund, and don't get me started on the sororities." She rolled her eyes.

Her mother's face went the color of puce. Through gritted teeth, she said, "I'll remind you that I'm an alumna of that college, and I was a sorority sister and we looked down on no one. Wherever you're getting your information, it's incorrect."

"But I want to come home. I miss everyone."

"And I want to be twenty-two again with my whole life ahead of me," Mrs. Walsh said, her voice rising. "But we can't always have what we want!"

"Maybe we could discuss this tomorrow after we've slept on it," Dr. Walsh said pointedly. "No sense in ruining dessert."

As if on cue, Agnes sailed in carrying what was left of the lemon meringue pie from the previous day. She set it down at Mrs. Walsh's right. "Be right back with the plates and pie cutter."

As promised, she returned within seconds carrying three dessert plates and a pie cutter, which she placed next to the pie.

Agnes looked over at Barb.

"It'd be nice to have you closer to home," Agnes said.

"Thank you, Agnes, we'll handle it from here," Mrs. Walsh said sharply.

"Just saying," Agnes muttered, and she headed out of the dining room.

The phone in the hallway rang, a loud trill, and they were silent as they listened to Agnes answering it.

"The Walsh residence." Agnes paused. "One moment, please." She appeared in the doorway and said, "Dr. Walsh, it's the answering service."

He stood, laying his linen napkin on the table. "Excuse me."

Mrs. Walsh didn't speak. She stood to cut the pie. Her movements were rough and jerky, and the lemon and meringue wobbled as she sliced it up and served it on the delicate floral plates. After the plates were passed around, she sat down, pulling her chair closer to the table, and announced, "There'll be no more talk of changing colleges. You can come back home after you graduate and not before then." She forked a piece of lemon meringue into her mouth.

Barb burst out crying, pushed away from the table, and ran from the room.

Chapter Thirteen

Isabelle

There was no further discussion amongst the three of them about Isabelle going in search of their father. Lily said nothing and neither did Alice, but Isabelle was not to be deterred. Once she made up her mind to do something, she usually followed through with it.

Both her sisters were at work when she made her way over to Miriam Monroe's house on a side street off of Erie, which led out of town and back to the main highway. She was feeling pretty good at this point and decided the walk and the fresh air would do her good. Plus, it was time to get reacquainted with Hideaway Bay.

She'd decided to go in the early afternoon in case Miriam was a late riser. She thought it odd that they had an aunt whom they knew nothing about and who'd chosen not to be a part of their lives. She wondered if her aunt had ever been curious about the three of them. As far as Isabelle knew, Miriam had lived all her life in Hideaway Bay, and Isabelle could recall no memories of her aunt after their father left. Before he'd done a runner, they'd see her from time to time, but always at her house, and the visits were infrequent.

The sky was a marbled blue, the sun a pale yellow orb radiating a decent warmth. Isabelle headed south on Star Shine Drive, toward the main center of town where all the shops were located. To her right, the lake was a faded blue, the horizon a thin dark blue line. Right before she reached town, she turned left onto Erie Street. The further away one traveled from Star Shine Drive and the lake, the smaller the houses became. There were no grand Victorians or farmhouses to be found here. Once the cottages of the tradesmen who built the grand houses at the beginning of the last century, they'd been converted into holiday homes or winterized for yearlong residency.

There was a variety of trees along her route. There was the maple tree with its distinctive leaf, and elm and oak trees, some of which, judging by their size, had borne witness to the town's inception. But Isabelle's favorite had always been the horse chestnut. As a child she'd collect the chestnuts, first with her father and then with Granddad, reveling in their smooth, glossy appearance.

As she turned off Erie, she saw Miriam's house in the distance of the dead-end street. She'd driven by the previous day to make sure her memory wasn't faulty. The name Monroe was on the mailbox in gold and black stickers you could get at any hardware store. But these stickers were faded, and the "E" was long gone. The house was covered in green asbestos siding, and the windows were trimmed in white. All the paint was peeling. There were no flower beds and the grass, if you could call it grass, had holes in it. It wasn't green, and Isabelle wondered if it ever had been.

As she neared the house, her courage wavered and her heart rate increased. But she continued putting one foot in front of the other until she was standing on the steps to the enclosed porch at the front of the house. There was an old-fashioned metal screen door with the image of a horse and carriage spanning the midsection. Once, it might have been a nice door, but parts of the metal were rusted and in one corner, the screen was rolled back. If she'd wanted to, she could have put her fist inside it. Peering inside, Isabelle gathered that the porch was mainly used for storage and not for sitting out. The street itself was too far away from the beach for this porch setting to be advantageous. There was no sound of the surf back here, although the people who lived on the street would still benefit from the breezes that rolled in off the lake.

Finally, Isabelle took a deep breath and pressed the bell. Her pulse pounded. She was aware that Miriam might not talk to her and could possibly slam the door in her face. Or she might not answer at all.

She waited a few minutes and when there was no reply or sound of movement from within the house, she rang the doorbell again. When there was still no reply, she knocked firmly on the frame of the screen door. She tested the door handle, but it was locked. She could easily slip her hand inside and unlock it, but decided that wouldn't be a good idea.

She banged on the door frame, deciding she wasn't going home until someone answered. Finally, the inside door opened and a large woman appeared, muttering, "Hold your horses!"

Isabelle backed down a step, giving the woman enough space to open the screen door.

But the woman did not open it. Instead, she peered through it, her eyes narrowing until they were skinny slits in her puffy face.

"What," she said.

"Miriam? Miriam Monroe?" Isabelle asked.

Miriam couldn't have been older than her mid-sixties; Isabelle knew she was older than her father, who hadn't been quite twenty when she was born. Miriam wore a voluminous pastel-striped, short-sleeved housecoat, and her thick salt-and-pepper hair was held in place by a pink headband.

"Who wants to know?" the woman asked.

"I'm Isabelle." When that didn't seem to register, she added, "Isabelle Monroe, Dave's daughter."

The other woman hesitated and said, "And?"

"I'm trying to find my father."

Miriam snorted. "Now? After all this time?"

"Yeah, now," Isabelle confirmed. She wondered if they'd have the rest of this conversation on the porch steps.

"You've left it a little late, don't you think?"

Isabelle did not answer that but said instead, "I'm here now."

"Yes, you are."

It was like a showdown. Neither woman budged, and they seemed to be at a stalemate. But Isabelle was a patient woman and could outwait just about anyone.

Finally, Miriam gave a put-upon sigh and opened the door. "Then I guess you better come in."

Following her, Isabelle allowed herself an indulgent smile. To cross the threshold of Miriam's home was a huge success. The woman ahead of her smelled of laundry detergent and body odor. Isabelle looked around as she followed her aunt inside her home. The enclosed front porch was stacked with newspapers and books and magazines. There was nowhere to sit on the furniture as it was all occupied by reading material.

Was her aunt a hoarder? She followed her inside to a living room. Beyond it was a dining room and at the back of the house, a kitchen.

There was a faint hint of disinfectant about the place, and it didn't appear as cluttered as the front porch.

As if reading her mind, Miriam said, "I like to keep newspapers and magazines for future reference. But I don't like clutter. If I don't want to deal with it, I put it on the porch, out of sight."

Isabelle wondered if this applied to Miriam's life in general.

Miriam sat in a recliner parked in front of a large wall-mounted flat-screen television. A table stood to the right of the recliner, and it held an assortment of medical equipment including a nebulizer, a couple of inhalers, and various medication bottles. There was also a box of tissues. At her feet was a small wastebasket that overflowed with used tissues.

When Miriam sat down, she picked up her nasal cannula and slipped it around her ears, parking the prongs in her nostrils. Behind the recliner, an oxygen concentrator sounded a low hum.

"Do you smoke, Isabelle?" she asked.

Isabelle shook her head.

"Good, because this is what happens when you smoke. You destroy your lungs," Miriam said. "But don't feel sorry for me as I've got no one to blame but myself." Her voice was loud in the small space.

Isabelle had nothing to add to that.

"Clear a space off the sofa and sit down," Miriam directed.

On the sofa were stacks of magazines and newspapers, indicating she didn't get a lot of visitors. Isabelle lifted one of the stacks at the end of the sofa, set it on the coffee table, and sat down. She sank so far into the cushions her feet lifted off the ground.

Miriam chortled. "You picked the wrong side."

Isabelle laughed too. "I guess I did." She remedied the problem by inching closer to the edge of the sofa and leaning forward.

A striped feline strolled in from the other room and meowed loudly.

"That's Roxie, pay no attention to her. She's just nosy."

The cat jumped up on the recliner, getting comfortable on the arm of the chair, never taking her eyes off Isabelle. Miriam stroked the cat's back and asked, "All right, what would you like to know?"

Isabelle didn't know where to start and she said with a shrug, "Anything. Where my father is, why he left. What his childhood was like."

"You want the unabridged version then?"

Isabelle nodded and smiled. "If you don't mind."

"It's not that I mind, I just don't know what good it will do," Miriam said. "Sometimes, it's best to leave things as they are."

"Dad leaving us affected my whole life," Isabelle said.

"As our father leaving affected us," Miriam countered.

Isabelle had heard that her father was raised by a single mother, but the details were sketchy. Her own mother had not been forthcoming, either due to lack of knowledge or because she'd decided it wasn't important. It was too late to ask her now.

"I'd offer you something to drink, but all I have is Ensure," Miriam said.

"Don't worry about it," Isabelle said. "Do you know where my father is?"

Miriam answered with a question. "Why is it so important that you find your father now?"

"I would like some closure."

"That's one of the most overrated words in the English language if ever there was one," Miriam replied. She continued stroking her cat.

"I feel like there are certain aspects of my life that are closed off because of my father leaving us," Isabelle explained.

"Like what?"

"For one thing, I never married or had children."

"Neither did I."

"I don't know if that was by choice or if it was a subconscious block," Isabelle said.

"You know what I think, Isabelle?"

"No, what?"

"I think you think too much," Miriam said. "I think you should move on with your life and take the good with the bad."

"That's what Lily thinks too."

"She sounds sensible," Miriam said.

Isabelle shrugged. "Maybe. But I can't move on."

Miriam had no answer for that.

"Is my father still alive?"

Miriam hesitated, and Isabelle wondered if she was holding something back.

"To my knowledge, he is."

"Do you keep in touch with him?"

"Not really," Miriam said, and she looked away. She hadn't said no, and Isabelle was buoyed by that. "Dave and I were never really close. Our own father left us when we were young—maybe there's a gene there for paternal abandonment or you live what you learn—and the two of us spent our time vying for our mother's attention, what little she had to give."

It all sounded sad.

"Do you know why he left us?" Isabelle pressed.

Miriam shook her head. "I was as surprised as you were. Like I said, we weren't close. He would not have confided in me."

"How was life growing up for the two of you?"

"Being raised by a single mother on welfare was not ideal. Sometimes, I think our mother resented our existence. We surely held her back. She could have taken off too, as she reminded us several times, but Dad beat her to it and she was left to raise two kids by herself."

No matter how torn up Isabelle felt about their father leaving, at least she knew their mother had never resented them. Nancy Reynolds Monroe tried and did her best.

"Do you have any idea where he is?"

Miriam shook her head. "No. There was a time I thought he'd gone up to Buffalo, but I really don't know. I can't picture him anywhere else but here."

Funny, Isabelle thought. She pictured her father everywhere else but Hideaway Bay. But the city was only an hour away, and there would have been work there. Although a long shot, it might be a possibility. "Any connection to Buffalo?" she asked.

Miriam shrugged, the oxygen concentrator behind her humming along and giving out rhythmic, short puffs.

Feeling discouraged, Isabelle asked, "Would you have any photos of my father? When he was younger . . . before he left?"

Miriam rolled her eyes. "You would want to see photos." She huffed and said, "I'd have to find them. If I do, I'll give you a call." She rooted around for a piece of paper and a pen for Isabelle, who stood to take them.

Isabelle scribbled down her phone number and handed it back.

"Are you still at the house on Star Shine Drive?" Miriam asked, looking up from the piece of paper.

"I—we are. The three of us inherited the house when Gram died."

"I saw her obit in the paper. Dave said she was always decent to him." Suddenly, Miriam said, "Can you show yourself out?"

"Um, sure," Isabelle said, standing.

"Please lock the door behind you." Miriam picked up her remote and turned on the television.

"All right, thanks, anyway," Halfway to the front door, Isabelle stopped, turned, and asked, "Would it be all right if I stopped in to see you from time to time?"

Miriam regarded her for a moment and then screwed up her face. "That's probably not a good idea. Why start something now?"

"Of course. Best of luck, Miriam," Isabelle said, walking hurriedly to the front door.

"Yeah, you too," Miriam said without looking at her.

It was curious that her aunt had no interest in Isabelle or her sisters. She hadn't even asked about them. A memory of Gram came to mind. No matter where she was in the world, Isabelle stayed in touch with her grandmother, even more so after the death of her mother and Granddad. And Gram would tell her everything that was going on in Hideaway Bay and want to know all about Isabelle's work and travels. She'd been curious about people and things, and liked nothing more than to stay up-to-date on her granddaughters' lives, especially as they all lived out of town.

Isabelle left without looking over her shoulder. She pulled the door shut behind her, twisting the handle to make sure it was locked.

A dead end.

CHAPTER FOURTEEN

1963

Barb

The cherry blossoms were in full bloom as Barb made her way to class, her mind elsewhere. The sun dappled the trees, throwing darts of sunlight and shade over the sidewalk. She hugged her books to her chest and tilted her face up slightly to feel the weak warmth of the sun. This was her last class of the day, and when she returned to her dorm room, she could put a big "X" on the calendar. One more day down, one more day closer to the semester being finished. And then she could go home for the summer.

Despite the prospect of being reunited with Junie and Thelma, returning home was fraught with its own problems. First, Junie and Thelma had seriously busy lives. Junie worked at the drugstore and was planning her wedding to Paul

Reynolds in the fall. Thelma worked full time in the cardboard box factory and was seeing someone named Bobby Milligan, although Barb didn't know how serious that was. Also, she spent most of her summer in Hideaway Bay. Her best friends were hardly in a position to entertain her all summer either in the city or at the beach.

Second, the rift between her and her mother had never properly closed since that day when Barb had asked to return home. Her mother seemed to resent the fact that Barb had not settled in and had not had the wonderful college experience she'd had. It was as if they were standing on opposite sides of a chasm that neither could cross or get around. She wondered what it would take to close it, or if it could be closed at all.

Resentment was a funny thing. It simmered just below the surface, not acknowledged, yet brewing, steeping into something much stronger, like a grudge.

Her thoughts were interrupted by a crowd of students gathered around the corkboard of notices posted in the main hall. There was a buzz of excitement. Curious, she elbowed her way through them to see what the big deal was. She edged her way closer until she could read the notices. There were the usual ones about summer internships and available jobs, but then a headline in bold, typewritten print caught her eye:

Would you like to work in New York City for the summer?

She scanned the advertisement, her lips moving silently as she read the posting. It was for a paid internship for an advertising company during the summer months, and it included room and board at a local women's hotel. She stepped back and cast a furtive glance around, studying the reaction of the other girls. No one seemed to be scribbling down the number and the address posted at the bottom of the page.

A few girls giggled—although Barb didn't see what was so funny—but some sniffed and lifted their noses a bit higher, and others shrugged and kept on walking. Her contemporaries did not need jobs; they were in receipt of hefty allowances from trust funds. And even Barb had her own money, but it was the thought of working in New York City that excited her. She'd gone on several trips there with her mother to visit two of her mother's sorority sisters over the years. The trips had revolved around shopping, visits to the Metropolitan Museum of Art during the day, tickets to Broadway plays in the evening, and expensive lunches and dinners.

She mulled it over as she went to class. The idea excited her. Living in New York City for the summer? How could it not? But her mother would never allow it, and her father would go along with whatever her mother suggested. Quietly, she seethed at the thought of it. *I'm twenty, she really can't tell me what to do anymore.*

As the bell rang, she hurried to her class and slipped in with a gaggle of loud girls ahead of her. She took the seat nearest to the door.

"Barbara Walsh, would you mind running this down to the office and mimeographing it for me?" Mr. Lange asked, holding up a sheet of paper. "I seem to have misplaced my copies." To add emphasis, he patted the pockets on his sweater vest, though Barb highly doubted they'd be found there.

She stood, leaving her books and purse behind, and took the sheet from Mr. Lange, exiting the classroom and walking down the hallway. She loved the school like this: the hallway empty, its floor polished to a sheen so that the daylight cast a thin band of shine down the middle of it like a narrow river. Her shoes echoed along the cool corridor. At the far end, the doors were wide open, and a light breeze blew through.

Halfway to the office, she paused at the corkboard and reread the notice. She untacked it from the board, thinking she'd copy it at the office, but Pearl Gasson, the secretary, was the nosy type, and she'd want to know exactly what Barb was copying. Barb glanced up the hallway and then down. Satisfied that she was alone, she folded up the advertisement and tucked it safely into the pocket of her cardigan. She carried on to the office, humming "It Might as Well Be Spring" from the film *State Fair*.

Later that evening, Barb waited for Bunny to go to the student lounge before she sat down at her typewriter, a gift from her father. Bunny only said, "Bye," as she sailed out the door. She no longer asked Barb to join her as Barb's answer was always no. In the beginning, she'd tried to fit in with the other girls, but she felt out of place and lost, as if they had nothing in common. She was lonely and missed Junie and Thelma. She never thought she'd say she missed Thelma, but there it was. At least Thelma was real. You got what you saw. Over the last two years, Barb had spent her time at the library, in her room listening to albums, or walking the campus during the daytime.

She waited ten minutes before pulling out a sheet of onionskin paper for the typewriter. If Bunny was going to return, it was usually within ten minutes of leaving, coming back to pick up a lipstick or a sweater if she thought the air was cool.

Carefully, Barb typed up her curriculum vitae, leaning back in the chair and frowning at one point, thinking it was woefully inadequate. She'd never worked anywhere, never even babysat as a teenager, and she was only halfway through college. She tried not to be discouraged and after a long sigh of resignation, she finished what she'd started, rereading her CV and her cover letter several times, making sure there were no mistakes and that it was perfect. Satisfied, she pulled the sheet out of the typewriter, added it to the CV, and folded them into a trifold before tucking them neatly into a business envelope. She slid the top drawer open, pulled out a stamp, and adhered it to the envelope. In her neat scrawl, she addressed it and put her own name and return address at the school in the upper left-hand corner.

She stood, smiling, the letter in her hand, and pulled on her cardigan for the quick walk to the mailbox in front of the main office. The night air was cool, and she walked briskly to the main administration building. She looked up at the night sky, sighing at the swath of bright stars, and wondered if somewhere in the world, the love of her life was glancing up at the same sky.

She kissed the back of the envelope for good luck before she dropped it into the chute of the mailbox. Feeling more hopeful than she had in a long time, she walked back to her dorm room, smiling and humming a tune.

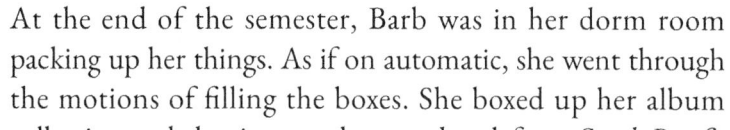

At the end of the semester, Barb was in her dorm room packing up her things. As if on automatic, she went through the motions of filling the boxes. She boxed up her album collection, only leaving out the soundtrack from *South Pacific* as she was listening to that one again.

Bunny sailed through the room, her ponytail flying behind her. When Barb had first met her, she had a bob, but had quickly tired of it. She was packed up and ready to go spend her summer in the Hamptons at her boyfriend's summer home.

"Someone is in a good mood," Bunny said, collapsing on her bed, her legs hanging over the end of it. "I can't wait for this semester to be over with. What a drag!"

Barb smiled benignly at her.

Bunny eyed her and frowned. "*Why* are you in such a good mood?"

Barb shrugged, not wanting to share her good news with her. She'd received a letter from Welch, Stine, and Cross advertising in New York City stating they'd be delighted to offer her the position for the summer. After three weeks of no response, she'd kind of given up on it, a fog of malaise settling around her at the thought of returning to Buffalo and being holed up all summer with her mother.

But New York City! This would be an adventure, and she couldn't wait. Initially, she thought she'd go home and tell her parents her plan for the summer but after careful consideration, she realized once she stepped foot in the house on Coolidge Avenue, she wouldn't be going anywhere.

There were all sorts of instructions in the letter along with the addresses of the workplace and the women's hotel. There was also a telephone number to arrange transportation. Barb planned to call them on the pay phone in the outer hall first thing in the morning and arrange train fare. As soon as her last exam was over, she'd head to the city. It wasn't that far by train.

Within minutes, Bunny was dozing on her bed. She did this, nodded off wherever she stopped. Probably because she kept such late hours studying and doing homework.

While her roommate slept, Barb snuck off to the hall and dialed her parents' phone number. She'd rather not do this on a public phone, but she had no other choice; it wasn't like she had a phone in her room. No matter how unpleasant the conversation was going to be, she would tell her parents she wasn't coming home for the summer.

It was answered on the third ring.

"Dr. Walsh's residence," Agnes said in her nasal voice.

"Hi, Agnes, it's Barb."

"Hello, Barb," Agnes said. "Everything all right? It's unusual for you to call on an afternoon."

Barb knew her mother would not appreciate the housekeeper hearing her news first, so she replied, "Everything's fine. I'd like to talk to Mother or Father if they're around." Her voice came out sounding higher-pitched than she would have liked.

"Your father isn't home yet, but I'll get your mother," Agnes said and set the phone down, the sound of her footsteps receding through the house traveling down the phone line.

Barb had hoped to catch her father, but maybe it was best to tell her mother and get it over with. Even if she spoke to her father, she'd still have to contend with her mother. She drew in a deep breath and held it.

"Barbara, this is a pleasant surprise," her mother said brightly.

"Hello, Mother," Barb started. "How are you?"

"I'm well, thank you," she replied. "Agnes and I have your room all ready for your return."

"Yes, that's what I wanted to talk to you about," Barb said.

"Oh?"

"I've been offered a paid internship at an advertising agency in New York City for the summer," Barb said. She tried to convey enthusiasm in her voice instead of the dread that filled her at having to tell her mother. Her voice shook as she spoke. She squeezed her eyes shut, trying to control the tremor.

"What?" her mother asked. Barb could picture her standing in the heavily wallpapered front hall with its black-and-white harlequin tile floor and gilt mirror. Those two lines would furrow between her eyebrows, she'd pale slightly, and she'd place her hand with its smooth, pink-polished oval nails against her throat.

Barb repeated what she'd said, her heart hammering against her chest, waiting for the backlash.

"Oh, Barbara," her mother finally said. "I don't think so. We don't *do* paid internships."

And Barb could imagine her mother scrunching up her nose as if there were a bad odor lingering in the room. For her mother, the purpose of her daughter going to college was to catch a successful husband. But for Barb, the purpose was to read more books and become more educated.

Barb summoned her courage and said, "I've already told them I'd take the position. I'll be heading to New York after my last exam."

"You've already told them? I don't recall you discussing this with your father or me," her mother pointed out.

It was her tone that irritated Barb. It always had: entitled and expecting to be obeyed at every turn.

"I'm over eighteen now," Barb said coolly. Technically and legally, she did not have to heed her mother's command. Just because she'd always been the dutiful daughter in the past didn't mean that she had to continue that into her future. She could think of nothing less desirable than living her life on other people's terms, or worse, their expectations.

"We'll discuss it when you come home," her mother said with a hint of finality that indicated the topic was closed. For *her*.

After Barb hung up, she held onto the receiver in the pay phone's cradle, seething. She was tired of being the obedient daughter and living her life as her mother expected. She was not going to meet the love of her life in her hometown. If that were so, she would have met him by now.

When she pivoted on her heel, she came face to face with two girls whom she knew by sight and who were freshmen at the school. Without taking their eyes off Barb, they huddled and covered their mouths with their hands, whispering and sniggering.

Barb rolled her eyes and headed back to her room, anxious to get out of there and as far away as possible.

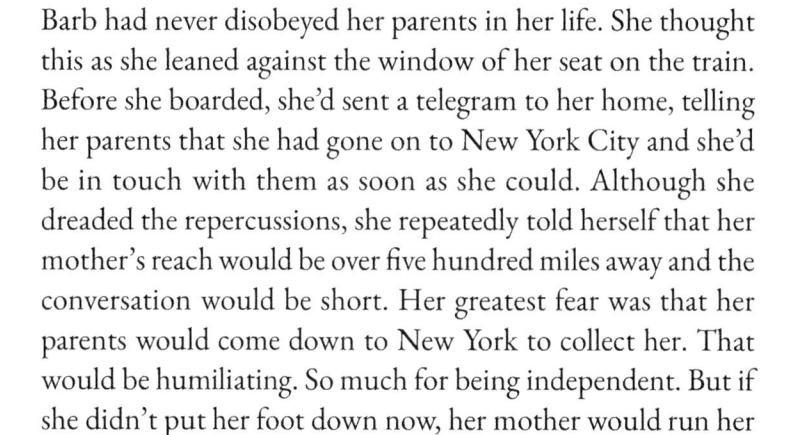

Barb had never disobeyed her parents in her life. She thought this as she leaned against the window of her seat on the train. Before she boarded, she'd sent a telegram to her home, telling her parents that she had gone on to New York City and she'd be in touch with them as soon as she could. Although she dreaded the repercussions, she repeatedly told herself that her mother's reach would be over five hundred miles away and the conversation would be short. Her greatest fear was that her parents would come down to New York to collect her. That would be humiliating. So much for being independent. But if she didn't put her foot down now, her mother would run her life for the rest of it.

Her belongings had been stored in cargo, which she had to pay extra for. It hadn't been too much of a drain; after all, the company had paid the train fare.

The previous evening, with all her worldly possessions packed up and ready to go, she'd called Thelma. Not Junie but Thelma. Junie probably wouldn't know what to say, but Thelma would give it to her straight.

"I'll be a son of a gun," Thelma had said when Barb told her of her plans. After she recovered, she said, "And your parents went along with this?"

Barb traced her finger along the side of the pay phone in the corridor of the women's dorm. "No, not really. They think I'm coming home. My mother didn't want me to take the job."

"Barbara Walsh, you dark horse, you," Thelma said. Barb could practically see her friend shaking her head and grinning.

"Do you think I'm making a mistake?"

Thelma didn't hesitate. "Not if it's what you want to do."

"But is it the right thing to do?" Barb asked as doubt crept in.

"Only you can be the judge of that," Thelma replied. "If you're going to New York because you want adventure and an opportunity, fine. But if you're going to spite your parents, you'll be miserable."

"When did you become so wise?" Barb asked with a laugh.

Thelma snorted. "It comes with life experience." Her voice faded away.

"Is everything all right, Thelma?"

"I don't know," Thelma said, but then she added with urgency, "Nothing that needs to be discussed right now. Look, Barb, you've got to live your own life. Do you think I want to spend the rest of my life cooking and cleaning for my father and my brothers? Not on your life!"

This led Barb to inquire after Thelma's boyfriend. "How's Bobby?"

She could practically hear the shrug down the line. "Oh, the same. He's all right."

When Thelma didn't elaborate, Barb dropped the subject.

"Look, Barb, only you know what will make you happy. You're not a kid anymore," Thelma said, her voice gruff.

They spoke for a few more minutes before Thelma ended the call with: "Send me a postcard from New York!"

Barb would miss her friends, but she wanted to do this one thing. She'd be back at college in September. After replaying the conversation in her mind, she felt more confident about her decision. If her parents didn't like it, there was nothing she could do about it. All she knew was she was spending her summer in New York City. She wanted something totally different from Buffalo, Hideaway Bay, or college. And this was it.

Chapter Fifteen

Isabelle

The arrival of warmer weather did nothing to dispel the pall that had settled around Isabelle after her visit with Miriam Monroe. She'd thought for sure her aunt would impart to her some nugget of wisdom or at least an address. She remained spiky and snappish, and it resulted in Lily and Alice giving her a wide berth.

"Why don't you go for a swim?" Lily suggested one morning before she left for work.

Isabelle scoffed. "It's a little cold."

"The lake might be chilly, but the air is warm. It won't be long before the water warms up," Lily said brightly.

Her sister might be trying to distract her or, worse, cheer her up, but Isabelle wouldn't budge. "No thanks."

"Since when has Isabelle Monroe been afraid of anything?" Lily asked, hands on her hips. Charlie circled her, whining, anxious to leave. Lily looked down at him and said, "Hold on, bud."

"Who said anything about being afraid?" Isabelle shot back. "And what does me not wanting to go swimming have to do with it?"

"Then what's the problem?" Lily pushed.

Isabelle looked pointedly at the clock. "Aren't you going to be late for work?"

"I make my own hours."

When Isabelle offered nothing to further the conversation, Lily said, "Come on, a little cold water is nothing to you. You've trekked across deserts and climbed mountains."

"Okay, I get the drift, I'll think about it," was all Isabelle could promise.

"Great, I look forward to hearing all about your first swim of the year when I get home tonight."

"Yeah, can't wait," Isabelle said sarcastically.

Lily laughed as she headed out the door with Charlie following her.

The truth was, Isabelle should be heading out of Hideaway Bay by now but since her visit with Miriam, she'd remained inert, unable to get moving. And the way she reacted with her sisters reinforced her belief that she operated best as a solitary creature.

She took her coffee out on the porch and sat down, looking around. It was hard for her to believe that she and her sisters owned this house. Isabelle had never wanted to be tied down by ownership of anything. Everywhere she traveled, she relied on public transportation, a rental bike, or her own two feet.

As she sipped her coffee, she took in the sad state of the flower beds in front of the house. *What would a homeowner do*? She glanced around, looking at other projects to be done. She wondered how Gram had kept up with it all.

After she finished her coffee, she carried her cup inside and rinsed out the dregs in the sink before loading it into the dishwasher. She just might go for a swim. It was too early in the season to swim in the evening, but the beach wouldn't be too crowded at this time of day.

She went upstairs, tidying up as she went, straightening the newspapers and magazines on the coffee table. She dug out her swimsuit from the bottom drawer of her dresser and tugged it on. After gathering her sunglasses, a beach towel, and a bottle of sunscreen, she threw the stuff into a straw bag. The last thing she did before she left her bedroom was to pull a sundress over her head. She darted down the staircase and went out the front door, closing it behind her and checking to make sure it was locked. She threw the house key into her bag and headed across the street.

The sun was hot, and she hoped the lake wasn't too cold. She looked around at the strip of brown sand that ran as far as the eye could see. The lake was a wide, shimmery stripe of blue. The horizon was clear and bright, and the shoreline of Canada was visible. The beach was all but deserted. There were a few walkers, some by themselves, some with friends, most of them retired and elderly. One mom had set up her beach chair in the sand while her two toddlers played on a blanket beneath a blue-and-red striped umbrella.

Isabelle set her stuff down on the sand, her towel draped carefully over her bag. She stood and stared out at the lake. Maybe Lily was right, maybe a swim would perk her up. She pulled her sundress over her head, folded it up, and stuffed it into her bag.

She tucked her hair behind her ears, donned her swim goggles, and stepped forward toward the shore. At the edge, she braced herself for the possibility that the water might be frigid. She was pleasantly surprised when it wasn't. Although cold, it was tolerable.

She walked further into the lake until she was waist-deep, and immediately the tension rolled off her body and she was reminded why she loved the water so much. Miriam came to mind, along with the ensuing let-down she'd felt afterwards having learned that her aunt had no information on her father and that she did not want to pursue a relationship with Isabelle or her sisters. When Lily and Alice had asked how the meeting went, she'd shrugged and said, "Just as you'd expect. She had no information on Dad." She didn't share with them her bitter disappointment as she didn't want to deal with their looks of sympathy or hear an "I told you so." She kept it to herself and licked her wounds in private, as the saying went.

Unable to resist, she dove into the murky water, letting that first exhilarating rush envelop her. She swam a few strokes, her body rotating gently side to side so she could lift her head out of the water and take a breath. After a half hour of this, she felt pleasantly exhausted and rolled over onto her back and floated, her arms out, looking up at the white orb of sun in the bright blue sky. It was a beautiful day. The water lapped gently at her ears and around her, the sounds from the beach and the cries of the gulls overhead became muffled. The only noises were the sounds of her breathing and her heartbeat. As she drifted, her body felt languid and relaxed. She observed any thoughts that came to her like clouds floating by in the sky, and that included any thoughts about her father. After a while, the cold that was at first invigorating became uncomfortable, and she swiveled onto her front and swam back to shore.

As she emerged from the lake, she spotted a group of elementary school children with their teacher, a man around her own age. She thought he looked familiar, but she couldn't be sure. He was on his haunches not far from Isabelle's belongings and the children, a group of twenty-five or so, were circled around him. He showed them something and explained it to them, but Isabelle couldn't see what was in his hand or hear what he said.

When he spotted her, he did a double-take as if he'd recognized her as well, and the children's gazes followed his, landing on her.

To the kids, he said, "And this, class, is a prime example of a modern-day mermaid." He wore a grin as he stood and placed his hands on his hips.

All the kids giggled, some clamping a hand over their mouth.

With a nod toward the group, Isabelle said, "I see they're easily amused."

"They're out of the classroom, so that helps."

She nodded.

One of the kids, a girl about nine, shielded her eyes against the bright afternoon sun and looked up at Isabelle with one eye closed. "She doesn't look like a mermaid. Where's her tail?"

"I forgot it," Isabelle said quickly.

"Some mermaid," muttered another child.

"Tough crowd," she said to the teacher.

He shrugged, his palms up, a gesture of defeat. "Sorry."

"No problem," Isabelle said. She picked up her belongings and headed in the direction of the house. Lily had been right; the swim had done her good. Closer to the sidewalk, she spread out her beach towel on the sand and sat on it to dry off a little bit. She leaned back, supporting her weight on her arms stretched out behind her. Surreptitiously, she watched the teacher with the students off in the distance.

The man seemed a natural with the kids. Sometimes he gestured wildly, or his voice was loud, bits carrying over to Isabelle, and the kids laughed. When they weren't giggling and guffawing, they were outright rapt, hanging on every word he said.

After twenty minutes, he gathered his students, told them to stick together, and led them along the beach toward the boardwalk, which would take them back to town and to the elementary school. She studied his form in his jeans and T-shirt. *My teachers didn't look like that when I was attending school.*

When the teacher and his students were out of sight, Isabelle stood, picked up her beach towel, and shook it out. She draped it over one arm and carried her bag with her belongings in the other. The house was directly across the street, the walk back short. She realized she was smiling, and she thought the swim, the students, and the beach had been a good distraction. However, by the time she reached the front porch, her thoughts had drifted back to her long-lost father. Even though Miriam had been no help, Isabelle thought she might hang around in Hideaway Bay a little bit longer as she was still determined to find him. How hard could it be to find someone, even if they were dead or didn't want to be found. Most of her blog posts and the articles she wrote on commission involved intensive research, and this would be no different.

Feeling better about her decision, she took another look at the flower beds in front of the house. If she was going to be staying, she might as well clean up the garden. She went upstairs to change, deciding a trip to the nursery was in order.

Chapter Sixteen

Summer 1963

Barb

Barb's parents hit the roof when she finally made contact with them. The journey on the train had been long and sweaty. She'd taken a cab to the women's hotel and was escorted to a room and told she'd have a roommate within two days. She planned to relish having the room to herself until her roommate showed up.

The hotel was quiet. The matron had informed her that most of the residents were either at work or out for the afternoon. Barb dumped her items in her room and headed to the communal bathroom at the end of the hall. She wanted to take a quick bath to freshen up after the train ride. After, she puttered around her room, removing items from her suitcase and hanging them up in the shared closet. She took half of the hangers, leaving the rest for her roommate. Having first pick of the beds, she chose the one by the window. As the afternoon lengthened, she realized she was putting off the inevitable and finally, realizing she'd want to make that phone call before everyone returned to the hotel, she made her way down the hall to the pay phone, her legs as heavy as lead. She slipped her coin into the slot and dialed her home phone number, slowly as if she had trouble remembering it.

Her mother answered on the first ring.

"Mother?"

"Barbara? Where are you?" her mother demanded.

"I'm at the Abigail Adams Hotel for Women in Manhattan," Barb replied as if her mother had asked about the weather.

"The Abigail Adams Hotel for Women in Manhattan," her mother repeated. "Don't go anywhere. We'll wire you the money to get the next train home."

Barb squeezed her eyes shut. But she found her voice and said, "No, I'm not coming home. I'm staying here for the summer, I already told you that." Her teeth clenched.

"You can't stay in New York City by yourself. It's no place for a young woman."

"Mother, I'm in a nice neighborhood, and I've got a job within walking distance."

"This is all nonsense. Stop dreaming and wake up," her mother said.

"I'm not dreaming," Barb said. "I'm living it. I'm going to do this, and you can't stop me."

"Don't be so foolish, Barbara Walsh. You'll come home right away, and we'll talk no more about it."

"I will not," Barb said, her voice rising. She had never raised her voice to her parents before. Her mother went quiet. Barb wasn't sure if she'd gone into shock or had laid down the phone and walked away.

She was about to hang up when her mother finally spoke. "Here, I'll put your father on."

She heard her mother say to her father, "You try. She won't listen to reason."

The sound of Dr. Walsh grappling with the phone came next.

"Barbara, what on earth is going on with you? Have you lost all sense of reason?" he demanded.

In her life, she'd never heard her father so angry. Her mother, yes, but not her father. He was always calm.

"You've scared us half to death traipsing down to the city. Have you no regard for your safety?" he demanded.

It upset her that she'd angered her father. Only then did she realize maybe her plan wasn't so great. But her father continued to speak.

"To be honest, Barbara, I'm disappointed in you," he said quietly.

Barb's chin quivered. Her father had never said those words to her. The thought that he thought a little less of her today than he had yesterday left her feeling squeamish and sick to her stomach.

"Why didn't you talk to us about it?" he said. 'The three of us could have sat down like grown-ups and discussed it."

Deep-seated fury welled up in her, and she snorted. "Really? I asked Mother about it last week and she said no. Would we discuss it like we did two years ago when I wanted to return to Buffalo to go to college?" On a roll now, she continued bitterly, "There would have been no discussion. You and mother would have told me no. This time, I made my own decision."

"Even though we disagree and disapprove?" he asked.

She let out a deep breath. "Dad, I want to do this. You can't stop me."

Her father didn't say anything for a moment and when he did, he sounded weary and resigned. "No, we can't."

In the background, Mrs. Walsh squawked about how they had to do something, how they had to go to New York City to retrieve their daughter. Barb pictured her father frowning and waving her mother off as she'd seen him do before.

"All right, stay there," he said. "but you'll call us the moment you want to come home. There's no shame if it doesn't work out."

Mrs. Walsh's volume in the background increased. Dr. Walsh ignored it and said, "I'll expect you to ring us a few times a week, Barbara. You promise me that you'll keep in touch. You'll write us a letter tonight with the address and phone numbers of your hotel and your place of employment. And you'll post this first thing in the morning. Understood?"

"Yes, Dad," she said, a smile breaking out on her face.

"And no more curveballs again like this one," he said finally.

"What about Mother?" she asked, her smile faltering.

Her father exhaled heavily. "Don't worry about that."

Barb said goodbye, relieved that she didn't have to speak to her mother again, and she practically skipped back to her room. For the first time in her life, she felt like she might have some power.

Barb settled into her paid internship at the Welch, Stine, and Cross advertising agency. She worked in the accounts department, where the two other employees spent their time wooing and keeping clients. She discovered she liked working, and even more than that, she liked receiving a wage. The routine and structure gave her a sense of purpose, a sense of doing something instead of waiting around for something to happen.

And she adored the Abigail Adams Hotel for Women. Most of the women, if not all of them, came from other parts of the country and worked in Manhattan. During the day, the residents of the hotel were gone, except for Sheila, who worked three to eleven as a telephone operator for Bell Telephone. In the evening, they'd open the doors to their rooms and amble back and forth between them. As Barb had a record player and a stack of vinyl albums, she provided the music. Gloria, who worked in the typing pool for a big multinational company, loved to do hair and nails, and most of the girls wandered in and out of her room, two doors down from Barb's. Judith, who was the tallest of them at six feet and with a towering beehive of brunette hair, always managed to smuggle in some alcohol.

And that's where Barb currently found herself, in Judith's room at the end of the hall, as far away from the elevator as possible. Someone always watched the elevator in case the matron or the night watchman should come stepping out of it.

"What can I get you, sugar?" Judith asked. She was from the south—Barb couldn't remember if it was Mississippi or Alabama—and she always called everyone some variation on 'sugar' or 'honey' or 'sweetie pie.' She was in her mid-twenties. Up close, she was quite pretty with a little nose, Cupid's bow lips, and eyes as dark as sapphires.

"Um, gee, I don't know," Barb said. She'd gone to one party at a frat house where alcohol flowed like a raging river, but she had never been one to partake.

"Leave it to me then, honey," Judith said as she mixed whiskey, sugar, lemon juice, and an egg white into a blender and pressed the start button. The machine whirred for about twenty seconds until Judith pressed stop. She lifted the glass pitcher off its base and poured the contents into two juice glasses.

"Now just a little bit, sugar pie. You don't look like much of a drinker, and we don't want you to get knocked on your tush," Judith said, handing Barb a glass.

"Thank you." Barb sipped it tentatively. It was frothy with a lemony taste. She liked it.

Judith took her drink and sipped liberally. With a nod, she said, "Sit down and tell me everything."

"Oh, okay," Barb said, unsure of what that meant.

She sat at the foot of the bed. Judith was the only one who didn't have a roommate. Barb wondered how she managed that. When questioned, Judith claimed she was a terrible snorer because of a deviated septum, and Barb made a mental note to ask her father about that. Barb's own roommate, a girl from Michigan, had terrible body odor. They had not hit it off. Not because of the other girl's lack of hygiene but because of her general surliness.

"Where you from, sugar?" Judith asked.

"Buffalo," Barb said, taking a bigger sip from her drink. "Um, what is this? It's delicious."

"A whiskey sour." Judith eyed her over her own glass. "Buffalo, Wyoming?"

Barb shook her head, licking froth off her lips. "No, Buffalo, New York."

Judith threw her head back and laughed. "Oh my goodness, I got that wrong. Somehow, I couldn't picture you out west with a bunch of cowpats. You seem too cultured for that." She regarded Barb thoughtfully. "What are you doing here in Manhattan, a working girl and all? I can picture you getting a four-year degree at a women's college then marrying someone with a future and Daddy's money."

Barb laughed, but at the same time she was disappointed that she was so easy to read and did not retain an air of mystery like Jackie Kennedy.

"Actually, I'm here on a paid internship. I go to college in Vermont. I'm only here for the summer."

"Where are you doing your internship?" Judith crossed one slim ankle over the other. She rested her left hand on the bed and held her cocktail in her right hand.

"I'm over at Welch, Stine, and Cross."

"And what is it they do?"

"Advertising," Barb said, finishing her drink.

"Want another?" Judith asked with a nod as she stood.

"Please, if it's not too much trouble," Barb said, handing her the glass.

"No trouble at all, sugar," Judith said easily. She made another round of whiskey sours and topped off their glasses before returning to the desk chair.

"These are delicious," Barb said truthfully. Drinking a cocktail after a day's work made her feel all grown up.

"Now tell me about this job of yours," Judith instructed.

"I'm an intern in the accounts department," Barb said.

"Is that so? I work at the Wendell Corporation, and we're looking for a new advertising agency to do business with. The last agency didn't work out. Their campaigns flopped." She scrunched up her nose at this.

Barb's eyes grew wide at the mention of the Wendell Corporation. They were a big national company, although what they did she wasn't sure. "What do you do there?" Barb asked.

"A little bit of this and a little bit of that," Judith said evasively with a bright smile that felt forced to Barb. "But I'm friendly with the boss."

Her last sentence implied a whole lot more than what Barb was used to.

"Look, why don't I have my boss call your department to set up a meeting?" Judith suggested before Barb could examine too closely the implications of her previous sentence.

"That would be great," Barb said. Judith handed her a scrap of paper, and Barb scribbled down her direct extension.

After she finished her drink, she declined another, thinking she was pleasantly buzzed and would leave it at that. Besides, she had to get back to her room to change the album. She knew her roommate wouldn't do it.

The following day at work, after Barb returned from lunch, her phone rang and when she picked it up, a man barked into the phone. "This is Wyler Wendell from the Wendell Corporation. I'm looking for Barbara Walsh."

"That's me," she said.

"Judith McCreary referred you to me. Said you work in the accounts department at Welch, Stine, and Cross."

"That's right."

"Can I speak to your boss?"

"The accounts manager?"

"That would be the one."

"One moment, please." She put the phone call on hold and ran to her manager's office. Her boss, Ger, was in a meeting with another member of their department, Sal. Both looked up at her when she rapped quickly on the doorframe, a little breathless, her heart a rapid drumbeat.

"Barb, I told you not to disturb us," Ger said. He sat behind his desk, leaning back in his chair until he was almost horizontal with the floor.

"I'm sorry, but I've got Mr. Wyler Wendell from the Wendell Corporation on the phone, and he wants to speak to you."

Both Ger and Sal jumped up. "Why didn't you say so? Transfer him immediately to my office phone."

Barb transferred the call, praying that she didn't disconnect Mr. Wendell in the process. Ger took the call, gave Barb a thumbs-up, and remained standing. When Judith had said she'd put her boss in touch, Barb had thought she was only being polite. She didn't think she'd actually do it. She was kind of excited. It was a big company. And with big companies came big ad campaigns and lots of money. That much she had learned in her short time with the agency.

She tried to keep busy, but her gaze was riveted to Ger's office, where the door had been closed by Sal, who remained inside. Through the glass window, Barb could see that Ger was still on the phone. She forced herself to concentrate on her work. Fifteen minutes later, she heard hooting and hollering, and her attention was pulled to the office. Ger was laughing and shook Sal's hand, and they were congratulating each other with slaps on the back. Barb smiled to herself. The door was flung open, and Ger made his way over to Barb's desk.

"Barb, you beautiful blonde angel! Do you realize what you've done?" he asked. His broad grin stretched across his face.

Barb thought he seemed effusive, but the question indicated wrongdoing.

"That was Wyler Wendell," Ger marveled. Barb didn't want to say she knew that as she had answered the phone. She waited. "We've been trying for eighteen months to get a meeting with this guy, and someone named Judith, who you know—"

"She lives at the Abigail Adams Hotel for Women, that's where I'm staying. Our rooms are on the same floor," Barb explained.

Ger stood there with his hands on his hips and looked at Sal. "Their rooms are on the same floor." And with that, he burst out laughing.

Barb looked from Ger to Sal and then back again, not clearly understanding.

Ger lowered his voice, toning down his excitability. "Apparently, this Judith—and I don't even know her position at the Wendell Corporation—told Wyler she thought, and I quote, 'you were a class act.'"

Heat surged up Barb's neck and spanned her cheeks. She wasn't used to this attention, although it felt like much more than attention. More like a glaring spotlight.

"Anyway, thank you, Barb, for being a class act and for your networking skills," Ger said and bowed before her.

This caused her to laugh nervously.

"We've got a lunch meeting with him tomorrow at their downtown offices. One sharp. The three of us," Ger announced.

She put her fingers on her chest. "Me too?"

"Of course. You're definitely going with us. It's because of you that we have this meeting in the first place. And we're going to need a class act at that meeting."

CHAPTER SEVENTEEN

Isabelle

Isabelle pushed a wheelbarrow full of mulch over to the furthest garden bed on the front lawn. The previous day, she'd spent the morning clearing out the flower beds and edging them to give them a neater appearance. Earlier that day, the garden center had delivered four yards of mulch as promised, dumping it onto the driveway. As she shoveled the dark, rich mulch onto the flower bed, Lily pulled up in her car. She parked it against the curb, got out, and opened the back door. Charlie bounded out and dashed to Isabelle. Isabelle leaned the shovel against the wheelbarrow and removed her garden gloves, shoving them into her back pocket. She lavished the dog with attention, and he wagged his tail furiously.

"What are you doing there? I thought you weren't supposed to be doing any heavy lifting," Lily remarked, looking around. "Although the flower beds do look wonderful."

"When I saw my surgeon last week, he said I could resume my previous activities."

Lily arched an eyebrow. "I didn't know you were a gardener."

Isabelle smiled. "Actually, I spent a few weeks working in the gardens at a manor house in England."

"You never cease to amaze me," Lily said with a smile.

"I thought since I'm going to be here for a while, I'll do what I can to spruce the place up a bit."

"Gardening is a good pick. I'm not very good at it, and I think Alice is too busy with her baking."

As she said this, Alice pulled up and parked her car behind Lily's. She walked over to them and lifted her sunglasses onto the top of her head. "The place is really shaping up. It looks great, Izzy."

"Thanks."

"Look, I don't know about you guys, but I'm beat, and I have no interest in cooking. Why don't we go out to eat?" Alice suggested.

"Sounds good to me," Lily said.

Isabelle looked around. "Let me finish up here and take a shower. I'll be ready in an hour, okay?"

The conversation turned to what kind of flowers they would like out front. Isabelle wanted geraniums, Lily wanted pots of pansies, and Alice put in a vote for daisies. Isabelle told them she'd make it all work. Her sisters disappeared into the house, leaving Isabelle to finish spreading the mulch.

Later on, the three of them walked over to Cabana Sally's, a bar slash restaurant on the water. Isabelle liked the relaxed, easy atmosphere of the place. Inside, the walls were dark, distressed wood paneling hung with all sorts of paraphernalia from Hideaway Bay over the last one hundred years. There was even a picture of old Mr. Lime when he was young—and when his back was straight—standing outside Lime's Five-and-Dime. There was a mixture of booths and high tables, and the chrome around the bar shone. The mirror that ran the length of the bar was backlit to showcase all the various bottles of liquor. The televisions mounted high on the wall showed three different baseball games.

But the three sisters bypassed the dim interior and found a place to sit outside. The back patio was more relaxed, furnished with generously spaced black wrought-iron mesh tables and chairs. On top of each table sat a collection of condiments in plastic bottles and an orange citronella candle. Alice grabbed a table near the railing with a great view of the lake, just as a couple vacated it.

The sun began its descent into the horizon, painting the sky with brushstrokes of scarlet, orange, and purple. Isabelle pulled out her chair and looked around. The weathered timber flooring ran on a slant. Pastel-colored Chinese lanterns and fairy lights were strung around the perimeter of the seating area, giving it a whimsical feel. In the background, music with calypso undertones played just quietly enough to allow for conversation.

The server approached and told them that only bar food was served outside and if they wanted the full menu, they'd need to go back in. They reassured her that was fine, and Isabelle got the sense she would have preferred if they'd gone inside.

"Someone doesn't want to be here," Lily whispered with a giggle when their server was out of hearing range.

"I know, right?" Alice said, her eyes widening.

Isabelle sat back and took in the view of the lake. She could get used to this: hanging out with her sisters, enjoying the view and good conversation. Amazing views were something she never tired of.

It was a beautiful night. A small group of people were huddled around a bonfire down on the beach, and their laughter floated over to where the sisters sat. Isabelle had always liked a good bonfire.

Her reverie was interrupted by the distant rumbling of a train, possibly going full speed down the tracks, its whistle muted and forlorn. She glanced at her phone and smiled.

"I see the train is right on time," she said. They were locomotives of the Norfolk Southern Railway, and Granddad used to say you could set your watch by them.

"It's nice how some things haven't changed in Hideaway Bay."

All three of them studied their menus. Isabelle wasn't hungry for a heavy meal, especially as she thought she might go for a swim later, and opted for an appetizer with a glass of wine instead. Her sisters ordered meals: fish tacos with a glass of white wine for Alice, and a burger and fries with vodka and iced tea with a splash of pineapple juice for Lily.

"It's nice that we're together," Alice said, raising her wine glass once the server had brought their drinks. "To the Monroe sisters."

Lily and Isabelle lifted their glasses and clinked them against Alice's.

Isabelle was all too aware of Alice's eagerness for them to reunite and stay together. And as sweet a notion as that was, for Isabelle any true sense of family disintegrated the day their father left. She realized that that was a warped way of thinking, but she couldn't help how she felt.

"You've decided to stay on," Lily said over the rim of her glass to Isabelle.

"Yeah, I think so," she said. Then she wondered if she was intruding. Lily and Alice had grown pretty close. "You don't mind, do you?"

"Of course not," Lily said.

"God no," Alice said. "You know how I feel."

"We know!" Isabelle and Lily said in unison, which caused them both to burst out laughing.

Alice fiddled with her napkin and her silverware, rearranging them and then lining them up against the edge of the table. "I always felt as a family we were kind of adrift, despite Mom's and Gram's best efforts."

Isabelle didn't know what to say to that.

Lily spoke up. "It wasn't ideal Dad leaving us, and I wish he hadn't left, but I think Mom did her best to raise us and instill in us a sense of family."

"With the help of Granddad and Gram," Alice piped in, lifting her wine glass to her mouth.

"We were lucky, actually. We were loved, and we belonged to a great family," Lily concluded. Her gaze drifted over to the beach, and it was as if she didn't see what was right in front of her but was looking at something in the past.

Isabelle sighed, swirling her wine around in her glass and staring at the contents as if she could divine some mystery from them. "I've always felt that there was something missing from our family—namely Dad—that we were incomplete as a family once he left." She raised her gaze, waiting for the inevitable blowback from her sisters.

"Of course you would feel that way," Alice said softly. "You were the oldest and had the most memories of Dad. You were close to him. I was three when he left, so I don't really have any memories of him. All I have are impressions."

"I was closer to Mom, and I've put Dad and what he did in a box and closed it up," Lily said.

Isabelle marveled at her sisters. It amazed her how one significant event in their lives had affected each one of them so differently. The server set their orders down in front of them. Alice tackled one of her fish tacos, and Lily took a bite of her burger, chewing thoughtfully, then swallowed.

"I think family is what you make it," she said. "I'm not downplaying what kind of effect Dad's leaving had on you, Isabelle, but we did have a good family with Mom, Gram, and Granddad."

"Then why did we grow apart?" Isabelle pressed. *Why, if it was so great, did everything crumble?*

Lily shrugged and wiped ketchup from the corner of her mouth with her napkin. "I don't know."

"But does it matter?" Alice asked. "Yes, we've all gone our separate ways and haven't been close, but we've managed to circle back to Hideaway Bay."

"But it took Gram's death to do it," Isabelle scoffed. A ribbon of guilt wound its way through her that though it had been their wish, her mother and grandparents hadn't lived long enough to see the three of them reunited.

"Don't do that to yourself, Isabelle," Lily said softly. "Don't live in a world of regret."

Isabelle tugged on her bottom lip with her teeth and pushed away her plate. Her appetite had abandoned her.

"I know all about the woulda, coulda, and shoulda regarding the past," Lily said. Isabelle knew she was probably referring to her late husband, who'd left her mired in debt. "Don't get sucked into that vortex. You're my big sister. I've always thought of you as independent and with a strong sense of self. I mean, you've traveled all over the world solo."

Isabelle laughed. "Outside of Hideaway Bay, I am all those things. It's when I come back that I revert into that eleven-year-old girl who was abandoned by her father."

Her sisters cast sympathetic glances toward her.

"If it's that important to you, then keep looking for him," Alice said. "But I'll sit this one out."

Isabelle nodded and swung her gaze over to Lily.

Lily bit her lip, stared at the table, and when she lifted her head, she said, "You already know how I feel about the whole thing. I don't want to dredge anything up. And though I understand that this is important to you, I don't want any part of it."

Isabelle had to respect that. In regard to what happened with their father, they were each in a different place.

Buoyed a bit by her sisters' somewhat begrudging support, Isabelle decided that no matter what the answer to her father's disappearance was, she was going to find out what happened to him.

CHAPTER EIGHTEEN

Summer 1963

Barb

A memo circulated from the boss with a list of names of people who were to meet in the conference room after lunch. When Barb saw her name on the list, she panicked, wondering if she was getting fired. Her stomach lurched and rolled. She'd been with the company for two months, and she loved the job. As the calendar days flipped closer to the end of August, she dreaded returning to college. She'd grown to love New York.

As she made her way to the conference room, dread made her legs heavy. She'd scanned the other names on the memo, seeing one of the account managers on the list but not the other. She could not imagine what this meeting was all about. Her gut told her it might not be good. Why would they include the intern with the other names? By the time she reached the conference room, she'd worked herself into a frenzy, sure she was about to witness and be part of a mass firing.

But when she entered the conference room with its plush gold carpet and its sleek, blond, Danish-inspired furniture and abstract artwork, she caught sight of her account manager, Ger, and he gave her a reassuring smile. She relaxed slightly. Ger indicated the empty seat beside him, and she took it and sank down into the chair.

She cleared her throat, pulled her seat closer to the table, and looked around. There appeared to be one or two people from every area of the ad agency: accounts, creative, production, and more. Curiosity swelled inside her. What was going on?

She was about to lean over to Ger and ask, when the double doors to the conference room opened and Mimi, secretary to one of the partners, wheeled in a cart carrying urns of tea and coffee and plates of cookies. Mimi was followed by Mr. Welch, one of the three founding partners of Welch, Stine, and Cross. More than once, Barb had been asked if she was related to Mr. Welch, with the implication being that she must have secured her position due to a family connection. In the first weeks at this job, she had been forced to explain, patiently and repeatedly, that she was "Walsh" and not "Welch." Surprisingly, there were some who viewed her suspiciously, as if even having a name sounding close to the boss's left a question mark. Barb had chosen to ignore it.

Mr. Leo Welch was tall, almost six four, with salt-and-pepper hair that he wore short. It was said that he'd fought in World War II and had saved his platoon from certain death. He wasn't married, never had been, and this created a wealth of additional gossip about him, which Barb also chose to ignore.

Mr. Welch took his place at the head of the long table and pushed his square black glasses up on the bridge of his nose. He smiled pleasantly, which brought to life a lone dimple on the left side of his mouth. His suit was Italian and handmade. He clapped his tan hands—golf four days a week—and his gaze scanned those seated at the table.

"Great, it looks like everyone is here." He nodded toward Mimi, who was in the process of setting the urns of coffee and tea in the middle of the table. "Help yourselves to coffee, tea, and cookies. We're going to be here a while."

Barb thought his mood appeared effusive and light, and was convinced she would not be let go that afternoon. No fear then of being served a cup of tea only minutes before being ushered out the door. She decided that this must involve some company project. Feeling a bit more relaxed than earlier, she leaned back in her chair and clasped her hands over her abdomen.

"All right, you're all probably wondering why I've called you here and what the hell is going on." There was a flash of another brilliant smile, Mr. Welch's teeth appearing whiter because of his tan.

Everyone waited. Barb helped herself to tea and whispered to Ger, asking if he'd like a cup. When he nodded, she poured him one and handed it to him. She caught the attention of Gail from accounting and mouthed to her to pass the sugar and creamer. She had lunch sometimes with Gail when their schedules permitted. She was a fellow summer intern, from a college in Pennsylvania. Although hardworking and nice, Gail had no hobbies or interests and was quite dull.

"We have some news regarding Welch, Stine, and Cross," Mr. Welch continued. "We've had phenomenal growth here in the agency in the last three years, which is a credit to each and every employee here. After deliberate consideration and research, we've decided to open another office in California, not far from San Francisco, in a town called Menlo Park."

A low murmur of excitement buzzed around the table.

"We've already acquired office space, and we even have our first client," Mr. Welch enthused. He paused, looked at the expectant faces gathered around the table, and added, "Now we need to relocate some of our staff to the west coast office."

Gary from creative thrust his hand in the air. When Mr. Welch nodded to him, he asked, "Wouldn't it be easier to hire locally?"

"It would, but we want to replicate our success in New York. And who better to do that than staff who currently work here? We're going to send out a skeleton crew and then hire locally," Mr. Welch explained. "Which is why I've brought you here. Along with Guy and Chuck, I've handpicked a team to go out there. That team is everyone sitting at this table."

Barb wasn't sure she heard correctly. There must be some mistake. They certainly didn't want her there. She looked around the room nervously, feeling like a fraud. She was tempted to raise her hand and remind Mr. Welch that she was only an intern and would be returning to Vermont at the end of August. But curiosity bested her, and she quelled the urge to interrupt him, deciding to stay and listen.

For the next hour as they drank tea and coffee and nibbled on cookies, Mr. Welch spoke about what was going to be required. There was an accompanying slide show, the white screen pulled down at the front of the room and the projector rattling to life. It was not lost on Barb how the slide show was all glitz and glamour about how wonderful a life in California could be. After all, it was an advertising agency. If they couldn't sell to their own employees, they were in trouble. Barb had to admit that all that sunshine was enticing. It sounded wonderful, but it still involved a cross-country move.

At the end of the meeting, Mr. Welch looked around the room once more. "I realize the ask here is large. It involves moving to the other side of the country. I ask you to think about it, but I must know by July 31st whether you're on board or not. Should you decide not to take this opportunity, it will not affect your employment here at Welch, Stine, and Cross. But we felt that each one of you would bring value and expertise to our new west coast office. Take your time, think about it, and get back to me."

Everyone was excited except Barb, who was sure a mistake had been made, and Gail, the girl from Pennsylvania. But with her you didn't know. She always looked bored.

Everyone stood, pushing in their chairs and talking amongst themselves. It seemed as if the transfer was being received as a positive by the sound of the chatter. Barb hung back a bit to speak directly to Mr. Welch.

She waited as two other staff spoke with him with some enthusiasm, and it wasn't difficult to guess which way they were leaning.

When they finally left, Barb gave a quick glance at her wristwatch, not wanting to return late.

"What can I do for you, Miss Walsh?" he asked, his smile inviting.

She had always liked Mr. Welch; of the three partners, he seemed the easiest to get along with. He wasn't intimidating in the way Mr. Cross was with his chronic scowl.

She looked around, relieved that the room had emptied out. "Mr. Welch, I think there's been some mistake."

He frowned slightly, a single groove appearing between his dark eyebrows.

"How so?"

"I don't think I was meant to be here," she said, realizing as she did that she sounded foolish. "I mean"—here she reddened, much to her mortification—"I don't think I was supposed to be on that list."

"Why do you think that?"

"Because I'm only a summer intern. I'm going back to college in August."

Mr. Welch smiled, and Barb thought how handsome he was and how he possessed movie star quality. Internally, she scolded herself, telling herself to stay present and not float off in a daydream.

"We realize that, Barb. In a short period of time, you have proven yourself to be an invaluable asset to the agency. And we also think you have a lot of potential to grow with the company. We think you'll be a good fit for the west coast office."

"You do?" she asked, unable to hide her surprise.

Mr. Welch laughed. "Yes, we do. It's a bona fide offer, and we did not make a mistake adding your name to the roster."

Barb contemplated this.

"Now, we understand if you want to go back to college. And we would fully support that. Education is the one thing no one can take away from you. But you could do night classes out west and finish your degree there."

The opportunity to go to California was terrific by itself. But the idea of not returning to the college she hated made her smile.

"Would I be made a permanent employee?" she asked. She didn't want to go out to California as an intern. She'd need something more solid and stable.

"Of course," he said. "Sit down with human resources to discuss the salary and benefits to see if it suits you."

"Can I think about this?" she asked, barely able to hide her excitement. Like all the characters in the books she read, she was sure her eyes were sparkling at that moment.

"Like everyone else, you have until the end of July," he said.

"Thank you, Mr. Welch."

As she made her way out of the room, enthusiasm filled her. All sorts of thoughts went through her mind: how unexpected it was, how they'd chosen her to go out to the west coast and most of all, how exciting an opportunity for her. It also meant she wouldn't have to return to college in September. California might be a destination for her after all. But again, the same obstacle remained: her parents.

November 1963

Barb liked living in Menlo Park. It was an affluent suburb of San Francisco, and the office was equidistant between the bigger city and her apartment. There was a lot to do in San Francisco. She'd expected the weather to be warmer, like Florida almost, but she soon grew to love its moderate, sunny climate. There wasn't anything she didn't like about California.

Barb always arrived early to open the office and get things ready, which included making sure the coffee was brewing. Everyone in that meeting with Mr. Welch back in July had come out to California, except for Gail, who said California didn't interest her.

Barb was in the break room, setting up the coffeemaker and opening a box of pastries she had picked up on her way in to work. They had a fund they all chipped in to that allowed them coffee and pastries. Barb kept the money in an old Maxwell House coffee can. She heard the front door open as a few of her coworkers drifted in, ready to start the day. Thanksgiving was the following week, and they had a four-day weekend. It was too long of a trip to consider going home to Buffalo and besides, things were still tense between her and her parents. They had not wanted her to drop out of college and move to California. There had been multiple phone calls fraught with anger and tears. To this day, she still couldn't believe her parents had driven to NYC to try to drag her home.

Ger and his wife, Bea, had invited her over for Thanksgiving dinner, and she'd offered to bring a dish. She'd wait until Christmas to go home to Buffalo, when the atmosphere was sure to be more festive. Her brother, Mark, and his wife were coming home with the new baby, and that was sure to be a buffer.

"It was cold last night, wasn't it?" Donna asked, coming into the break room and eyeing the pastries. Donna lived locally and had been hired as a secretary. Barb liked her. Everybody did. She was young and cheerful.

After a few minutes, Donna said, "Oh, I almost forgot, I've got those recipes for the pecan sandy bars and the green bean casserole." She pulled the folded-up recipes out of the pocket of her skirt and handed them to Barb.

While she was enthused about the bars, Barb was skeptical about the green bean casserole, even though Donna had guaranteed it would be a hit. Barb glanced at the paper, scanning the instructions to determine the level of difficulty before tucking it into the pocket of her sweater.

"Thanks, Donna."

They chatted for a few more minutes before going to their desks. Barb's desk was right outside Ger's office. She'd been promoted to his assistant.

She settled in, her list of tasks to be done that day written out on a legal pad on her desk. In the background, Ger had a radio playing in his office. He always listened to it but kept it low enough that it didn't disturb her. He was a fan of rock and roll and by extension, Barb rather was now as well.

Going for eleven in the morning, Barb crossed one more thing off her list, satisfied with her productivity rate that day. In the background, a song was cut off midway through, the announcer's voice cutting in. Barb glanced in the direction of Ger's office but made little of it, the words only murmurs for the low volume.

A moment later, Ger came out of his office and stood at her desk, blinking and appearing dazed.

Barb looked up at him, smiling, about to make a crack that if he added one more thing to her list, she'd quit. His expression, unnaturally pale and stunned, made her hold her tongue.

"What's wrong, Ger?" she squeaked, instantly alarmed.

He blinked several times, and his Adam's apple bobbed up and down. His voice was a ragged whisper when he spoke. "It's the President. He's been shot."

"What?"

As if on cue, there was a scream from another office, and one of the guys stepped into the main room and shouted, "Kennedy's been shot in Dallas!"

Barb sat there, unable to move, stupefied. Soon everyone gathered around Ger's radio in his office. The details were sketchy coming out of Texas. Something about JFK being shot while riding in the motorcade.

"I thought the presidential cars were bulletproof," someone said.

"They are," someone else replied.

Ger looked around the crowd that had pushed their way into his office. "Let's go to that bar on the corner. They have a television."

Everyone filed out of Ger's office quickly, quiet and somber, some teary-eyed, grabbing their coats and pulling them on as they exited the office.

Barb had worn her heavy wool winter coat to work, and she was glad she had. Now she not only felt cold but numb as well. They made their way to the bar on the corner. She had passed it every day but had never been enticed to go inside. It looked like a watering hole for regulars.

She pulled the collar of her coat closer, unable to shake off the sudden chill that had nothing to do with the weather.

Ger led the way, and one of the guys held open the door as they all poured into the bar. It was dimly lit inside, and the long bar was occupied by a few elderly men. All eyes were glued to the black-and-white screen of the television resting on a shelf above the bar. Even the bartender didn't seem to notice them come in. He stood in the corner, the glow of the television screen illuminating every detail of his aged face. A blue-and-white striped dish towel was slung over his shoulder. There was a strong scent of pine-scented disinfectant.

"What's the news on Kennedy?" someone from the office asked.

The bartender folded his arms across his chest and leaned against the bar and shook his head. "He's been shot in Dallas. That's all we've heard."

Murmurs rumbled through the crowd as people began to speculate.

"Maybe it's only a flesh wound."

"It might have missed him."

Barb had a sick feeling in her stomach. Not even aware of what she was doing, she bit her lip until she tasted the metallic tang of blood in her mouth.

"It's horrible, isn't it?" asked a voice beside her.

Barb swung her gaze up to the owner of the voice. He was tall, with a dark blond crew cut and blue eyes. Her eyes zeroed in on the deep cleft in his chin. It reminded her of Kirk Douglas.

She could only nod. The idea of the President being shot was so horrific that she couldn't make it fit properly into her frame of reference. He was so young and vibrant, with a beautiful wife and children. Stuff like this wasn't supposed to happen.

"I'm Jim Eckhert," the stranger said, and he thrust forth a large hand that clasped around hers.

"Barb. Barb Walsh," she said.

He swung his gaze to the bar and then back to her. "Can I get you a drink?"

She'd like a whiskey sour, but somehow it seemed inappropriate to be sipping a cocktail in these circumstances and at this time of the day. She saw he held a beer in his hand. "I'll have a beer. Whatever you've got there."

He leaned across the bar and in a low voice ordered two beers, setting his empty bottle down. His dress was conservative: khaki pants, a checked shirt, and a jacket. Despite the jacket, she could see his bicep pushing against the fabric.

He handed her a bottle of beer. As they waited for news, all the voices hushed inside the bar, Barb and Jim spoke.

"Are you from around here, Barb?" he inquired, taking a gulp of his beer.

She shook her head. "I'm from Buffalo but I work at Welch, Stine, and Cross. It's an advertising agency."

"Do you like it? Working and all?" he asked, his eyes never leaving her face, his gaze speculative.

"I do," she said. "What about you?"

"I'm in the Army. I graduated from college two years ago, and I'm stationed at the Oakland Army Terminal."

She nodded but had no idea where that was. "What are you doing in Menlo Park?"

"A group of us were out here for work and we were driving back to the base when we heard the news. We stopped at the first bar we found."

The fact that there had been no further news bulletins gave Barb hope.

"Is Oakland far away?" she asked.

He shook his head. She could see he'd had a recent haircut as evidenced by his tan line, and she concluded he must spend a lot of time outdoors.

"No, about an hour. Have you been to San Francisco yet?"

"A few times," she said. For the most part she preferred to spend her evenings and weekends at home, reading and listening to her albums. But there'd been a few occasions where she'd gone into the city with some of the girls from work for lunch or dinner. She'd ridden the trolley car and gone to the Wharf and picked up some postcards to send to Junie and Thelma.

"I was hoping I could show you some sights," he said.

Barb arched one eyebrow at his confidence. He didn't seem smug, but he did appear self-assured. She liked that about him.

"What sights would you show me?" she asked, looking up at him from beneath her lashes.

Before he could answer, their attention was diverted as the current programming was interrupted and Walter Cronkite appeared. The low murmurs of the crowd in the bar disappeared and there was total silence, all faces glued to the television screen, expectant. The newsman sat at a desk, and in front of him were black rotary phones. Barb thought it would be odd if one of those phones rang. The things you thought of during times of trauma. Cronkite, his voice gruff, announced that the President had died. Barb stared at the screen as a few of the women screamed around her and someone, a male voice, shouted, "No!" Someone must have fainted because Barb heard a heavy thud behind her and then a clamoring. Stunned, she didn't move. She was unable to take her eyes off the television screen. Walter Cronkite struggled to maintain his composure.

A groundswell began deep within her, moving up and out, building slowly until it was a feeling and an emotion that she could no longer control. She put both hands to her face, trying to find some privacy. First she whimpered, and then a low keen escaped her lips. Immediately, the man beside her, the one with the cleft in his chin—Jim Eckhert—took her into his arms. She buried her head into his shoulder, soaking his shirt with her tears. He rubbed his hands along her back as she shook with sobs, resting his chin on the top of her head. But she needn't be embarrassed by the show of emotion, as it was replicated by everyone in the bar. People either stared in outright shock and horror at the screen or they cried openly, unashamed.

After a while, Ger told everyone from the office to go home, that he was closing the agency for the day. Barb was relieved; she knew there'd be no way she'd be able to concentrate on work. It would seem trivial and disrespectful.

Jim suggested they step outside and get a breath of fresh air. They were blinded by the bright daylight. Barb looked up at the sky and then around her. Why did she think it would be dark out? With his arm around her shoulders, careful and protective, Jim walked her three blocks until they found themselves in front of a diner. He thought a cup of coffee would do them both some good. Barb was glad someone else was making the decisions. The place smelled strongly of freshly brewed coffee and bacon and onions. The customers there also appeared to be in shock. Waitresses moved as if they were on autopilot, and customers sat in booths and sipped coffee and ate in silence. Barb and Jim joined them in their universal shock as they drank several cups of coffee. Barb wanted to call home. More than anything, she wanted to hear the voices of her parents. She would do that as soon as she got back to her apartment.

As the months went on and she saw more of Jim, the relationship budded and then blossomed quickly. It had not happened as she'd imagined it. There'd been no wonderful backdrop of a pink sunset or a waterfall. No fragrant scent of roses lingering in the air. There'd been no instant chemistry, no knowing at first glance. It had been a hug during a dark, inescapably horrific moment of life and national tragedy. But that hug had tethered her to earth, prevented her from flying away like a lost balloon. Funny, she thought, how of all the imagined scenarios as to how she might meet the love of her life, never in her wildest dreams or fantasies did she think she'd meet him during a presidential assassination. At the far reaches of her mind, she hoped it wouldn't cast a dark shadow.

CHAPTER NINETEEN

Isabelle

The three sisters had different routines when it came to the beach across the street. Isabelle preferred to swim at night beneath the moonlight now that the weather was warmer. Lily was out on the beach at daybreak to collect beach glass that the tide had swept in overnight, and Alice was more casual, going over at various times throughout the day. But the three of them enjoyed the pastime of sitting on the long porch in the evenings, watching the sunset.

It was almost nine as Isabelle strolled over to the lake. Lily had insisted she take Charlie with her to keep an eye out. Isabelle wanted to point out that he was a dog and not a lifeguard, but she did like his company. The Great Dane would sit on the shore, watching her in the water. He only barked when she disappeared below the surface, and when she emerged from the lake, she'd wave and call out to him and he'd settle down, resuming his sitting position, sentinel to the lake and her in it.

Since that night at Cabana Sally's, Isabelle had started searching for her father via the internet and had turned up basically nothing. She'd narrowed the search to Buffalo in hopes that he had ended up there, but that had proved to be a dead end. She searched Facebook and although that yielded a lot of Dave Monroes, none matched the description or age of her father. She searched the public records and came up empty. The thought that he might have died occurred to her, the worst possible outcome as it would leave her with absolutely no answers. On a whim, she wrote to the New York State Department of Health, searching for a possible death certificate and supplying her father's full name, date of birth, and birthplace. She enclosed the fee and waited. They sent her a refund, saying they could find no death certificate.

And as she searched, she kept busy. She planted red geraniums and daisies out front in the flower beds. She put yellow and purple pansies in red clay pots she bought at the garden center and set one on each porch step. Once a week, she cut the grass using Granddad's old push mower. She still didn't know what she was going to do with the backyard, but not everything had to be done this year. After discussing it with her sisters, she planned to create a flowerbed that ran parallel to the driveway and if she was still here in the fall, she'd plant bulbs of red, yellow, and orange tulips.

She thought of all these things as she floated on her back and stared at the night sky above her, the lake water lapping gently at the sides of her head. The sky was a large haze of twinkling stars. She did some of her best thinking in this position. It had cooled down considerably from the mid-afternoon, but it was not unpleasant by any means.

Half an hour later, she forced herself out of the water. The lake was calm. As she emerged, Charlie pranced around, whining.

"Hey, Clumsy, it's okay, we'll go home," she said, reassuring him with a stroke along the top of his head.

Isabelle gave a quick perfunctory dry-off with the beach towel she'd grabbed from the cupboard, and picked up her shift and pulled it over her head. After she rolled up the beach towel and tucked it beneath her arm, she headed in the direction of home with Charlie loping easily alongside her.

As they neared the sidewalk, a man walked by with a small dog, a Jack Russell terrier who, upon seeing Charlie, launched himself like a rocket at the Great Dane, barking and growling. Charlie whimpered and scurried behind Isabelle's legs.

"Hey, Luther, knock it off," the man said, pulling on the lead. The dog immediately stopped barking and sat at the man's side.

Charlie, meanwhile, remained behind Isabelle, his head lowered. Isabelle gave him a reassuring pat.

"I'm sorry about that," the man said.

Isabelle looked at him in the spotlight of the streetlamp and recognized him as the teacher who was at the beach a few days ago with his class.

"Oh, I remember you," she said.

He tilted his head, grinned, and said, "And I you."

Isabelle was glad for the cover of darkness because she could feel herself blushing. For a distraction, she nodded at his dog and said, "He's fierce."

"Yes, for someone so small he is mighty," the man agreed.

Luther walked gingerly around Isabelle and sniffed at Charlie, who remained stationary but gave in and sniffed the smaller dog. Satisfied, Luther returned to the man's side.

"I'm Joe Koch," the man said and held out his hand.

She shook it. "Isabelle Monroe."

"You live over there in that house?" he said with a nod toward the house across the street. Realizing how it sounded, he added quickly, "I walk my dog every night, and I've seen you on the porch."

Isabelle smiled, thinking his discomfort was cute.

"I'm staying there for the time being," she said.

"Where do you live?"

She hesitated and said, "I have no permanent address." When he didn't say anything, she felt the need to qualify her answer. "I'm a travel writer and I, well, travel a lot."

"Sounds interesting," he said.

"It is. I love it," she said.

"Good, I'd like to hear more about it," he said. He looked over his shoulder in the direction of town. "Would you like to go for ice cream at the Pink Parlor?"

"Is it open this late?" she asked with a frown. It had to be almost ten by now.

"In the summer, they're open until midnight," he said.

"All right. I need to get my purse," she said.

He shook his head. "No, you don't. This one's on me. I'll even throw in a couple of pup cups for the dogs."

Isabelle laughed. "When you put it like that, I can hardly resist."

"Great, let's go," he said, and he turned and walked in the direction of Main Street with Isabelle and Charlie at his side.

Across the street, Isabelle's sisters sat on the porch. She gave them a quick wave and when they returned the gesture, she looked in the direction of town, pretending their eyes were not wide with speculation. She braced herself for lots of questions when she returned home.

There was no one out except a few walkers, so she and Joe strolled down the middle of the street with the dogs. When he'd asked, she'd been in the mood to do something spontaneous, but as they neared the Pink Parlor, she saw with relief that there were no other customers inside. She only had a swimsuit cover over her bathing suit and sandals.

They tied the dogs to a lamppost, and Joe held the door open for her as she stepped inside into the bright fluorescent lighting of the ice cream parlor. *Yes, I should have thought this through a little more*, she thought to herself. And she admitted as much to Joe: "I should have at least gone home and brushed my hair."

He paused and looked at her. Up close his eyes were clear and bright green, reminding her of the beach glass that Lily collected. "I think it looks beautiful," he said.

"Thank you," she stammered.

"Come on, let's get some ice cream," he said with a smile. He had beautiful teeth and when he smiled, it lit up his face. Deep lines framed his mouth and the corners of his eyes, and Isabelle thought he might be older than she originally suspected. Maybe mid-forties. But still, she liked the look of him.

"What would you like, Isabelle?" he asked.

Quickly, she scanned the glass case. "Coffee on a waffle cone." She peered through the large front window to make sure Charlie was all right. He was seated in front of the lamppost, still secured. He stared at her and she waved back at him, causing him to stand up and bark.

Joe leaned against the counter, and the teenaged boy working there approached them and smiled. "Hi, Mr. Koch."

"Hey, Jeff, how are you? Working here for the summer?"

"I am. Going off to Buffalo for college in the fall."

"Are you going to dorm?"

The boy had blond hair and acne in his T-zone. He smiled and said, "Yes, I want the full college experience."

"Have you decided on a major?" Joe asked.

"I'm thinking about aeronautical engineering, but I'm not sure yet," Jeff said with a squint.

"The good news is you don't have to make that decision tonight, you've got time before you declare a major," Joe said. "Keep an open mind."

"Will do, Mr. Koch."

An older man stepped in line behind them. Isabelle felt self-conscious standing there in her cover-up and wet hair.

"What can I get you?" Jeff asked.

"A large coffee and a large pistachio, both on waffle cones, and two pup cups," Joe said. He reached around to his back pocket to pull out his wallet. From his billfold, he retrieved a twenty and paid for the ice cream.

Jeff got their orders and handed them over.

"If you take the ice cream cones, I'll handle the pup cups," Joe said to Isabelle.

She nodded and reached for the cones, and they headed outside to where the dogs were tied up. Joe set down a pup cup in front of each of them. By the time he stood back up, Charlie had already wolfed down the entire contents of his in one go.

Joe regarded the Great Dane with a laugh. "He's going to have brain freeze in about thirty seconds."

Isabelle handed Joe his ice cream cone and began to eat hers. "That's Charlie for you. He gulps his food down. Life's too short for chewing."

Joe laughed, and their attention was diverted to the terrier, Luther, who licked his ice cream. His mouth was covered in white. Charlie, his own ice cream gone, looked longingly at Luther's.

"Come on, let's sit down," Joe said, and they found seats at one of the white bistro tables. From down the road, music floated out from Cabana Sally's, and the sounds of conversation and laughter drifted out on the gentle night breeze.

"How long are you staying in Hideaway Bay?" he asked.

Isabelle shrugged. She leaned back in her chair, folding one arm across her chest and holding her ice cream cone with the other hand. "I don't know. I've got a few things to do before I leave again."

"Like what?" Immediately, he smiled and said, "I'm sorry, that was an intrusive question and none of my business."

"Not at all," she said. She didn't mind. Besides, she found him easy to talk to. "While I'm here, I'm trying to find my father."

Joe didn't say anything. Waited for her to expound, which she did. "My dad took off when I was eleven. I'm trying to see if I can locate him if he's even still alive."

Joe nodded and appeared thoughtful. "It's tough being raised by one parent."

She didn't want anyone feeling sorry for her; that wasn't who she was.

"We did all right. Our mother loved us, and our grandparents were there to help raise us," she explained. When she said it out loud, it sounded all right.

"Do you want any help?" he asked.

She laughed at the direction the conversation had gone. "I think I'm good." She realized she didn't know anything about him. "You haven't always lived in Hideaway Bay, have you?" She certainly would have remembered him.

He shook his head. "Transplant. Met my wife at Ohio State and followed her back home here."

Isabelle froze mid lick at the mention of the word "wife."

Joe caught her expression and gave a sad smile. "Tracy passed away a few years ago from leukemia."

"I am so sorry," Isabelle immediately said.

"It's been a bit rough, but we're making our way through it."

This statement led her to ask, "You have children?"

He nodded. "Three kids, one dog, and two cats."

Isabelle's heart sank. Just when she was beginning to enjoy his company.

"Does that scare you?" he asked, then said with a laugh, "Because sometimes it scares the hell out of me!"

Isabelle burst out laughing. She eyed him and said, "Not yet."

CHAPTER TWENTY

1965

Barb

Barb surveyed her bedroom; the refuge of her childhood had been all but emptied out. Her room was bare except for the bed, dresser, bookshelves and desk. All her things had already gone out on the moving van to California. She viewed her childhood room through the eyes of an adult. An adult who'd been living in California for almost two years.

Her wedding dress hung on the back of the door. This weekend, she was marrying Jim, and the reception was to be held at the Saturn Club downtown. She couldn't wait to start her new life with Jim out in California. First there was to be a honeymoon in Hawaii, and then they'd live in California in officer housing. She'd seen the house—it was nice, and she couldn't wait to decorate it. But more than that, she couldn't wait to have children with Jim and start their family.

This was the very beginning of her happily ever after, the life she'd always dreamed of.

The weather was beautiful for mid-June, and Barb hoped it would hold for Saturday. The weather forecast was the first thing she and her mother looked at when *The Courier Express* arrived in the morning.

The tension and disagreements that had erupted during her college years and her moves, first to New York and then to California, had settled down as Barb matured and was able to view things from several points of view. When she became engaged to Jim, her mother had risen to the occasion as if she'd been destined to plan a grand wedding for her daughter. And surprise of surprises, Barb had enjoyed wedding planning with her mother; they had finally found something they had in common. And being out on the west coast until last week, she'd been grateful that her mother was home, able and eager to do any of the wedding-related tasks that needed to be done from Buffalo.

Her parents had liked Jim from the start. They'd thought he was polite and well-mannered with a good future ahead of him. But it wouldn't have mattered if they liked him or not; she was marrying him. She loved Jim Eckhert. Of that there was no doubt.

She headed down the stairs, her footfalls muted by the lush runner on the staircase, and found her mother in the dining room. The table was covered with all sorts of wedding gifts that her mother would pack up for her after the ceremony and ship out to Barb's new home.

"Look what my cousin Meredith sent," Mrs. Walsh said, holding up a pair of crystal candlestick holders.

Barb took one, marveling at the weight of it. "Wow, they're heavy."

"That's the lead. Beautiful though. It's a shame she couldn't come to the wedding," her mother said. There was a slight hint of derision in her voice.

"Mother, she's going through treatment for breast cancer," Barb reminded her. It didn't bother her that her cousin wasn't coming to the wedding. She understood. Meredith needed to look after her own health. That should be the priority.

"She could have flown in for the weekend," Mrs. Walsh said. She kept a mental scorecard.

"It's fine, Mother, there'll be plenty of guests," Barb said. They had sent out almost four hundred invitations.

"I suppose," her mother said, finally turning her attention to Barb. She frowned when she spotted the handbag looped over Barb's arm.

"Where are you going?"

"I'm going over to Junie's to see the baby, and Thelma will be there with Donny," Barb explained.

"I know you had to have them in your wedding party, but do you really need to keep seeing them?"

"Mother, they're still and will always be my best friends," Barb explained for what felt like the hundredth time.

There was a grim set to her mother's jaw, and Barb hoped they wouldn't get into an argument about it. Before it could escalate, she decided she was not going to let it bother her.

"Before you go, I want to talk to you about something," Mrs. Walsh said.

Now what? How am I failing her now? Why couldn't they just enjoy this time together?

"I spoke to Helen last night and you know her brother is high up in the chain of command in Washington."

Barb scowled. She wanted to say, *So?* but said instead, "Chain of command?"

Her mother pursed her lips. "Army. He's a one-star general or something. Been in Washington for years."

"And?" Barb could not imagine where this conversation was going.

"I thought maybe Helen could speak to her brother and see about getting Jim transferred to a base closer to home."

Barb's mouth fell open. Of all possible topics, she'd never imagined this one.

"What?"

"California is too far away, Barb. We'll hardly ever see you." Mrs. Walsh put the crystal candlestick holders on display next to the other gifts and propped the card up against their empty box.

"Don't you dare interfere in Jim's career," Barb said through gritted teeth. "I won't have you meddling in my marriage or in my life."

"I want to help get you closer to home."

Seething, Barb took a step closer to her mother. "If you interfere and try to manage Jim's career with your connections, you will never see me again."

Her mother blanched and reared back as if she'd been slapped.

Barb headed toward the door, furious.

"I thought you'd like to be closer to home," Mrs. Walsh stammered behind her. "Near your father and me."

Barb stopped and stared straight ahead and counted to five. She wouldn't explode. She couldn't. Finally, she pivoted half a turn and said over her shoulder. "I wanted to come home once, remember? And you said no."

"Barbara, that was for the best," her mother said.

"For whom? You? Because it wasn't best for me," Barb said, turning around and facing her mother.

Mrs. Walsh staggered and grabbed the back of the dining room chair. Quickly she regained her composure and straightened her posture, and while she gripped the chair, she said evenly, "You'll never be first in his life, my dear. The military will always come first. You'll be second."

Barb processed those words for a moment. Quietly, she said, "After we're married, we're moving into our new house in California. If you want to see me, you can come out and visit me." She rushed out of the dining room and out the front door, slamming it behind her.

Six months later

Barb arrived home, dropped her purse and bags on a chair, and waited anxiously for Jim to get home.

They had plane tickets to head home to Buffalo a few days before Christmas, returning after New Year's. She hadn't seen her friends and her parents since the wedding, and she was anxious to reunite with them. She only wished she were pregnant as that would have been wonderful news to share. She hadn't thought it would take this long. But hopefully, it would be soon.

After work, she'd gone to several stores, finishing her gift buying. She headed to the spare bedroom, where she'd set up a little card table that served as a wrapping station. Colorful tubes of holiday wrapping paper lay across the table along with spools of red and green ribbon, a pair of scissors, and some tape. Most of her gifts were wrapped and positioned beneath the Christmas tree in the living room. She knew she'd have to box them up to take them back with her, but she liked looking at them under the tree. She set the bag of presents she'd purchased next to the table leg. She'd wrap them after dinner.

She placed a quick call to her mother, who picked up on the second ring.

"Mother?" Barb asked.

"Hello, Barb, this is a pleasant surprise."

"Are you busy?"

Barb had spoken to her mother only the previous week. Since she'd married and begun running her own household, she'd done a little growing up. She felt bad at how she'd left things with her mother after the wedding and now that she was a married woman, she wanted to mend the fence. Frequently, she rang her for advice—advice her mother was only too happy to give—and sometimes she called her on the premise of looking for advice when all she wanted was to remain connected to home.

"No, I was decorating the tree, but it'll be nice to sit down and have a chat and catch up," Mrs. Walsh said.

"How's Father?"

"Busy as ever. But we're really looking forward to having everyone here for Christmas. Mark and Nancy are flying in with the children," Mrs. Walsh said. Barb could practically hear the happiness in her voice. "Barbara, not to sound crass, but I moved your bed to the attic and bought a double bed for you and Jim."

Barb couldn't picture her mother actually moving the bed herself; she had probably slipped money to Agnes's husband to do it. "Thanks, Mother, I hadn't even thought of it."

"*The Sound of Music* is still playing at the show. We could go see it together if you'd like," her mother said.

"I'd love that." She'd seen it a couple of times already and knew that her mother had seen it too, but she'd love to go to the movies with her mother again like they used to do when she was young.

"Are you all finished with your shopping?"

"Almost. One question though. I'm stumped about what to get Nancy," Barb said, referring to her sister-in-law.

"That's easy enough," her mother said. And she went on to list several items to consider, all of which Barb thought were good ideas. They spoke for several more minutes and before they hung up, her mother said, "I'm counting the days, Barbara."

"Me too, Mother."

Jim would be home soon, and Barb had a simple dinner of steak, baked potatoes, and a salad planned. A glance at the clock said she had to get the potatoes in the oven. First, she put on the stereo. She'd purchased the Supremes' *Merry Christmas* album with her last paycheck, and she really enjoyed it. She decided she'd buy a brand-new Christmas album every year; that way, by the time their children were grown, she'd have a variety of holiday albums.

Jim was unusually quiet during dinner and when Barb pressed him, he said nothing was wrong. Once they'd eaten, she began to clear the table of the dishes, but Jim reached up and took her gently by the wrist.

"Put them down for a minute, Barb, I need to talk to you," he said.

What alarmed her was how grave his expression was. Jim was so easygoing and relaxed that she loved being married to him. It was easy being his wife.

She set the dirty plates down on the table and sat. "This sounds serious."

"It is," he said.

She wondered if he was being transferred. It turned out she would like to be closer to home, but she was trying to create a life for herself and Jim. They were friendly with other officers and their wives, and they usually got together on Saturday nights, taking turns at each other's houses. Or worse, maybe he'd been called up to Vietnam.

"My leave has been canceled." He rubbed the inside of her wrist, his gaze circling her face.

Barb blinked. "What?"

"We can't go back home for Christmas this year. They canceled my leave," he said.

She slouched in her chair like all the air had leaked out of her. "Why?"

He shook his head. "It has to do with sending the increased troops to Vietnam."

Barb frowned, feeling in a fog of confusion. "But what does that have to do with you?" You work in an office."

He laughed, humoring her. "That may be, but I do work in logistics."

"We can't go home at all?"

He shook his head.

"Can't you tell them that we have our plane tickets already? That we're going home to see our families for the biggest holiday of the year?"

He scoffed. "The Army doesn't care about our plans, our personal life."

"They should if they want happy soldiers," she said, her voice rising.

He laughed at her, and that irritated Barb. She squared her shoulders. "Just tell them you can't do it. That you'll be back after New Year's." She did not want the military dictating her life.

Jim looked at her, his mouth opened slightly. He closed it, then opened it, then closed it again. There was a tight set to his jaw. Finally he said, "You're serious, aren't you, Barb?"

"I've never been more serious," she said. She straightened in her chair, leaned back, and folded her arms across her chest.

"Unfortunately, it doesn't work that way," he said stiffly. "I can't march in there and tell them, 'Oh sorry, you can't cancel my leave because my wife wants to go to Buffalo for Christmas.'"

She wanted to ask, *Why not*? but refrained. Her emotions plummeted from anger to depression. It would only be the two of them for the holiday. Thanksgiving and Christmas were family holidays to her. They didn't go home at Thanksgiving because the plan had been to go back to Buffalo for Christmas. They'd spent Thanksgiving with other couples they'd made friends with. Barb had made the pies: pumpkin, apple, and lemon meringue. It was nice, and it was better than spending it alone, but it wasn't the same as going home.

Jim pulled his chair closer to her, leaned forward, and took her hand in his. He massaged her knuckles. As he spoke, he lowered his voice and stared at her hands. Absentmindedly, he moved the rings of her wedding set on her finger. "I'm sorry you're disappointed. I know how much it meant to you to go home."

Tears filled her eyes. "Christmas is a time to spend with family."

"I know it is," he said. "But I'm in the Army and they own me."

"Is it worth it, Jim?"

"It's disappointing, but Christmas is one day, and the Army is a whole bunch of days. It's my career. It's what's going to support us and give us the kind of lifestyle we want for our family."

Barb knew all this. She had a career too, with the advertising agency. Granted, she didn't make the money Jim did, but she earned her own wage. The military was his life. Not hers. But once she'd married him, it became hers. And although she knew it in a sense when they married, she hadn't really known what it would entail.

"Look," he said, "we can drive down to Monterey or anywhere you want to go, and take a few days for ourselves over the weekend."

Deep down, she understood it wasn't his fault, but she couldn't help but be disappointed. Determined to make the best of it, she smiled, leaned forward, and kissed his forehead. "Okay, we'll see."

CHAPTER TWENTY-ONE

Isabelle

Isabelle had told Joe not to bother walking her back to the house as he lived on the other side of town, but he said he didn't mind. It was their fifth time going for ice cream in two weeks. She'd go for her swim at dusk just as the moon was rising in the sky and by the time she emerged from the lake, he'd be waiting there for her at the shore with Charlie and Luther.

The idea of a man with motherless children held little appeal to her, and yet she continued to see him. He was male company who was engaging, who made her laugh, who could talk about a variety of subjects, and who was someone to hang out with other than her sisters. Not that she minded sitting on the porch in the evenings, watching the sunset, chatting with her sisters about everything and nothing. But she was trying to keep boredom at bay, and this helped.

As they walked back to her house, she said, "It must be hard raising children by yourself."

He shrugged, his hands in his pockets. "It has its challenges, that's for sure, but they're my kids and after Tracy died, I decided I was going to make the best of a terrible situation. I had three children who were grieving in different ways, and I didn't have the luxury of being swallowed up by my own sorrow. In a way, they've given me a reason to carry on."

Isabelle wondered if her mother had ever felt like that when they were growing up. She'd been left but managed to soldier on, raise them without complaint.

Luther and Charlie walked on ahead of them. Or rather, Charlie loped forward and stopped, waiting for Luther to catch up.

"You know, this is a great little town," Joe said enthusiastically. "After my wife died, my parents moved here and they love it too."

Isabelle supposed it was a great little town. Situated right on the beach with a thriving community, it had a lot to offer. *Funny, how we take our hometowns for granted.*

In front of the house on Star Shine Drive, she said goodnight to Joe and walked up the driveway to the front porch, Charlie loping along at her side. She glanced at the new solar lights she'd installed in the landscaping, appreciating the way they glistened among the flowers.

Lily and Alice sat on the wicker furniture with an open bottle of wine on the table in front of them. Both wore broad smiles, and Isabelle braced herself for an onslaught of questions or some innocent ribbing.

As she stepped up onto the porch, she ran her fingers through her damp hair. She sank into an empty chair and leaned back. Along with the bottle of wine there was a charcuterie board that held black and green olives, slices of cheddar and pepper jack cheese, pepperoni, and crackers.

"Do you want wine?" Alice asked.

Isabelle shook her head. "No thanks, I just had ice cream."

"You're eating a lot of ice cream these days," Lily said. There was a slight lift to the corner of her mouth.

"I didn't know you loved ice cream *that* much," Alice said with a grin.

"You're doing great for someone with no gallbladder," Lily teased.

Isabelle tilted her head and smirked at them. "Ha-ha." She crossed one leg over the other.

"You seem to be seeing a lot of him lately," Lily said.

"You want to pursue this, don't you." Isabelle said. She stared at the charcuterie board and, unable to resist, reached for a piece of cheese and popped an olive in her mouth.

"Of course, we want to know everything," Alice gushed.

"I've told you *everything*," Isabelle said pointedly.

"You've given us a fact sheet," Lily said with a laugh. "He's a widowed teacher with kids and pets. That's it."

"What more do you want to know?"

"You must like him if you keep meeting him," Alice said.

Isabelle looked away. "I suppose. He's nice. But my relationships are never long-term. I'm not built that way."

"Maybe you haven't found 'the right one' yet," Lily said, making air quotes with her fingers.

Isabelle leveled her gaze at her sister. "I've met a lot of interesting men during my travels."

"No one that had 'forever' written all over them?" Alice asked.

Isabelle looked at her youngest sister, ever the romantic. "No, not really. After the novelty wears off, I move on."

"Do you want to be alone for the rest of your life?" Lily asked.

"I don't mind. I like my own company. I'm used to traveling alone. To add another person to the mix would be a hassle."

"At least you're honest," Alice said.

What could she say?

"But what about Joe?" Lily asked.

"What about him?"

"What happens after the novelty wears off?"

Isabelle shrugged. "I guess I move on. I've told him I'm not staying in Hideaway Bay for long. Besides, it's only ice cream. We're not rolling around in the sand and making out on the beach or anything like that."

Alice leaned forward, her eyes sparkling with mischief. "Would you like to do those things with him?"

Isabelle laughed. "I wouldn't refuse, let's put it that way."

They had a laugh and when they quieted down, she added, "We're coming at life from different angles. He's got kids! I wouldn't know what to do with them."

"Who said you have to do anything with them?"

"And he has three," Isabelle said, wincing. "I dated a guy once down in Texas. I liked him a lot. He had a horse farm. And he also had a nine-year-old daughter who made it her life's work to make my life miserable."

"What'd she do?" Lily asked, stretching her legs out in front of her and kicking off her sandals.

"She poured orange juice in my shoes, and let me tell you how fun that was to slip them on. Then she threw my custom-made pair of cowboy boots into a bonfire. I loved those boots; they cost me over a thousand dollars."

"Charming," Alice said with a grimace.

"Tex thought if I—"

"Whoa, hold up," Lily said, grinning and raising her hand. "Tex?"

"His name was Sean, but I always called him Tex because he always wore this big Stetson and he was a Texan," Isabelle explained, thinking it might sound foolish now. "Anyway, Tex thought if we spent some time together alone, Anna and I, that we would start bonding. One day, I took her for a manicure and a pedicure and to the movies. She asked to go to the concession stand during the movie and then disappeared! When she didn't come back, I went searching for her and she'd left the theater. She was nine! I almost had a heart attack."

"Where'd she go?"

"She started walking home. Through the woods! I called Tex and he had to call the police. I was in a state by the time they found her."

"That little beast," Lily said.

Isabelle sighed. "It had only been her and her dad since her mother walked out, and she didn't want anyone coming between them. I get it. But let me tell you, that broke us up. I seriously considered getting my tubes tied after meeting her."

Lily and Alice burst out laughing.

She didn't want to force love. It should be easy and effortless, or at least that's what she'd always thought. Not only should they want to stay, but they should also not want you to go. Silence descended, and it was Alice who broke it first:

"Do you find it odd that none of us have any children?"

"Jamie and I wanted to have children," Lily said, "but I thought we needed to get his gambling addiction under better control before we brought a baby into the mix. Sadly, that wasn't meant to be."

"I'd love to get married and settle down," Alice said. "And have kids."

"Things seem to be going well with you and Jack Stirling," Isabelle said. You'd have to be blind not to see the way Alice lit up any time the Colonel was around.

Alice smiled and even in the darkness, her eyes shone. "I really like him and am interested in seeing where it goes. Luckily, he feels the same way."

"I'm happy for you, Sparrow," Isabelle said, using her sister's childhood nickname.

"What about you, Isabelle?" Lily asked.

Isabelle appeared thoughtful for a moment. "I guess I never had strong maternal urges. There were fleeting ones"—here she chuckled—"but I quickly recovered. It never bothered me that I didn't have children. I was too busy enjoying my work and my life and travel." She paused, her gaze diverted by an elderly couple across the street, walking along the sidewalk with what appeared to be a group of grandchildren around them. "Now that I'm almost forty, the opportunity to have children is decreasing."

"For me as well," Lily said. "I'm over thirty-five."

"You're only thirty-eight, you've got time," Isabelle reassured her. She eyed their youngest sister. "No pressure on you either, Alice, you've got plenty of time."

Alice nodded. "I do, but anything can happen."

"Think positive," Isabelle said, sounding cheerier than she actually felt. Secretly, she thought not having children felt like a missed opportunity, and she hated missed opportunities. Instead, it would have to be filed under "not meant to be."

After a spate of silence, Isabelle said, "In saying all that, I'd love to be an aunt. I think I'd make a great aunt." That she truly believed.

Lily smiled. "I think you'd be a great aunt too."

Chapter Twenty-Two

1967

Barb

Barb lowered her head and wept. The day she knew would come had arrived.

The weather outside matched her mood. Gone were the perpetual sunshine and blue sky. Instead, it had been morning fog, gray skies, and steady rain for the past two days. It seemed appropriate.

Jim pulled her into an embrace and rubbed her back. "Honey, we knew this was going to happen." He pulled back and lifted her chin, wiping away her tears. "Honestly, I'm surprised I wasn't called up sooner."

Vietnam. If she never heard the name of that country mentioned again, it would be too soon. Within the last year, the subject had come up with increasing degrees of alarm.

Being married to an Army man did not help. It was all that was talked about at all the parties and gatherings. She knew men whose wives she was friendly with who had gone off, done their year, and returned. And she knew some who hadn't returned. Their wives looked thin and hollow-eyed. She did not want to be one of those wives.

The tenor of the parties with other military couples had changed. When they first moved out to California the parties were fun, and it was a great way to socialize and meet people, especially other families in the Army. But now, the men tended to huddle in the corner of someone's living room or outside around the grill, talking in hushed voices, while the women leaned against the kitchen counters, some smoking cigarettes, speculating about when their husbands would head over to Asia.

"Do you have to go?" Barb asked, knowing it was a stupid question but feeling a sense of desperation.

He laughed and pulled her close, hugging her and kissing the side of her head. "More than anything, I hate leaving you."

Then don't leave.

But she said, "I'll be worried about you."

"Nothing to worry about. I'll be in an office, far away from any of the fighting. In one year, I'll be home."

There was that small bit of comfort, knowing that he wouldn't be on the front lines. She bit her lip and wrapped her arms tighter around Jim's waist, always loving the feel of him. More tears pooled in her eyes at the thought of him leaving. She was missing him already.

He pulled away and said, "After Vietnam, there's a strong possibility I'll be posted in Europe. How would you like to live in Germany for a while?"

Barb's eyes widened, her fears about him going off to war momentarily forgotten. "Germany?"

"I have it on good authority that when I come home from 'Nam, Germany is there if I want it." He looked into her eyes and asked, "Do we want that, Barb?"

She nodded, and he smiled.

"That's my girl. Listen, why don't you go home for a bit. Your parents will be opening up the cottage down in Hideaway Bay, and I'm sure they'd love to have you. I know how much you love the place."

"Maybe I will," she said.

"You can meet up with Junie and Thelma," he said. "It's a shame they can't come out here to California."

Barb shook her head and laughed. "No, it's too expensive now that there are children involved." Junie had looked into it once, but the cost of flying was so prohibitive she never mentioned it again. And when Barb first raised the idea of her friends coming out for a visit, Thelma had snorted and said, "What? Are you kidding? Bobby and I don't have two nickels to rub together!"

Still, she'd love to see them. And it would make more sense for her to go there than for any of them to come out to the west coast. She'd hoped to have been pregnant by now, but even after two years of marriage, it didn't seem to be happening. And now with Jim going away for a year, starting a family was definitely on the back burner. Her mother had reassured her, reminding her that she herself hadn't gotten pregnant until she'd been married for almost four years. Barb tried not to be disheartened, but it was just about impossible. Doubts crept in late at night, worries that there might be something wrong with one of them.

Jim said something to her.

"What?" she asked.

"How about that? Go home for a bit, stay with your mother, go out to the lake, go swimming and everything," he said. "I don't want to think of you moping around here."

Barb nodded. Although she'd be sad and miss him terribly, she didn't want him thinking that she was sitting around, depressed, waiting for him to come home. He didn't need that.

"I'll be fine," she said, straightening up. She sniffed and blinked, wiping away the tears from beneath her eyes with her forefingers. "Will you write?"

He laughed. "Do you have to ask?"

She flung her arms around his neck, kissing him. Already she was making plans, determined to keep busy while he was gone for the year. If she filled her days and nights with work and activities, the year was sure to fly, wasn't it? And maybe he was right; a trip home to Buffalo was a good idea.

Barb carefully unwrapped the pineapple upside-down cake she'd brought to Marilyn's home. There was a going-away party for Jim and Roger Darren, who was shipping out with Jim. Marilyn and her husband, Ron, were throwing the party at their home not far from the base. Ronald was almost a colonel and Jim's direct boss. Barb liked them and did a lot of work with the Army wives under Marilyn's expert direction. Marilyn stood at the counter with another wife, whose name might have been Tammy, but Barb wasn't sure. She'd only just arrived. Marilyn and Ron's home was all done up in blond Norwegian furniture. It wasn't to Barb's taste, but she admired it.

"That looks delicious, Barb," Marilyn said, peeking over her shoulder and holding a bowl of potato salad. Through the sliding glass doors, Barb spotted Jim standing around the grill with Ron, who flipped hamburgers with a spatula. There were other guys she recognized, the usual crew. "I'm surprised you're speaking to Jim," Marilyn said with a laugh. Marilyn was in her mid-forties, had had four children, and was short, barely five one, with ample curves and dyed blond hair.

Barb frowned at her, confusion clouding her expression. "Why wouldn't I?"

"Because he's going to Vietnam," Marilyn said.

Barb chuckled. "I can hardly fault him for going over there and doing his duty." She tried to sound bright about it—after all, what choice did she have?

"You're taking it better than I thought you would," Marilyn said, setting the bowl of potato salad on the table.

Did they think she'd fall apart just because her husband was shipping off to a war zone? Their situation was hardly unique. Every day, women watched their men go off to war. She didn't want special treatment; she only wanted to get through the year.

"If my husband asked his commanding officer to go over to Vietnam—to volunteer—I'd kill him," Marilyn said with a laugh. "But you must be made of sturdier stuff."

Barb tilted her head to one side, her eyebrows knitting together. "Marilyn, what are you talking about?"

Marilyn's mouth grew slack, and she went pale. "Oh gosh, I've put my foot in it."

"Tell me," Barb said firmly.

"All right, but you didn't hear it from me," Marilyn said. She looked around to make sure no one was in close range and lowered her voice. "Jim was anxious to get over to Vietnam.

Kept asking Ron to fill out the paperwork and send him over there."

Barb blinked several times, gape-jawed, trying to process what Marilyn had just revealed to her. "He volunteered? You mean he wasn't called up?" she repeated quietly, her voice almost a whisper. She felt the fury growing inside of her.

Marilyn laid her hand on Barb's arm. "Don't feel bad. You know how men are, especially soldiers. They all want to be where the action is. Don't say anything. You don't want to part on angry terms with him."

Barb pressed her lips together and nodded. If she started talking, she might spew. She pulled away from Marilyn's grasp and headed to the bathroom. She stared in the mirror; her face had gone blotchy from her anger. She splashed cold water on it and buried her face in a towel to dry it off, not caring if her mascara ran.

For the rest of the evening, she smiled politely when spoken to but somehow managed to stay out of Jim's range. Marilyn's home was not the place to fight with her husband. And she didn't care whether he was shipping out or not; she was furious. By ten, she tugged on Jim's sleeve, stating she had a headache and was ready to leave.

Quickly, she made her goodbyes, hugging Marilyn tightly and avoiding her gaze when she caught the other woman studying her. She gave her a tight smile, but Marilyn's expression looked as if she was unconvinced.

Barb rushed down the driveway with Jim following her. There was a slight mist, and one side of the moon peeked out from behind heavy cloud cover.

"Hey, honey, slow down," he said with a laugh. He placed his hands on her shoulders, but she shrugged him off and pulled away, out of his grasp. "Barb? What's going on?" he asked.

"Nothing," she said tightly.

The drive home was quiet, and Jim looked over at her in the passenger seat and asked several times, "What's the matter?"

But Barb remained quiet. This was an argument that could wait until they got home. Apparently he hadn't even noticed that she'd been avoiding him all evening.

When he pulled in to the driveway of their modest home, Barb jumped out of the car before he had it in park, anxious to get inside. She waited at the front door while he unlocked it, and he allowed her to step inside first. He followed her in and closed the door behind them, locking it.

"Barb, tell me what's going on," he demanded, throwing the keys on the console table.

She spun around, her eyes filled with hot, angry tears. Surprised at her expression, he took a faltering step back.

"Was it your turn to go to Vietnam, or did you volunteer?" she spat.

Jim paled and fumbled. "What?"

"Answer my question!" She crossed her arms, her heart thumping against the inside of her chest.

He took a step toward her, reaching out for her. "Let me explain."

She took another step back and threw up her hands. "Don't touch me!"

"Just listen for a minute," he said quietly. He didn't move, just stood there in the middle of their living room with its new gold carpet and new furniture.

She snorted. "I can't wait to hear this."

"I volunteered—"

"Why?" she said. She circled around the living room until she reached one of the easy chairs and stood behind it, as far as possible from him.

Jim remained where he was, altering his direction to face her.

"Because there's a war going on, and I don't want to be stateside," he said.

"Yes, why would you want to be stateside with a wife who loves you?" she asked, her voice rising. The ground shifted beneath her. What she thought of Jim and their marriage had been shattered. To Barb, this was a huge betrayal.

"Don't twist this," he said.

She narrowed her eyes at her husband, and she couldn't help the snideness in her tone. "You couldn't even confide in me. I had to hear it from Marilyn."

"I am sorry about that," he said. "It wasn't her place to say anything."

"Were you ever going to tell me?" When he didn't respond, she said, "Then I'm glad Marilyn did. It makes me wonder what other secrets you're keeping from me."

Jim blanched and stepped closer, reaching out for her, but then dropped his arm when she took a step back. "I don't keep any secrets from you. You know that."

She put her hand up. "But I don't know that, do I. Don't come any closer, Jim."

"Barbara Eckhert, if you don't know anything else about me, then know this: I am a soldier. I can't stay here while the front line is in Asia."

Her mother's words from years ago about how Jim would put the military first echoed in her mind.

"I know that. But I would have preferred for you to discuss it with me instead of you doing it without consulting me. I would have liked to be given the chance to support this big decision, but you left me out of it."

"I am truly sorry for that," he said. "I won't do that again."

"And now I'm pissed because you're leaving for Vietnam in a few days and I'm angry."

"You don't have to be," he said quickly.

Barb regarded him. "Do you think I can just shut it off like a switch?"

He shrugged. "I hope you can."

She wished he wasn't so damn handsome. But she wasn't going to be left out of the major decision-making of their marriage, even if it had to do with the military and his career.

She walked past him and didn't look at him. In the bedroom, she grabbed the pillow from his side of the bed and an extra blanket from a shelf in the closet. She carried them out and tossed them onto the sofa.

Jim blew out a ragged breath. "Come on, Barb! Really? I'm going off to war in a few days and you want me to sleep on the couch?"

She spun on her heel. "I trusted you and you betrayed me. I'm sorry. Make better choices next time."

And she marched off to the bedroom and slammed the door behind her.

The following night, realizing she'd made her point, she allowed him back into the bed. No matter how angry she was, she wouldn't send him off to war with the two of them fighting. There was no way she could do that; she loved him too much. She put her hurt aside and tried to keep their last few days together as normal as possible. In that time, Jim couldn't do enough for her and by the time she went with him to the base to see him off, things were somewhat back to normal. But it seemed as if there was a snag in the fabric of their marriage and Barb was afraid if she worried it or pulled at it, the whole thing would come apart.

"This is it then," he said, setting his duffel bag down beside him.

She nodded quickly, words lost and feeling inadequate. The place was packed with soldiers heading off. Couples clung to each other, and mothers and fathers kept hugging their sons.

Barb stood there, her arms wrapped around Jim's waist, burying her head in his shoulder, breathing in the smell of him—a combination of aftershave, soap, mint gum, and laundry detergent—and committing it to memory.

"I'll write you a lot. I'll try to write every day," he whispered into her hair.

"I understand you'll be busy, so write when you can," she said. She didn't want to be a ball and chain.

He rubbed his hands along her back, and she tried not to think of the fact that she wouldn't see him for a year. It was too awful to contemplate.

"Go home, stay with your parents, visit mine. Hang out with Junie and Thelma. Go to Hideaway Bay. Do things, Barb. Do things for me," he said.

She nodded and lifted her chin, and his gaze circled around her face as if he was memorizing her features. He brushed her bangs aside and kissed her forehead. She leaned into it.

"How lucky am I to have married you?" he whispered.

Tears filled Barb's eyes. She'd promised herself she wouldn't cry, but he was leaving and taking her heart with him.

He bent down and crushed his lips against hers. She slid her arms up along his back, wanting to hold him tight and not let him go. She lingered in his kiss until he pulled away.

With a grin, he said, "When I get home, we're going to start a family hot and heavy."

She looked down and blushed.

"You're killing me. You're so beautiful when you do that," he said, his voice husky.

The signal to depart went off, and Jim looked toward the military plane and then back at Barb. A steady stream of soldiers headed toward the transport plane with duffel bags over their shoulders. Every once in a while, they'd turn and wave to a loved one.

"This is it." Jim swept Barb into his arms and kissed her again. She stood on her tiptoes to kiss him. When they pulled apart, he picked up his duffel bag and joined the stream of soldiers marching toward the ramp up to the belly of the plane.

She couldn't bear the sight of him walking away from her. Racing after him, she cried out, her voice cracking on a sob. "Jim!"

He turned to her and pulled her into his arms one last time.

"Promise me you'll come back to me," she whispered in his ear.

He looked into her eyes and whispered, "I promise."

He let her go and headed off, turning once to smile and wave.

It was the last time she would see him alive.

Two months after his arrival in Vietnam, Jim Eckhert was killed in a motor vehicle accident on his way to his desk job. Later in her life, as Barb reflected on her first marriage, the irony was not lost on her that their short-lived relationship had begun and ended with death.

Chapter Twenty-Three

Isabelle

Lily and Alice were gone to work by the time Isabelle woke up. She'd had an early night; she'd gone for her swim and returned home as Joe hadn't been able to meet up. One of his kids needed help making a volcano for an end-of-year project. *Better him than me,* she'd thought at the time.

She took a quick shower, threw on a maxi sundress in the colors of orange, pink, and turquoise, and swept her hair up into a messy bun. She made her way down to the kitchen. The wind was strong, and a good breeze blew through the open windows downstairs. First order of business was a leisurely breakfast of yogurt and fruit. Alice had made cinnamon rolls with cream cheese frosting, but Isabelle resisted, thinking of her missing gallbladder. After she cleared her breakfast dishes, she poured herself a large mug of black coffee, settled in at the kitchen table, and turned on her laptop. It was time to get to work. She had a few articles she was working on and of course, a new installment for her travel blog. She loved her work, and it gave her a sense of purpose. With her sisters gone all day, the house was a perfect place to think, research, and write. If it hadn't been so breezy outside, she would have set up on the front porch, but that would be a hassle with the wind. Content, she worked away all morning until lunchtime. There was only one interruption: a text from Joe inviting her to dinner. It had taken her more than an hour to respond. She wanted to go to dinner with him, but then she didn't. She liked Joe and was certainly attracted to him—how could you not be with those magnificent clear green eyes and his sense of humor. In the end, she texted *yes* and asked for a time and place. It was only dinner, she told herself. It was a night out. Something different with some pleasing male company.

At lunchtime, she stood and stretched, reaching for the ceiling and trying to work out a kink in her lower back. Although it was still windy, she opted to go for a walk into town, if only to move and take a break from work and have a change of scenery. Alice had mentioned they were out of olive oil and balsamic vinegar, and she thought she might head over to the Hideaway Bay Olive Oil Shop and pick up some supplies.

Halfway to town, she was sorry she hadn't brought her cardigan as the air was cool with the breeze, despite it being June. Just because it was summer didn't necessarily mean there'd be summer weather. She hoped this was only a fluke. Some people waited all year for summer.

As she neared the end of Star Shine Drive, she spotted Martha Cotter exiting her house on the corner. The woman was hunched over her walker and gingerly made her way down the long asphalt driveway. Isabelle waited so she could say hello. It had been many years since she'd seen Mrs. Cotter, and she doubted she'd remember her.

"Hello, Mrs. Cotter," Isabelle said as the older woman neared the mailbox.

"Is that you, Isabelle Monroe?"

"Yep, it's me," Isabelle said, unable to hide her surprise.

Mrs. Cotter picked up on it. With a smirk, she said, "Although my body is seventy-six and feels every day of it, my mind is still twenty-two."

Isabelle remembered her old neighbor as being a bit domineering and felt like she was eight years old again and being cussed out for running across her lawn.

"We haven't seen you around here in a long time," Mrs. Cotter said.

"I travel a lot," Isabelle explained.

"That's what Junie said." Mrs. Cotter pushed past Isabelle to get her mail out of the box.

"How have you been?" Isabelle asked. It seemed impolite not to ask, but she also was under the impression the older woman didn't want to engage in small talk.

"I've got a list of physical ailments as long as your arm," Martha Cotter said. "None of which you'd be interested in hearing about."

Sensing the old woman wanted to wrap it up, Isabelle said, "Look, if you ever need anything, Lily and Alice and I are all at Gram's house."

"It took your grandmother's death to bring you all back."

There it was: the neighbor's legendary abrasiveness.

"It did," Isabelle agreed. "Like I said, if you need anything at all, let us know."

"I won't need anything, but thank you," Mrs. Cotter said with a slight tilt of her head, and she began to push her walker up the driveway.

Isabelle watched for a moment and then made her way to town.

The Hideaway Bay Olive Oil Shop was located halfway along Main Street, next to Lime's Five-and-Dime. It had a distinctive burgundy-colored awning. The sandwich board placed out front on the sidewalk listed the day's specials, and Isabelle noted there was a sale on popcorn toppings. She made a mental note to take advantage of the three-for-two offer to stock up for when she and her sisters dragged Gram's old VCR out and had a movie night, which was happening with more frequency. *Was she becoming domesticated*? It could happen quickly, and she might not notice it until it was too late. What was it that Gram always said? It was very easy to get into a rut and much harder to climb out of it.

The owner, Della, asked Isabelle how she was doing after her surgery, and Isabelle told her truthfully that she was doing fine. They exchanged a few more words, and Isabelle took a small wicker basket and began to browse.

On the other side of the shop, she spotted Sue Ann Marchek. Sue Ann was the only child of Gram's friend Barb, and had moved back to Hideaway Bay in the last eighteen months after a divorce. When they were younger, Sue Ann used to babysit Isabelle and her sisters. She was in her late forties now with two grown sons. As Isabelle made her way over to Sue Ann to say hello, she thought the other woman looked lost in thought. Normally, the best way to describe Sue Ann's personality would be sunny. She was outgoing and warm, and always waved and smiled, but today she seemed far away. Isabelle hoped everything was all right.

Forgetting her short list of items she needed, she headed straight over to Sue Ann, who hadn't even noticed her.

"Hey, Sue Ann," Isabelle said in greeting as she approached her.

Sue Ann looked up, startled, but immediately broke into a smile that didn't quite reach her eyes.

"Isabelle. It's good to see you," she said.

"You too. I came in to get a few things," Isabelle said. "How are Noah and Josh?"

Sue Ann shrugged. "Good. They'll be dropping in at different times over the summer. I'm really looking forward to seeing them."

"Hey, are you all right?" Isabelle asked, reaching out and placing a hand on the other woman's arm.

Sue Ann bowed her head for a moment and pressed her lips together. She looked up quickly at Isabelle and smiled. But it was a smile that was there for show; it didn't convince Isabelle.

"What's going on?" Isabelle pressed. She hoped her friend was all right.

Sue Ann made a dismissive gesture with her hand. "It's nothing."

"It must be something because you're not yourself today," Isabelle said.

Sue Ann drew in a deep breath. "Today's the anniversary of my mother's death."

Isabelle's expression morphed into one of sympathy. "Oh, Sue Ann, I'm so sorry." Having lost her own mother at a young age, she could certainly understand how Sue Ann felt. You never stopped missing the people you loved. "How long has it been now?"

"Twenty-eight years. I was nineteen," Sue Ann said. "It still hits me hard."

"Your mother was such a lovely person," Isabelle said.

Sue Ann smiled, the first genuine one Isabelle had seen on her today. "She was, wasn't she. I'd give anything to talk to her again."

Isabelle sighed and pursed her lips. "I know the feeling."

"It's not easy being motherless, is it." Sue Ann said.

"No, it is not. I think no matter how old we get, we always want our mothers," Isabelle replied.

"Truer words were never spoken."

"Are you doing anything tonight? You could come over and hang out with Lily, Alice, and me, and we could reminisce," Isabelle said, thinking she'd change her plans with Joe.

"Isabelle, that's so thoughtful and I appreciate it. But Dylan knows this is a tough day for me and has made plans for us," Sue Ann said, referring to her next-door neighbor and boyfriend, Dylan Sattler.

Isabelle gave her a warm smile, relieved that her friend wasn't going to be alone tonight. "He sounds like a keeper."

"He is," Sue Ann agreed.

"All right, but let's get together sometime soon," Isabelle said.

"Let's do that."

After ringing up her purchases at the counter, Della handed Isabelle a brown paper shopping bag, and Isabelle said goodbye and headed home.

She took a leisurely walk back to the house, contemplating Sue Ann's sadness after so many years—a lasting sadness Isabelle knew all too well. She'd once heard that it took seven good or positive things—events or times or people—to counteract the effects of one negative thing. She wondered now if she could even name seven good things, knowing she would need four or five times that amount to offset the losses in her life. But what was to be done about all those wounds left open?

Isabelle retrieved the mail from the box at the end of the drive and went into the quiet house. It took her less than five minutes to put away her purchases, and she folded the brown paper bag and stowed it in the pantry. She poured herself another mug of black coffee and popped it into the microwave to reheat it. As the glass table inside the microwave turned and the clock counted down the time, she quickly leafed through the pile of mail. Aside from circulars, there were a few pieces for Lily and Alice, which she set on the kitchen table, and there was one small envelope addressed to her.

The microwave beeped, and Isabelle removed her mug and carried it to the kitchen table. Once seated, she powered up her laptop and took a tentative sip of her coffee. It was blistering hot, and she set it aside to let it cool. Using her fingernail, she slit open the envelope and removed a small piece of paper. As she unfolded it, a photo fluttered away, landing on the floor.

Bending over, she retrieved the old photo from the floor. She studied it. It was a colorized Polaroid picture from the early seventies, showing a boy and a girl maybe ten or twelve years old with longish hair and sweaty faces, wearing shorts, sneakers, tube socks and T-shirts.

Isabelle froze. Her heart rate picked up. Immediately, she recognized the boy as her father. And the older girl must be Miriam. She set the photo down on the kitchen table and picked up the note. There were only a few short sentences in large, loopy handwriting.

Dear Isabelle,
This is the last address I have for your father.
Miriam

Isabelle's gaze traveled further down the page:

Dave Monroe
135 Hewley Avenue
Buffalo, NY
It was a start.

CHAPTER TWENTY-FOUR

1968

Barb

Barb sat on the porch out at her parents' cottage in Hideaway Bay. Three empty teacups sat on the table in front of her. Barb's tall frosted white-and-turquoise glass was half full of lemonade, the ice long melted. In her direct line of vision was the town green with its war memorial and gazebo and then beyond that, the lake. She couldn't look at the war memorial without thinking of Jim. That block of granite in the middle of the green was a constant reminder of what she had lost.

It was late August, and you could feel the shift in the air at the edge of summer: cooler nights and the days, although still hot, were no longer sweltering.

On either side of her sat her parents, her mother to her left on the two-seater lounge with its stiff floral cushion, and her father on her right in a turquoise-colored metal chair. They reminded her of bookends, which seemed appropriate as it felt as if they were propping her up.

She'd come home last week, the first time she'd been able to make the journey back since Jim's death. He'd been gone almost a year, and time had tempered the rawness of it. But Barb felt she still had a ways to go. This time, her father had come out to the cottage and had stayed longer than he usually did. He'd be here during her entire visit, not only on the weekends. She hadn't seen them since they'd come out to California for Jim's funeral, although her mother called her several times a week.

This was what they did in the morning. The three of them sat together outside after breakfast, drinking tea or lemonade, and sometimes they talked and sometimes they didn't. The easy companionship was a buoy, keeping her afloat, keeping her head above water. Her mother, with her practicality and her no-nonsense attitude, proved to be exactly what she needed at this time. Mercifully, her parents hadn't insulted her by saying she was young and eventually she'd move on and settle down with someone else. She'd been told that more times than she cared to admit. As if being young inured a person against death and grief. She didn't want to settle down with someone else. In her mind and heart, she was still married to Jim.

In front of them on the sidewalk, a small boy, maybe four or five, had let go of his balloon and it floated away. His mother chased it, the effort futile, and after a few seconds, she stopped, peering up at it, shielding her eyes from the dazzling sun. The child beside her threw a tantrum, lay right down on the ground, kicking and screaming, his angry shouts piercing the summer morning idyll. His mother bent over and lifted him up, although his kicking continued, and whispered something to him. She carried him off like that as if he were a sack of potatoes.

It was a bitter reminder to Barb that she and Jim had had no children. It made her sad.

"Barbara," her mother started as she examined her thin-boned hands and seashell pink–polished nails. "Would you think of moving back to Buffalo?"

Barb slowly looked at her but remained silent.

"You could live with us, and you'd have no problem getting a job," her mother said.

"We'd love to have you back home," her father added, puffing on his pipe.

The air around him was scented with cherry tobacco, which Barb always found comforting.

"We hate the thought of you all alone out in California," her mother said.

Barb knew her parents meant well, and she didn't know how to explain why she felt compelled to stay in California. It was true; she was alone. She'd moved out of base housing and gotten an apartment closer to work. The close-knit military family she'd been a part of and had become used to had slowly drifted away. In the beginning they were supportive, at her house every day with casseroles, but soon the invitations to dinners and barbecues tapered off as if she served as a painful reminder of what could happen to them and their own husbands.

"California is the last link I have with Jim. I don't think I'm ready to come home yet." Back in California, her job at the advertising agency was the one good thing that kept her not only distracted but moving forward. It kept her mind occupied during the daytime. Besides, she liked working and making her own money.

"But—" her mother began to protest, but her father held up his hand.

"Grief is a funny thing, Barbara," he said, removing his metal-rimmed glasses and wiping them with a clean handkerchief. "Each person must find their way through it as best they can. You'll find your own way in your own time."

Mrs. Walsh opened her mouth, always ready to add her own thoughts on any matter. Strangely, she hesitated, and then clamped her lips tight and said nothing.

The three of them went quiet and Barb stared out at the lake, marveling at how it looked different every time she was here. In the stillness of the summer morning, it was flat and silver like a mirror, the sun glinting off it in places.

"I thought we could drive up to the farmer's market and get some peaches," her mother said. "I used to make a peach cobbler a long time ago."

Barb nodded. She didn't care what they did, she just went along with her mother's suggestions. Keeping busy was a distraction. In the evening, they'd go for a walk into town to the Pink Parlor for ice cream, or she and her mother would go to a movie.

"I can't remember the last time you made peach cobbler," Dr. Walsh said with a smile. "1947?"

"Oh, you," Mrs. Walsh said in mock offense, but she grinned.

Barb swallowed hard. Why couldn't she have had that with Jim? That growing old together and the easy banter.

A red 1961 Rambler Classic station wagon with a white top pulled up in front of the cottage, hovering in the street just at the edge of the lawn.

Recognizing Thelma's vehicle, Barb smiled with some relief. Her friends were here.

Mrs. Walsh's lips thinned as Thelma and Junie got out of the car and pulled their kids from the back seat. Thelma's little boy, Donny, was four now, and Junie's daughter, Nancy, was only half a year younger.

Junie and Paul had bought a house on Star Shine Drive, which they were in the process of renovating. They'd come to pick up Barb, since Junie wanted her to see the house.

Thelma gave a wave and called out, "Hello!"

"I'll put the kettle on," Mrs. Walsh said. "I suppose Thelma will want instant coffee."

"Most likely," Barb said.

As Dr. Walsh regarded the women coming up the walk, Thelma holding Donny's hand and Junie with Nancy balanced on her hip, Barb stood and leaned against the railing. This was exactly what she needed.

"Old friends are the best friends," he said quietly.

She couldn't agree more.

1968

Fall

It was the first week in October, and the weather had been warm. There'd been a dip in the temperature the previous week but now the mercury had gone back up to the low seventies, although the nights remained cool. As Barb exited the movie palace, she pulled her cardigan around her to ward off the nip in the air. She'd just seen *Funny Girl* for the second time. It was something to do in the evenings. She found the nighttime the hardest part of the day. During the day she kept busy at work and thoughts of Jim were fleeting, but in the evening when she was home alone in her apartment, there was more time to ruminate, and it was too easy to slide into the black hole. She'd probably see *Funny Girl* several more times before it was replaced with the next big hit, she loved it that much. When Barbra Streisand sang "My Man," Barb had twice now bawled all the way through it.

Sometimes grief was buried deep and needed to find a way out. Barb knew the symptoms by now. Restlessness would set in, an agitation she couldn't shake. She'd pace her apartment, her skin feeling prickly, trying to find some relief but succor was not forthcoming. When she cried at some movie—she couldn't remember which one it was—she'd found some of the temporary relief she'd been seeking. There weren't as many musicals as there were ten years ago, which was a disappointment. And she avoided comedies as they irritated her. For the last year, nothing seemed funny. But she had not expected to have a good cry with *Funny Girl*.

Maybe her parents were right. Maybe it was time to go home. Go back to Buffalo and Hideaway Bay. Despite their encouragement, sometimes Barb felt as if she wasn't finished with California, and maybe California wasn't finished with her. Besides, Jim was California and California was Jim, and to leave for good would be to close a chapter in her life that she was not ready to shut the door on.

Her apartment building was in view. There were curbside restaurants and clubs along the street. Pots of chrysanthemums and monkey flowers adorned the exterior spaces. Through the windows of one of the restaurants she could see couples sitting at tables with candles in small, frosted glass bowls. Quickly, she looked away. It made her feel alone.

But she was in no hurry to go home, so she walked slowly. She dreaded returning to her apartment. The silence was heavy and had lately begun to feel suffocating. At least it wasn't long until bedtime. She thought briefly about stopping at one of those curbside cafés and getting a coffee, but she didn't want to sit alone in a sea of couples.

"Barb?" a voice called out.

She slowed her pace, turned around, and came face to face with Tony Sebring with a girl on his arm. Tony was a new ad executive from New York who'd transferred out to the west coast office. The girl on his arm was young, early twenties, with flame-colored hair teased high and wearing a bright orange form-fitting dress and a pair of white go-go boots. Barb felt dowdy next to her.

She waited until they caught up with her. Tony was everything Barb was not: dark-haired, outgoing, and confident. Sometimes she overheard him at the coffeepot, talking about the girl he'd taken out the previous night. It sounded like he dated a lot of girls. He was tall and muscular with bright dark eyes that illuminated his face. He truly looked like a movie star. She was surprised the office Adonis even knew her name.

"What are you doing out here at this time of night?" Tony asked.

The redhead had her arm looped through his. She regarded Barb with curious disinterest.

Thinking it might sound pathetic to admit having gone to the show by herself, she lied casually. "It was a nice night and I thought I might take a walk."

"Are you alone?" he asked.

"I am," she answered, "but my apartment is close by."

She flicked her gaze again over the redhead, which prompted Tony to perform introductions.

"Oh, excuse me. Barb, this is Chrissy Montcrief. Chrissy, this is Barb Eckhert. I work with her."

The girl's frosted pink lips curved slightly. Her eyes were a deep, dark brown and reminded Barb of chocolate. She gave a slight nod to Barb.

"Nice to meet you."

"Look, where do you live?" Tony asked.

"Right there," Barb said, pointing to the apartment building that dominated the corner two blocks away on the opposite side of the street.

"We're going in that direction; we'll walk you home."

"That isn't necessary," Barb protested, not wanting to intrude on their date.

"Come on, let's go," he said, grinning. He offered her his left arm as Chrissy had her arm hooked through his right.

Barb hesitated and slid her arm through his, and Tony smiled down at her, though he wasn't much taller than she was. Chrissy stared straight ahead, either oblivious to Barb or deciding to ignore her.

"A guy could get used to this every night: a beautiful girl on *each* arm," Tony said with a laugh.

Barb smiled perfunctorily, and Chrissy tittered.

The walk wasn't that long—her apartment was only two blocks away. But it was long enough for Barb to notice Tony's cologne—something different than the usual Old Spice. This smelled pleasantly of sandalwood. She liked the feel of his suede jacket against her. It was so soft.

Tony continued in the same vein. "I've got a blonde and a redhead tonight. Who says I'm not lucky?"

He was like this at work too: always joking and lighthearted. But his work ethic was a different story. There was no lighthearted approach there. Since he'd been hired, he'd quickly become the top sales executive at the agency. He was ambitious, and Barb admired that about him. Wasn't that what the American dream was all about?

Not wanting to exclude or alienate his date further, Barb looked across Tony and asked the other woman, "What do you do for a living, Chrissy?"

"I'm a flight attendant with Pan Am," she said.

"That must be very exciting, traveling all those different places," Barb said enthusiastically.

Chrissy shrugged, the gesture noncommittal, and added nothing further. Her posture was stiff, and Barb wondered if she resented her presence. She wanted to reassure Chrissy that she had no interest in Tony or any man, for that matter.

Tony turned to Barb and winked.

"This is me," Barb said, removing her arm from Tony's. Chrissy's posture relaxed when she did so. They'd arrived at Barb's apartment building, a six-story blond stone affair. She'd been drawn to it because it reminded her of the Abigail Adams Hotel for Women in New York City. The building stood in stark contrast against the night sky. The moon was visible over the top of the trees.

"Nice place," Tony said, looking up at the building.

"It is nice. I moved here when I had to move off base," Barb said, clearing her throat.

Tony nodded. It was no secret at work that she was a widow. The people she worked with had become like family.

Chrissy latched on to her statement and eyed her with curiosity. "What base?"

"I lived in officer housing with my husband at the Oakland Army Terminal," Barb replied.

"Were you in the Army?" Chrissy asked, confusion clouding her features.

"No, she wasn't, but her husband was," Tony said with a trace of impatience. "Her husband was killed in Vietnam."

Chrissy's eyes widened. "I'm so sorry, I didn't know." She reached out and laid a hand on Barb's arm.

"It's all right," Barb said, her throat thickening. "I better go up. Good night."

She turned, grateful that her back was to them so they couldn't see her eyes filling with tears.

"Goodnight, Barb, see you at work," Tony said.

"It was nice meeting you, Barb," Chrissy called after her.

Barb said nothing but hurried into her apartment building, relieved to be alone and anxious to get to her apartment on the fourth floor so she could close the door on the world.

Chapter Twenty-Five

Isabelle

Isabelle debated showing her sisters the photo and, in the end, decided it would be better to wait. As she was leaving to meet Joe up at Cabana Sally's, Lily and Alice were coming in from work. There was no time to get into it and show them Miriam's letter and the accompanying Polaroid. This wasn't something that could be done as she was passing them in the doorway. It would have to wait until the next day.

The three of them had a quick catch-up at the front door before Isabelle headed out. She put the letter and Polaroid in her purse and walked into town. Joe had offered to pick her up, but it wasn't that far, and the wind had died down to a gentle breeze. The exercise would be good for her, she decided.

Joe stood outside waiting for her at Cabana Sally's, watching the pedestrians walking up and down Main Street. Isabelle smiled to herself. He was so intent on what he was looking at that he didn't notice her approach.

"Hey."

"Oh, hey," he said, a smile breaking out on his face. He leaned in and kissed her on the cheek.

"How was your day?" she asked.

"Great. Took the class on a birdwatching expedition," he said.

"Nice. See anything good?"

"Lots of cardinals and blue jays, and we did spot a cedar waxwing over on Lakeview Terrace."

Isabelle really liked this man. He didn't do anything by half measures. She had an image in her head of him walking around Hideaway Bay with a pair of binoculars, looking for various birds. It led her to ask, "How did you keep a group of schoolchildren quiet long enough to look at birds?"

Joe arched an eyebrow. "I can't tell you all my secrets, Isabelle." She laughed, and he held the door open for her. "I don't know about you, but I'm starving."

"I am hungry," she said. The letter and photo had occupied most of her afternoon, and she only now realized she hadn't eaten lunch.

"Did you want to eat inside? It's kind of breezy outside," he said.

"That's fine."

They stood at the hostess station, waiting on a server to gather menus and lead them to a booth at the back of the restaurant. It ran along the side wall, and Joe encouraged Isabelle to take the side that had a view of Lake Erie out the back window. The server laid the menus on the table and asked if they'd like anything to drink. Isabelle chose a red wine, and Joe asked for a bottle of beer.

"How's your week going?" Isabelle asked.

Joe nodded. "Good. Casey lost her first tooth, Aiden hit a home run for his baseball team, and Kyle is reading a book on hurricanes."

"Lost her first tooth? That's exciting," Isabelle said. Or was it? She had no idea; she'd spent so little time around kids. "And Kyle is reading a book on hurricanes?"

"He loves natural disasters."

"Lucky you," she said with a laugh.

Although she'd never met Joe's kids, he talked about them, and she had a general idea. Kyle was the oldest and a sophomore in high school. He'd taken his mother's death the hardest. Aiden, the middle child, played baseball and soccer and ran track. The youngest was Casey, who was five and who Isabelle had to admit, sounded as cute as a button.

"What about you, Isabelle? What's been going on with you?" he asked.

The server reappeared with their drinks, and Joe informed her they'd need a few more minutes to look at the menu. Once the server was out of earshot, Isabelle told Joe about the letter from Miriam that contained the Polaroid and address. She pulled it out of her purse and handed it to him.

He studied the photo and looked up at Isabelle with a smile. "I can see the resemblance."

She gave him a quick smile.

"Are you planning on driving up to Buffalo?" he asked.

She nodded. She hadn't even had to think about that. "Yes. Even though he may no longer be at that address."

"Do you want some company? I could drive," he offered.

She smiled, touched at the gesture. "I really appreciate that, but this is something I have to do alone."

"Understood. What did your sisters say?"

"I haven't told them yet as they were only coming in the door as I was going out," she explained.

"When do you think you might go?"

"I don't know," she said, sipping her wine. "Maybe the day after tomorrow. I want to tell Lily and Alice first."

"Speaking of families, how would you like to meet mine?"

Isabelle's mouth opened and stayed that way as her brain scrambled to come up with an excuse for why she didn't want to meet his kids, without hurting his feelings.

To her surprise, Joe laughed. "I guess that's a solid no."

Before she could rebut him, the server appeared to take their order. Something as simple as perusal of the menu provided Isabelle with both relief and distraction from the topic. She decided on a falafel panini, and Joe opted for the pulled pork sandwich and fries. The server gathered their menus and disappeared. Isabelle leaned slightly forward and folded her hands on the table. The varnish was sticky with the summer humidity.

"Joe, I really like you. And I've enjoyed the time we've spent together," she started.

Even though he winced, he was still grinning. Isabelle began to suspect that he might not be that easily put off. She supposed being a widower with three young children, he'd have to be made of sturdy stuff.

"Ouch," he said. "The start of the brush-off."

Even she had to laugh. He was so good-natured about everything it was hard to feel uncomfortable.

"I won't be staying in Hideaway Bay," Isabelle said.

"You've said."

The problem was she liked Joe. A lot. He was easygoing and chill and didn't take things too seriously.

"I thought you might want to meet my kids because they're a part of who I am," he said, his hands out, palms up. He did not remove his gaze from her face.

She understood his point of view but said, "It wouldn't confuse them?"

He cocked his head to one side and asked, "How?"

"If they meet Dad's new lady friend—"

"Oooh, lady friend, I like that," he interrupted with a laugh.

Again, she couldn't help but smile; that's what happened when she was with him. Admittedly not knowing the first thing about children, she asked, "Wouldn't they jump to conclusions, and wouldn't that upset the balance in your household?"

"You mean would they think you're there to replace their mother?"

"Yes, exactly," she said. His youngest, Casey, was only five. Isabelle had no idea how the mind of a five-year-old worked, but she suspected there might be some magical thinking involved. And she didn't know if she wanted to find out. Meeting his children indicated an investment in Joe and—well, his children.

"No one can replace Tracy," he said seriously. "Honestly, I've never been out with a woman since she died. I didn't think I'd ever be interested again. But then I saw you, and there was a shift in my perspective."

How could she not feel flattered? She could feel her attitude softening and not because he'd complimented her but because she genuinely liked him. She liked being with him. She said with a pretense of ease, "I'd like to meet them."

"Good. Maybe you could come over for a barbecue," he said.

"I like barbecue," she admitted.

Joe's posture relaxed and his expression brightened, and Isabelle wondered if he'd been nervous about asking her. This surprised her as he always seemed so self-confident, so sure of himself. It suggested a vulnerability that he kept well hidden. She might have guessed that having been widowed at a young age with young children would leave anyone raw and exposed.

Chapter Twenty-Six

1969

Barb

"Can I get you some coffee?" asked Tony, coming up behind Barb.

Startled, she put her hand, fingers splayed, across her chest. "You scared me."

He laughed.

She looked up from her desk and blinked. His thick, dark, wavy hair sported the new trend of sideburns, and he had grown a thick, healthy mustache. To boot, he had a pair of dimples that seemed to be working in overdrive.

The offer of coffee left her speechless. This truly was a modern man. It might be nice to have a man pour her coffee for a change.

Finally, she found her voice and said, "Yeah, sure, that'd be great."

"How do you take it?"

"One cream and one sugar," she said.

"I'll be right back," he said, and he disappeared.

Barb looked around to see if anyone else had witnessed their exchange, but the rest of the staff seemed oblivious. Through the glass window, she spotted Ger, who was dropping an Alka-Seltzer tablet into a glass of water. His ulcer must be acting up. At the desk next to her, Donna—who'd been promoted from secretary to a job share with Barb—placated a client in soothing tones and by the sound of it, promising them the world.

Barb put her elbow on her desk, placing her hand on the back of her neck and rubbing it. She told herself not to look too much into Tony's attention. Though it was flattering, surely it didn't mean anything. The office was full of pretty young girls. Likely, he was only being solicitous to the war widow. She'd listened to the talk around the water cooler and the break room. Tony was considered quite the catch. As for Barb, she wasn't so sure. Although he was easy to talk to and funny, she liked to keep him at arm's length, a safe distance. Tony was so vibrant and so very alive, and Jim wasn't. His robustness was like a magnet, and that scared her.

But she'd watched the other women in the office trying—and failing—to get his attention. To her knowledge, he didn't or hadn't dated anyone from the agency.

When he didn't return immediately, Barb thought he'd either forgotten or had been waylaid. But he showed up just as she was mulling over these thoughts, smiling and carrying two cups of coffee, one in each hand, in Styrofoam cups with lids.

He set her coffee down in front of her and sat on the edge of her desk so that his muscular thigh was within reach. It was oddly disconcerting. She hadn't thought of a man in that way since she was married to Jim.

"Thank you," she said. "You went out for it?"

He nodded, swinging his leg and sipping from his cup. "Little diner around the corner, they make the best coffee. You can get it to take out." He studied her for a moment, a smile on his face. His gaze was the type that didn't just flit over you, bouncing around, but bored into you, to the very depths of your soul as if he could read all your deepest, darkest thoughts.

She squirmed in her seat and focused on the coffee. It had been a long time since she'd had to make conversation with a man who appeared to be singling her out. Interested? Or only polite? "Hmm, not bad," she said, thinking it beat the instant coffee in the company's break room. "I've worked for the agency for almost six years, and this is the first time a man has ever gotten *me* coffee."

"I'll have to work on rectifying that imbalance. I'm a big believer in women's rights," he said.

"Good for you," she said. Suddenly she wished he'd leave her alone and be on his way. Talking with him like this—she didn't consider it flirting—made her feel disloyal to Jim. Like she was cheating on him. It was times like these and men like him that made her really miss her late husband.

When Tony made no move to leave, only stared at her with some expectation that she didn't understand, Barb stood, unnerved, and murmured, "Excuse me. I better get back to work."

"Ooh, I see you're going to be a challenge, Barb." He laughed, clearly not offended. And still not moving away from her desk.

With some effort, she tamped down the smile that threatened to emerge.

"I've got two tickets to see Blood, Sweat & Tears," he said. "Will you go with me?"

"Is it a good idea to go out when we work together?"

He shrugged and grinned. "Probably not, but then there are exceptions to every rule."

"Thanks, but no thanks," she said. Ignoring the coffee and unwilling to encourage him, she pushed her chair in, hoping he'd take the more obvious hint to leave.

Undeterred, he pressed on. "What about dinner? How about Chinese? Do you like Chinese food? I know a place," he said easily as if they were lifelong friends.

Barb was conflicted, finding his familiarity both refreshing and off-putting.

"What about Chrissy?" she asked. She was pretty sure the flight attendant from Pan Am wouldn't be too thrilled to know her boyfriend was asking another woman out.

For a moment, there was a blank expression on Tony's face.

"Oh brother," Barb said, rolling her eyes.

He laughed. "Sorry, we broke up. She wasn't the one for me."

The mention of "the one" made Barb think back to when she was a teenager in search of a fairy tale and the love of her life and had somehow ended up in a nightmare. She frowned at the recollection.

"Have I said something distasteful? Because I would never want to offend you, Barb," he said sincerely.

"What? No, no, I was only thinking about something."

He grinned his boyish grin, and the light in his eyes danced. "I hope it was about me."

Now she did laugh. "Let me go back to work, Tony, or we'll be here all day."

"I'd love to waste a day with you," he said simply.

Her cheeks went hot, and she didn't have to look in a mirror to know her face had gone scarlet.

"Again, thanks for the coffee," she said. She turned and headed out of the office to the ladies' room, the one place he couldn't follow her. When the door closed behind her, she set her hands on the sink and looked in the mirror, letting out a long sigh.

It was the first time since Jim died that she had a strong attraction to another man. And she didn't know what to do about it.

"Barb, you're killing me," Tony said with a laugh, pulling up a chair across from her in the break room a few days later.

Barb looked up from the sandwich she was eating. "You don't appear to be dying. In fact, you look quite healthy."

He burst out laughing. "Come on, go out with me. You know I can't resist your charms."

She snorted, recovered, and shook her head. As attracted as she was to him, he was too much. Too over the top, and she feared she wouldn't be able to handle him. He was wild in a way Jim hadn't been. Good old dependable Jim, who had always kept her on sure footing. Tony was the complete opposite, and that scared her sometimes. Still, he wouldn't leave her alone, begging her for a date. But his reputation as the office playboy bothered her. She knew he dated girls, took them out once, and then never took them out again. The last thing she wanted was to become a statistic. Still, his pursuit of her was relentless.

Despite her concerns, she was flattered by the attention. In the evenings when she was home alone in her apartment, Jim and Tony fought for space in her head.

An idea came to her. If she went out with him, maybe he'd leave her alone. One date and he'd be gone. Could she handle that? That type of rejection? She reminded herself that she'd handled Jim's death and therefore, she could handle anything, never mind rejection at the hands of the office lothario. Besides, it might be nice to go on a date for a change instead of sitting home alone in the evening.

She narrowed her eyes and regarded him. "If I go out with you—one dinner, that's all— do you promise to leave me alone and not bother me again? Not ask me out anymore?"

Tony's face lit up. "Yes, yes, yes. I promise."

"Really?" she asked, seeking confirmation. He was about the conquest, she was sure, the notch in the proverbial belt. He'd find out that she was staid and unremarkable, and that would be the end of it.

"But what if we have a really great time and want to go out on a second date?" he asked.

"Ugh!" she said. She dropped her sandwich and put her head in her hands. What was it with this guy?

He burst out laughing. "Barb, you're too much. I think we'd make a great pair."

"I don't know about that."

He leaned closer and whispered, "Oh, I do."

She dragged in a ragged breath and pulled herself together. "One date, Tony."

"I'll pick you up at eight tonight?"

"All right," she said, caving in.

At the end of the night, Tony drove Barb home to her apartment. He pulled up to the curb in front of her apartment complex and shut off the engine. He looked toward the building and with a nod, he said, "Can I come up?"

Barb wasn't so stupid that she didn't know what that was code for. Immediately, she shook her head. "No."

He smiled, his eyes twinkling in the darkness. He leaned across the front seat, the cushion protesting beneath him. Lowering his voice, he asked, "Can I kiss you goodnight?"

"Yes." She'd never kissed a man with a mustache, plus they'd had a great evening together. He'd taken her to dinner, told her about his childhood growing up in Kansas and how he'd wanted to see the world. It was two hours where she didn't think of Jim and their lost future. Two hours where she was able to focus on something other than her grief, where she hadn't dreaded going to bed for fear of crying herself to sleep. It had been a long time since she'd been this relaxed.

Sliding his arm along the back of the seat, he scooched closer and beckoned with a grin, "Come here."

A shiver went down her spine, and the baby-fine hairs on her arms stood up. She inched closer to him until he pulled her into his arms and began exploring her lips with his, passion building as their tongues connected. Breathless, Barb pulled away for some air. She was actually dizzy. Tony leaned toward her again, his kisses—warm, insistent, and possessive—making her body feel languid, like liquid, golden and warm.

Reluctantly, she pulled away from him, forcing herself over to her side of the car.

"Good night," she said, and it came out sounding breathier than she'd intended.

"A good night it was," he said with a laugh. "Barb, I'm a passionate guy. I don't do anything by half measures."

She laughed, still trying to catch her breath. She smoothed down her hair and said teasingly, "I'm happy for you."

He smiled. "That's what I like about you. You keep me grounded."

"That's romantic," she huffed.

"Let me come up to your place and I'll show you how romantic I can be."

Barb shook her head slowly, though she was still smiling. "You are too much."

"Am I? But not too much for you, right?" he asked with an arch of his eyebrow.

She laughed and leaned over and kissed him on the lips but before he could take it any further, she pushed away from him and opened the car door, jumping out.

"Good night, Tony," she said.

He leaned over the seat and asked, "You did have a good time tonight?"

She nodded and waved goodbye.

As she strolled up the footpath to the front entrance of her apartment building, she swung her purse, smiling, and thought, *I had a great time.*

And that's what scared her.

Chapter Twenty-Seven

Isabelle

A relentless pounding rain accompanied Isabelle all the way from Hideaway Bay to Buffalo. She'd taken the New York State Thruway until she hit the 190 north in the city, getting off at exit 9, which landed her on the west side of Buffalo, continuing north onto Busti Avenue then Niagara Street. Lily had lent her her car for the expedition, and Isabelle had dropped her off at work and had run a few errands before leaving Hideaway Bay. A mixture of feelings gripped her: determination, uncertainty. The closer she got to the city, the more the determination ebbed and the uncertainty rooted itself firmly, taking hold and growing.

The previous evening, she'd showed her sisters the letter with the address and the picture of their father with Miriam as young children. Alice had studied it before passing it onto Lily, who glanced at it quickly and then set it down.

The rain had decreased from drenching to a light drumbeat as Isabelle pulled in to the first restaurant she found on Elmwood Avenue, in search of some lunch and fortifying sustenance and perhaps, delaying the inevitable. Her emotions ran the gamut from excitement to fear. What if he was no longer there? What if he wanted nothing to do with her? What if he had died? Then what? Over a lunch of beef souvlaki—which was delicious—and a cup of black coffee, she decided she'd take it one step at a time. Let it unfold naturally and deal with whatever came up as it came up. She couldn't control everything, she reminded herself.

After lunch, she booted up her GPS in the car and cut over from Elmwood to Grant Street, then made a right onto Hewley Avenue, slowing down to study the numbers on the houses. The dwellings that lined the street were older and large. Some appeared to house multiple families. Some looked forlorn with their sagging porches and chipped paint, but others appeared to be rejuvenated, bought possibly by younger couples with an intent to get on the property ladder. These were optimistic with their colorful hanging baskets, fresh coats of paint, and newly mowed lawns.

As she neared the address, she slowed down and pulled over on the opposite side of the street, throwing the car into park and turning off the engine. Leaning back, she peered out the window and studied the house.

It was a grand affair, three stories. Or it had once been grand. The front yard had been converted into a parking lot, and various late-model cars lined it haphazardly. One car was missing its back tires. The house had been sided in pale yellow, and the replacement windows were too small for the size of the house. The front yard was devoid of flowers or grass. A row of garbage cans lined the curb. The house number had been spray-painted on the siding to the left of the front door beneath an exterior light whose glass dome was cracked. There was a porch railing that looked basic, as if someone had just nailed a piece of wood to two supporting posts. Overall, the place had an air of dismal neglect.

After a few minutes, she exited the car, looked both ways, and trotted across the street. The rain had stopped but the air was muggy, and her shirt stuck to her back. The steps to the front porch were steep, and she grabbed hold of the wooden railing, but it wobbled beneath her grip, not inspiring any kind of confidence.

She stood on the stoop for a moment, collecting herself, and rubbed her damp hands on her jeans. There was no doorbell, so she knocked. When there was no answer, she rapped louder. After a few moments, the door was flung open by a teenaged girl with greasy hair and a chubby baby on her hip.

"Yeah." It was said more as a statement than a question. The girl regarded Isabelle with heavy black kohl-lined eyes.

"I'm looking for Dave Monroe—" Isabelle started.

The young girl flung the door open to reveal a dark hallway with a wide staircase. A bike leaned against the wall, and the hallway itself smelled of stale cigarette smoke and old grease and boiled root vegetables, like cabbage or turnip. A smoky haze wafting about in the dim light suggested the residents ignored the no smoking sign posted on the wall.

"Dave's in apartment four," the girl said, and she disappeared behind the door of one of the ground-floor apartments.

Isabelle wandered over to the metal mailboxes on the wall. There were eight in all, marked with paper strips beneath a plastic cover. The number four mailbox had a yellowed paper strip written in pencil. *D. Monroe.* Beneath it was a bell Isabelle pushed, listening for a corresponding chime deep within the building but hearing none. She rang it again and when there was no answer, she walked down the hall.

There were only two apartments on the ground floor, and Isabelle stood at the foot of the wide staircase and looked up. Above, a bare light bulb hung suspended, flickering on and off. Tentatively, she made her way up the staircase, looking up and seeing that it continued onto a third floor. She reached out to the banister, but it was sticky to the touch, and she withdrew her hand. Slowly, she made her way up the staircase to the second floor. Like the first, it was dark. There were three rooms on this level. The fuggy haze continued, and now the hallway smelled of both old smoke and spilled alcohol. Outside of apartment four was an old milk crate filled with empties: beer cans and liter bottles of vodka and whiskey. The number four hung upside-down on the door.

Isabelle knocked loudly, the sound startling her. From behind the door, she could hear music playing. A radio? A stereo maybe? Had her father been interested in music? She couldn't remember.

She knocked again.

"It's open," came a voice from the other side of the door.

Isabelle's palms were damp, and her heart pounded against her chest at the thought that on the other side of the door was her father.

Slowly, she turned the knob and pushed the door open. The atmosphere inside resembled that of the dim hallway: hazy and airless. Her gaze traveled around the one-room apartment, the kitchen area sporting only one cabinet, a sink, and a two-burner stove. The edges of the upper cabinet were grimy with fingerprints. The sink was full of dirty dishes.

"Whaddya want?" called a voice from the other direction, startling her.

She turned to see a daybed pushed up against the wall beneath the only window in the apartment. She swallowed hard. The deep windowsill was lined with ivy plants, most set in glass jars with water and marbles, no soil. There was a thirteen-inch black-and-white television with rabbit ears propped on a wonky end table. Her eyes finally landed on the man in the bed.

He was gaunt to the point of emaciated and appeared to be swimming in his blue jeans and dingy short-sleeved T-shirt. He was in a supine position with his head propped up on a blue-and-white striped pillow that had seen better days.

"What can I do for you, darling?" he asked, waving his left hand toward her, holding both a can of beer and a cigarette, whose ash dangled precariously. The pads of his index finger and thumb were stained with tobacco.

"Dave Monroe?" she asked, her voice low.

His brown hair was longish and streaked with white, and he wore about three days' stubble on his face. Narrowing his eyes at her, he asked, "Who wants to know?"

"It's me, Isabelle," she said, her gaze fixed on his face, wanting to see his reaction. For clarification, she added, "Your daughter."

It didn't appear to register at first. He took a long drag of his cigarette and narrowed his eyes further through the stream of blue smoke. "You're all grown up, Isabelle."

"I'm almost forty," she said.

"Is that so?" he asked. He did not get up, did not even sit up on his bed. He took a swig of his beer and then a drag from his cigarette, which he then stubbed out in the ashtray on the floor next to the bed. Immediately, he lit another.

Isabelle remained standing, no invitation to sit forthcoming.

"What brings you here after all this time?" he asked. There was a slight edge to his voice. "I haven't heard from you girls in years." His eyes did not leave her face.

What? He thinks we abandoned him?

"Lily and I were only nine and eleven when you left. And Alice was a baby," she said. "We could hardly follow you, let alone search for you."

"I suppose," he said, his tone aggrieved. He did not look at her.

"May I sit down?" she asked, her voice rising slightly. Before he could agree or refuse, she removed a pile of newspapers stacked on a kitchen chair, set them on the floor, and pulled the chair close to the daybed. She set her purse on the floor next to the leg of the chair, sat down, and crossed her legs.

"Have a seat why don't you?" he said, waving his hand around, the cigarette smoke a trailing ribbon of bluish-gray.

"I have a few questions," she said.

"We all have questions, Isabelly," he said. He tipped his face up toward the ceiling, blowing out more ribbons of smoke.

She hadn't heard that nickname in decades, and it slammed her back to her childhood.

As much as she wanted to delve into his reasons for abandoning them, she opted for a softer approach. "Have you always lived here?"

He shrugged, his bony shoulders lifting underneath the T-shirt. "In this place? I've been here for the last ten years or so. I dunno, I don't keep track."

"Did you come to Buffalo from Hideaway Bay?" she asked. She tried to keep her tone neutral, like Switzerland.

"Nah. When I left Hideaway Bay, I went to Binghamton first. Bummed around there. Then went over to Cleveland and back to Rochester and then Buffalo."

"Did you not ever want to come back to Hideaway Bay?"

His expression was one of scorn. "Hideaway Bay? I hated that place."

"But we were there," Isabelle said quietly, and she hated herself because her voice wobbled.

He did not reply.

"What were you doing in all these places?" Was it work that drove him? Was it another woman? Had there been a second family? But she dismissed that idea with a quick look around. There were no personal photos of her or her sisters or even her mother. There was a framed photograph of a racecar and the Indy 500.

"I was bumming around, looking for a good time. Looking for work," he said.

"You didn't want to be married or be a father?" she put out gently.

"My old man left me when I was a kid. I didn't know how to be a father," he said. He glanced at her and then looked away, staring straight ahead without seeing, as if he was mentally somewhere else. He seemed to remember that she was there and added quickly, "I never wanted to get married in the first place." He took a liberal slug from his beer can, finished it, crumpled it up, and tossed it onto the floor with the rest of the empties. He picked out another can from the case at the bedside and popped the lid, the cracking noise slicing through the awkward silence. "Your mother was a beautiful girl. We were just having some fun," he said, smiling at the memory of Nancy Reynolds. "But then she got pregnant."

Isabelle knew the story. Her mother had told them when they became teenagers that if they were going to fool around, they needed to use birth control. She would point to herself and say, "I'm the cautionary tale."

Dave Monroe said something.

"What?" Isabelle asked.

"When your mom found out she was pregnant, I offered to pay for an abortion," he said easily. "We were way too young to be having a baby. Hell, we were still kids ourselves."

Isabelle felt herself go pale. The father she'd adored would have preferred if she had not been born. Of all the possible scenarios, she had not imagined this one.

"What made you change your mind and marry Mom?" she finally managed to ask.

He lifted his head and laughed. "Paul Reynolds changed my mind."

"Granddad?"

"The one and only. The almighty Paul Reynolds," he said, with a trace of bitterness in his voice.

"What happened?" It was important to Isabelle to fill in all the blanks. Her family history didn't have only gaps; there were large holes where her father should have been.

"After her parents found out that Nancy was pregnant, Paul came over to my house, where me and Miriam lived with my mother." He paused to take a puff off his cigarette. "Said as I'd gotten Nancy into trouble, I would have to marry her." He shook his head. "I was only eighteen or nineteen at the time. I'd like him to try and tell me what to do now."

"You married Mom because Granddad forced you, but you had no interest in marriage or a family." Isabelle blew out a long breath.

"At that age? How could I? My dream had always been to get out of Hideaway Bay. I hated the place," he said. His jaw was tight, and a vein pulsed in his forehead. "I did the right thing," he said, defending himself, "married your mother. But then we started having more kids."

Although he didn't say it, his tone indicated that had not been part of his plan.

"Did you regret marrying Mom?"

"Of course I didn't regret it. Once you girls came along, it was nice." He bent his elbow and placed his arm behind his head. "No, I didn't regret that at all."

"Then why did you leave?"

"It all got to be too much," he said. "We never had enough money. Paul was always trying to find me a better job."

"But you took off. It affected us," she pointed out.

He shrugged. "I figured you'd be better off without me."

"How did you come to that conclusion?" she asked, unable to keep the disbelief out of her voice.

Dave Monroe didn't answer that question. "My own father left me when I was young . . . and I turned out all right."

A quick glance at his current living situation and Isabelle disagreed. What was considered not turning out all right? The room reeked of cigarette smoke and stale beer. And her father looked and smelled as if he hadn't had a bath in a while.

The conversation faltered along, stumbling, staggering, trying to find purchase on uneven, rocky ground and failing miserably.

He felt around in the cardboard container for another can of beer and when his hand came up empty, he frowned and exhaled.

"Mom is dead," Isabelle said bluntly.

"I heard that. Miriam told me," he said without looking at her. He swung two skinny legs off the bed and set his feet on the ground. His sock had a hole in the big toe. "Isabelle, could you give me a ride up to the gas station? It's two blocks over."

Taken aback, she said, "Sure."

She stood from the chair and waited for her father. He was slow moving. Once upright, he waited a minute before he stood, and then he staggered and missed a step as he crossed the small room. There was a pair of shoes next to the door, and he picked them up and slipped them on. He patted his back pocket for his wallet and took the key off the hook by the door and palmed it. He regarded her for a moment.

"Boy, you're a real tall drink of water," he said, assessing her.

"I don't know where I get my height from," she found herself saying. Her mother hadn't been tall, and neither had Gram or Granddad.

"My dad was tall," he said. "Six four, I think."

"That's pretty tall."

He seemed to remember his purpose for getting up and opened the door. "Come on, let's go." Isabelle followed him out into the hall, and he closed the door behind him, making sure it was locked.

As she walked beside this man, it was hard to reconcile the fact that he was her father, her flesh and blood. If he'd remained in Hideaway Bay, would he have turned out like this? To speculate and think things could have turned out different for him and for them was dangerous. Delusional. Maybe this had been inevitable. Sadness and disappointment clothed her, and her posture slumped as she followed him down the stairs.

When they stepped outside, the bright light and fresh air made her dizzy. She could smell the cigarette smoke in her hair and on her clothes. The beach at Hideaway Bay came to mind and she wished she were there now, breathing in deep lungfuls of lake air.

"Where's your car?" he asked, squinting and taking a last drag on his cigarette before tossing it aside.

"Right there," she said, taking the keys out of her purse and clicking the fob to unlock the doors.

"Nice."

Without a word, he got into the passenger seat and pulled the seat belt over, buckling himself in.

"Make a left at the end of the street and the gas station is two blocks up on the left."

They arrived at the corner gas station in less than five minutes.

"I'll be back in a jiffy," he said, and the door slammed before she could respond.

She studied him as he went inside. Time had not been kind to him, and he appeared older than his actual age. He was skinny, not from genetics or dieting but from alcohol abuse and poor nutrition. She suspected her father might be his own worst enemy.

It was a few minutes before he emerged from the shop and when he did, he had a six-pack of beer cans in his right hand and a pack of cigarettes in his left.

When he buckled in, she asked, "Do you work?" She was doubtful but she didn't want to judge.

"Nah. I'm on permanent social security disability," he said.

"What happened?"

"Busted my knee real good on a job."

"What were you doing?" she asked, making a right onto his street.

He laughed, but it sounded more disgruntled than funny. "You sound like Paul. Always asking what irons I had in the fire. Listened to his lecture more than once about how anyone who wanted to work would always find work in this country," he said. He leaned against the window. "I sure don't miss that."

Something bristled inside of Isabelle, and she felt compelled to defend her grandfather. "Granddad was a good man." She didn't want to add that he'd been the only stable male influence in their lives.

Dave snorted. "St. Paul, I know. I lived it." Bitterness laced his voice.

She pulled up in front of his apartment building but left the car idling. She would not go in; the short visit had left her weary and exhausted.

He hesitated, not getting out of the car. Finally, he said with a smile that was meant to ingratiate but instead told Isabelle he was in desperate need of a dentist, "Can you do me a solid and lend your old man some money?"

Caught by surprise, Isabelle paused before saying, "Oh, of course. I don't carry much cash on me but let me see what I have." She pulled her purse into her lap and took out her wallet. There were three twenties tucked neatly in the fold. She pulled them out and handed them to him.

"Sorry, it's all I have," she said.

He lifted the bills up and said, "Hey, thanks for this. Good seeing you again. Take care." And he got out of the car and disappeared into the apartment building without once looking over his shoulder.

Isabelle stared after him, stunned. The entire encounter was surreal. He hadn't defended his actions, hadn't displayed shock at seeing her or even any of the embarrassment that should have been known to a man who'd abandoned his entire family thirty years ago. He'd stated his reasons for leaving with a tone that implied they were rational, completely normal. He hadn't asked a thing about her or her sisters, had known no shame in bugging her for a ride and money. Beer and cigarettes, apparently, were all he cared about.

After a moment of sitting there, staring blindly, Isabelle put the car in gear and drove away. Her shock evolved, turning quickly to anger. How dare he? No, she wasn't going to let it end like that. He needed to know, to be told precisely, what his leaving had done, and what an ass he was to have treated her arrival here today as if it were nothing.

At the end of Hewley Avenue, she pulled over, her anger building. Was that it? All these years of wondering about her disappearing father and he had nothing to say? *I don't think so.* She looked in her rearview mirror, turned and glanced over her shoulder for any oncoming traffic, made a U-turn, and headed back to her father's home.

She slid into her previously vacated parking spot, got out, locked her car, and trotted across the street to the apartment building. Without hesitation, she ran up the stairs to the dingy apartment on the second floor and rapped loudly on the door.

"Yeah," he said as he had before.

Isabelle stepped in. He was in the same position as he was previously: on the bed, sipping from a can of beer and smoking a cigarette. If he was surprised by her reappearance, he didn't show it.

"Don't you have anything to say for yourself?" she demanded.

He regarded her through narrowed eyes, a grim set to his mouth. "Like what?"

Her fury rose. "I don't know, let's start with the fact that you walked out on us all those years ago. Do you know what that did to us?"

There was no response at first. "I couldn't stay." He added as an afterthought, "You seem to have turned out all right."

"Yes, thanks to Mom and Gram and Granddad."

He shrugged. "See? You didn't need me after all."

"You're my father. I did need you. For a long time, I waited for you to come home," she cried.

"I don't know what to tell you, Isabelle."

"And don't you want to know about Lily and Alice? You didn't even ask how they were doing."

"Does Alice even remember me?" he asked.

"She has impressions—" Isabelle rubbed her forehead. "It doesn't matter whether she remembers you or not, you were still her father. And you weren't there. By choice."

"Lily was always closer to Nancy."

"So what? You were her father too."

"Like I said, I didn't have a great role model myself," he said. The defensiveness and the resentment and the bitterness and the accusations faded away to be replaced by something else, maybe disappointment, regret? She wasn't sure if he was capable of those emotions. He'd given little evidence of it thus far, and she didn't know him well enough to presume.

Finally, she said softly, "Your leaving us affected all our lives to some degree. Mine probably more than most."

"Why?" he asked, genuinely perplexed.

"Maybe Lily was closer to Mom, but I always felt closer to you."

"I wasn't that great of a father," he admitted.

"I thought you were a great father when I was a kid," Isabelle said.

"You did?" This seemed to surprise him.

"Yes! How could I think otherwise?"

Dave took a long gulp from his beer and appeared to consider this.

"Maybe you didn't have a high paying job. Maybe you didn't take us to Disneyworld or on family vacations," she started. "But I remember you teaching me to play Monopoly and buying me a CD player for my bedroom and my first CD. You painted my room orange when I was eight because it was my favorite color, even though Mom tried to talk me out of it." There were lots of memories of her father, too numerous to list. But maybe he didn't remember it that way.

"When you left, you took a part of me with you," she said.

Dave shifted on the bed roughly as if he were growing annoyed with the subject. He leaned over the side of the bed and tapped out a cigarette from the pack, lighting it with his current one before stubbing it out. Gingerly, he sat up, his elbows on his knees, and leaned forward. With his cigarette poised in his right hand, he used his thumb and fourth finger to remove a speck of tobacco from the tip of his tongue, wiping it on his jeans.

"Look, Isabelle, I'm going to give you some fatherly advice."

She scowled and folded her arms across her chest, expectant.

"It happened a long time ago. There's nothing that can be done about it now. It's too late for anything." He sighed. "Let it go and move on with your life."

They stared at each other for a few moments, neither one saying anything. Isabelle turned away, picked up her purse, and fumbled around for a piece of paper and a pen. She scribbled down her name and phone number then dropped the pen in her purse. She handed him the scrap of paper and said, "If you ever need anything, you can give me a call."

He said nothing and she left, doubting he would ever call her, supposing if he did, it would likely be only for a ride or money.

CHAPTER TWENTY-EIGHT

1972

Barb

Not for the first time, Barb wondered why Tony had married her. She kept coming back to the old adage about opposites attracting, and remembering his comment about how she kept him "real," whatever that meant. But why did that make her feel like a mother figure to him? Hardly romantic. More than anything, she wanted to be a mother, but not his.

"Ready, Barb?" he asked, standing in the doorway of their bedroom in his burgundy-and-white double-knit slacks and burgundy r shirt.

Shortly after they married, they'd purchased a nice ranch house out in the suburbs, which Barb hoped to fill with children. She had yet to fall pregnant and while this had begun to concern her, Tony didn't seem worried about it.

"Can you zip my dress?" she asked.

"With pleasure," he said. He came up behind her, planting both his hands on her hips, and leaned in and kissed her on her shoulder. "Mmm, you smell nice."

"Come on, zip me up or we'll be late." It wasn't that Barb was eager to go to this house party, but that she was in a hurry to get home. The party was being hosted by Tony's racquetball partner and his wife, people Barb had met only once. There'd be a houseful of people she didn't know. She would have preferred to put on the stereo, play some albums, and curl up with her book.

Tony zipped her up, the halter dress hugging her lithe figure.

"God, you're gorgeous," he whispered.

He pulled up her dress from behind and Barb stepped away with a laugh, pushing his hands away.

"Behave yourself," she admonished.

"Come on, little wifey of mine. How about a quickie before we go?" he said.

Tony Sebring's appetite was insatiable and sometimes, Barb felt as if she couldn't keep up. Their marriage seemed to revolve around sex, which in the beginning had been exciting, but she was ready to explore other things as a couple. Things like mutual interests and hobbies. So far, there seemed to be nothing they had in common outside the bedroom.

"Why not make it an all-night thing? Do we have to go out?" she asked with an arch of her eyebrow.

"Not this again," he said, blowing out a sharp breath.

Like a summer storm coming out of nowhere, his mood changed.

This was an ongoing argument that was happening with more frequency, which concerned her. Tony's calendar was full, and he expected her to accompany him someplace almost every night. She loathed all that social activity.

"I'm not a social butterfly like you, Tony. I prefer to stay in some nights and read a book or watch television," she said.

He rolled his eyes. "Read a book? How boring! Come on, Barb, sometimes you act like you're eighty years old."

She stiffened. "No matter how much we disagree on how we should spend our evenings, I don't think you should attack me personally."

"Oh, lighten up," he snapped. "We're not even thirty, let's live a little."

She softened and said, "I'd like to have a baby."

"And we will."

They didn't speak on the car ride over, and Barb's stomach felt like it had a brick in it. She hated going to parties where she didn't know anyone. And what she hated even more was attending a social function after she and Tony had fought; he tended to ignore her once they arrived. She missed the days when she and her first husband lived on base and were part of a military family.

As Tony turned onto the quiet cul-de-sac, the O'Jays song "Backstabber" played on the radio. The cul-de-sac held spacious two-story homes with mature trees and double-wide driveways. Barb didn't know much about their hosts except that the husband was an investment banker.

Tony found an empty space on the street and pulled into it and turned off the engine.

He leaned over toward her, his arm along the back of the seat. "I have a surprise for you tonight," he said, running his fingers along the top of her bare shoulder.

"Oh, I can't wait," she said, forcing an enthusiasm she didn't feel.

"All I ask is that you keep an open mind," he said.

A red flag popped up at the back of Barb's mind. "Oh boy."

"Come on, don't be such a stick in the mud," he said, pulling away from her, leaning back in the seat and sighing, unable to hide his exasperation.

"Tell me and let me judge for myself."

"It's called a key party, and I thought it might be fun for both of us," he said, and grinned. "Spice things up a bit."

"A key party?" she repeated, unable to discern what that might mean.

"Everyone puts their car keys in a bowl and at the end of the night, each guy picks a different set of keys and takes the wife home."

Barb's eyes widened. "What? I wouldn't be going home with you?"

He shook his head. "No, someone else would give you a ride."

"And then what? Where are you while this is happening?" she demanded. She felt sick inside. This didn't feel right at all.

"I'll be giving someone else a ride home," he said with a smile.

She blinked in disbelief. "And after you give her a ride home, then what?"

He shrugged. "I'm curious to see how it plays out."

Barb's mouth fell open. "So you might be having sex with another woman?" She couldn't believe this. This wasn't committed love between a man and a woman—not her idea of it, anyway.

"I told you when we got married that I wanted an open marriage."

It was like they spoke two different languages and neither knew what the other was saying. "When you said 'open,' I thought you meant in regard to communication," she said. How could she have gotten it so wrong from the get-go?

"You didn't know what an open marriage meant?" he asked. His tone rose, a signal that his anger was growing as well.

"No, of course not. It wasn't something that was discussed around the dinner table while I was growing up."

"Of course not. Not the perfect daughter of a wonderful doctor," Tony said with a sneer.

Barb bit her lip to tamp down a biting reply. Best to end it right here.

"Give me the keys. I'm going home," she said.

"You can't go home, we just got here," he protested. "Besides, if you don't come to the party, I won't be able to partake." He sounded like a whiny kid.

"I can and I will go home. Sorry, I don't want to stick around and be bartered," she said tightly.

"I don't believe you! You're so damn uptight!"

He threw the keys down on the bench seat and got out of the car, slamming the door.

Barb watched him walk up the driveway by himself, a queasy feeling overcoming her. Would he really sleep with another woman? Good heavens. Had he already slept with someone other than her during the course of their short marriage? And did she want him being the father of her children?

CHAPTER TWENTY-NINE

Isabelle

"It was a strange visit," Isabelle told her sisters. "It wasn't what I expected at all."

"How come?" Lily asked.

The three of them walked the beach on Saturday morning, each carrying a container or a pail. Their mission was to collect beach glass. Morning was the best time because the tide always swept in a new batch overnight. The previous year, when Lily had arrived in Hideaway Bay, she'd begun collecting and fiddling around with the lake-smoothed shards of tempered colored glass, creating holiday ornaments and other crafts to sell. At last year's Christmas bazaar, she'd run out of stock and, not wanting to run into the same problem, she'd already started production of this year's crafts. Isabelle and Alice were only too happy to help.

Isabelle relayed the events of the visit and described their father's physical state and apparent decline. She told them about his shifting moods, how his tone was all over the map from indifferent to flat to almost accusatory. The most difficult thing to explain was his lack of curiosity regarding his three daughters.

Lily had nothing to add.

"Maybe you caught him on a bad day," Alice suggested.

Isabelle stopped and stood, holding her pail at her side, almost half full of glass. "A bad day? It looked as if he's had a string of bad days."

"He sounds as if he's down on his luck," Lily said quietly. For all her posturing and saying she didn't care, Isabelle suspected that maybe deep down she did.

The three of them took turns speculating about what had gone wrong in their father's life. Was it leaving Hideaway Bay that was the beginning of a downward spiral for him? The beginning of an addiction to alcohol and cigarettes? Or was it the way he was raised? Isabelle recounted that Miriam was hardly doing much better. But in the end, they had no definitive, satisfying answers.

"Do you ever wonder if he thought he'd made a mistake and wanted to come back to Hideaway Bay but figured it was too late?" Isabelle asked, thinking out loud. She wished she'd asked him that question while she was there.

"To be honest, I've never wondered that," Lily said bluntly. She bent over, picked up a piece of beach glass, examined it, and tossed it into her pail. She muttered, "I've never given him much thought over the years."

The conversation dwindled as they moved quietly along the beach, gathering glass, each lost in their own thoughts.

It was early yet, and the sun was just coming up behind them, casting the shadows of the houses on Star Shine Drive out onto the street in front of them.

Aside from the sisters, there were several walkers on the beach. A middle-aged woman had a black lab puppy who jumped around, dashing in and out of the water. After oohing and aahing and fussing over the puppy for a few minutes and then lavishing extra attention on Charlie, the three of them resumed their task.

"It always amazes me how much beach glass the lake spits out overnight," Lily said with a shake of her head. The dog walked on in front of them, his gait a steady, rhythmic lope.

Isabelle looked at her own bucket and had to agree. It made her wonder what else lay at the bottom of the lake. Of all the Great Lakes, Erie was the shallowest, and it was also the graveyard of about two thousand shipwrecks.

The day was muggy, and Isabelle already felt sweaty. The early morning sun was hot, and everything was still, including the lake. The surface was gray and glassy, reminding her of a mirror. The burgeoning sunlight dappled along the surface, making it look like diamonds.

"Do you feel better now that you've seen Dad?" Alice asked Isabelle, bringing the subject back around to their father again. The rising sun glinted off Alice's red curls, highlighting the copper streaks.

"Not necessarily better," she said. She did feel something, but she wasn't sure what it was. She had yet to assign a label to it.

"Disappointed maybe?" asked Lily. She bent over to retrieve a bottle green shard. Green and brown were the most popular colors to be found along the beach.

Isabelle sighed. "Definitely."

"But maybe there's some closure so you can move on with your life," Alice said.

Was there closure? Somehow, Isabelle didn't think so. Maybe their father leaving was just one of those things that happened, and she had to create a life around the void that was his absence. Maybe you never got the answers you needed to the questions you had. You had to make the best of it and move on.

"For a long time, I thought if only Dad returned then we could be a happy family," she confessed.

"There's no such thing as a perfect family," Lily said softly.

Isabelle didn't point out that she'd said "happy," not "perfect." Things didn't have to be perfect for them to be happy.

Alice stood, her eyes on the horizon and the hazy outline of Canada across the lake. The three of them stopped in their tracks, forming a small semi-circle on the sandy beach.

Charlie nudged his way in, not wanting to be left out. A fart escaped.

Grimacing, Isabelle waved her hand in front of her nose and said, "What is he eating? He needs to change his diet or something."

Lily giggled as the dog let another one rip. "He's always been like this. They are powerful."

"Powerful? They're devastating!"

Alice dropped her pail and held her stomach she was laughing so hard. Pulling herself together, she said, "Look at his expression! Mr. Innocent."

The dog farted again.

Lily and Isabelle laughed and said in unison, "Charlie!"

"Come on, let's keep walking and get away from the smell," Lily said with a laugh.

"Now, where were we?" Alice asked. She swung her pail at her side. "Oh right, we were talking about perfect families. I always thought I did have a perfect family—Mom, Gram, and Granddad, and of course, you guys."

Alice had always had a tendency to view things through a rose-colored filter.

"I'm not downplaying the fact that we were lucky to have Mom and our extended family of Gram and Granddad, and even Thelma and Stan," Isabelle said. "But life back then in Hideaway Bay was kind of parochial. There weren't a lot of single mothers or kids from broken homes. I suppose I was in love with the idea of a nuclear family. Textbook style." This thought now seemed silly and archaic to her, and she laughed.

Lily shrugged. "It didn't bother me that we were from a one-parent home."

"It bothered me," Isabelle admitted.

"And I didn't know any better," Alice chimed in.

"I used to dread the father-daughter dances," Isabelle admitted. Her recollections of her childhood were not hazy. They were as clear as crystal. On Sunday mornings, her father used to take her swimming in the early morning before the beach was packed. Lily was too busy watching cartoons, and Alice hadn't been born yet. He'd taught her how to swim. Initially she'd been unsure, but he'd stood in the water and said, *I promise, I won't let anything happen to you.* When he taught her how to ride a bike, he'd said, *I promise you'll learn in no time.* And when he disappeared the first time, he'd pulled her aside and said, *I promise, I'll be back.* But when he left the second time, he made no such promises.

"But Granddad always went to those dances with us," Lily pointed out.

"I know that. He was great about those sorts of things, but those events shone a spotlight on the fact that I didn't have a father," Isabelle said. She wondered if she sounded whiny.

Maybe she spent too much time in her head, thinking about it. "Maybe I'm making a big deal over nothing."

"It's a big deal if this is how you feel," Lily said.

"Maybe," she said. She couldn't admit to her sisters that one of the feelings she'd investigated in therapy was this feeling that she wasn't good enough, which she knew was rooted in her father's abandonment of them. Why wasn't she good enough that he could stick around and be a father to her? But after seeing him, she realized that he had problems of his own, and maybe him leaving them had nothing to do with her or her sisters.

"Do you think you'll see Dad again?" Lily asked.

Isabelle shook her head. He'd issued no future invitation.

"What are your plans now?" Alice asked. "Now that you've found him?"

"I don't know. I was thinking of hanging around a bit longer in Hideaway Bay," she said truthfully. She'd grown used to her late-night swims in the lake, hanging out in the evenings on the porch with her sisters, and going out with Joe.

"That makes me happy," Alice said.

Chapter Thirty

1973

Barb

Barb's new job was a huge departure from her old one and after three months, the differences remained stark. She wondered if she'd ever adjust or if she should start looking for something else.

After almost ten years with Welch, Stine, and Cross, she was forced to relinquish her position when it became apparent that she and Tony could not work in the same place as they went through a bitter divorce. Ger, her usually easygoing boss, had words with Barb on more than one occasion, and it soon became apparent that the agency preferred if Tony stayed on. She might have been able to expertly soothe the ruffled feathers of clients, but Tony was the one bringing in those clients. She figured it was better to go before they fired her.

There hadn't been a plethora of jobs, and she ended up at Diamond Marine down near San Francisco Bay, a family-owned company that built boats and yachts. It was a big change. Instead of working in a nice office, she was now in a small, confined trailer that had been moved on-site to serve as office premises for the boatbuilders. The company was located near the docks, and boats in various stages of production filled the yard. There was a big marina building that was painted blue with white letters where most of the work was done. Barb sometimes found this place, the size and height of an airplane hangar, a refreshing change from the trailer where she currently worked with another woman named Heidi, who made no bones about the fact that she didn't like Barb.

Her desk was located right by the door and Heidi sat behind her, at the back of the trailer, her desk parked up against the wall. Every time the phone rang, Heidi rushed to answer it. She was so fast that Barb wondered if they were in a race no one had informed her about. Whatever the case or whatever Heidi's problem was—aside from the fact that she was forty-five years old, her husband had just left her, and her own children didn't seem to like her—Barb no longer bothered with the phone.

Except when it suited Heidi, such as when she was confronted by difficult or angry clients. These calls, she was happy to transfer to Barb.

Like now. Barb had barely paid attention to the ringing line until Heidi had answered it, put the caller on hold, and called out across the room, "Can you take this call?"

"Sure," Barb said through gritted teeth.

"Line one," Heidi said.

"Who is it?" Barb asked.

"Mr. van Dusen."

MOONLIGHT AND PROMISES 223

Heidi's smirk advised Barb that Mr. van Dusen, a long-standing and exacting client who called regularly for updates on the yacht he was having built, was not pleased about something. Barb ignored her and took the call.

"Good morning, Diamond Marine Boatbuilders, this is Barb." She tried to convey confidence and not the hesitation she felt.

"Barb, you're just the person I want to talk to," he said.

She shrank in her seat. This was how Mr. van Dusen started every conversation, which usually evolved into a list of complaints or concerns. She took a deep breath and braced herself.

"How can I help?"

"I got your Polaroids that you sent last week in the mail," he said. "That was pure genius on your level."

Often when Mr. van Dusen called to check on the status of his yacht, Barb found that her explanations were not helpful, as he had difficulty imagining the progress. The previous week, she'd brought in her Polaroid camera from home, taken some pictures of his yacht in progress, focusing on what was being worked on that week, and mailed three snapshots to him.

She smiled. "I'm glad to hear that, Mr. van Dusen."

"Will there be more Polaroids this week?" he asked.

She laughed at how childishly eager he sounded. For the first time, she wondered what he looked like. Thus far, she'd only spoken to him on the phone, hadn't ever met him.

"If you'd like," she said. "I can send a few pictures every week. That way, you can see the painstaking detail that goes into building your yacht."

"That would be great, Barb. I'd appreciate it," he said.

"Will do. Goodbye, Mr. van Dusen," she said.

"Goodbye, Barb," he said, and he hung up.

"What did he want now?" Heidi asked from her side of the room, not even bothering to pretend she hadn't been listening to one side of the entire exchange.

"He called to tell me he was happy with the pictures I sent him of his boat." She turned just in time to see Heidi's expression: narrow-eyed displeasure that erupted into a disbelieving snort.

"Mr. van Dusen happy? Did he hit his head or something?" She eyed Barb and added, "Don't get too comfortable over there, Barbie. There's still twelve months left on the build. Plenty of time for Mr. van Dusen to hit his head again and go back to being difficult."

Barb shrugged and said casually, "If you say so."

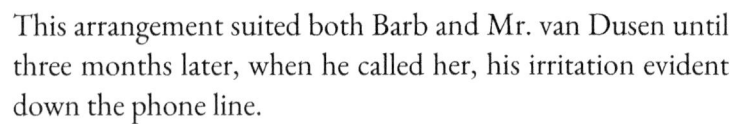

This arrangement suited both Barb and Mr. van Dusen until three months later, when he called her, his irritation evident down the phone line.

"I thought we had an agreement," he started.

"And we do," Barb said, confused.

"You are supposed to send me Polaroids every week of the progress made on my yacht," he said.

"And I am," she said. "I haven't missed one week."

"I never received them last week," he said.

"I mailed them on Tuesday, so you should have had them by Wednesday or Thursday."

"I didn't get them."

"No problem. I'll run to the boatyard, take some pictures, and drop them off to you personally," she said smoothly.

"Would that be acceptable?" Anything to avoid having him drop in unexpectedly. The builders would not appreciate that.

"That would be great, Barb," he said.

"Let me get a pencil and paper and you can give me the address," she said.

"It's the same address you send the photos to. I'll be expecting you. What time do you think you'll be here?"

She eyed the clock on the wall and did some quick calculations. "I take my lunch hour around noon, so twelve thirty?"

"Perfect, I'll see you then."

When Barb hung up, Heidi commented, "Doesn't that sound cozy."

"Just doing my job," Barb said through gritted teeth. Did Heidi have to comment on everything? It was relentless.

Trevor van Dusen ran a textiles company that he'd started from the ground up and that was now nationwide. His offices were located in a redbrick building in downtown San Francisco. She managed to find a parking spot on the street and threw coins in the meter before going through the doors of the Van Dusen Company.

When she informed the receptionist that she was expected, she was told to proceed to the top floor, where Mr. van Dusen awaited her.

The building was all old-world charm with high ceilings, intricate coving, and detailed woodwork. She rode up in a birdcage elevator, making a secret wish as she'd never ridden in one before.

She arrived at Mr. van Dusen's office. Outside was a single desk and two chairs in a small waiting area. His secretary, Miranda, a pretty woman in her early forties with a soft voice, advised her to take a seat while she informed her boss of Barb's arrival.

Barb had no sooner sat down than the door to the inner office sprang open and Mr. van Dusen—she presumed—appeared. He was not what she expected. He was maybe five six or five seven with short auburn hair that was receding. He was tanned and his shave was close. His oval nails were even and polished. His suit was handmade. Overall, a sharp presentation. Over the phone, she had guessed his age to be mid to late forties. But in real life, she could see that he was definitely in his fifties.

Mr. van Dusen's office was like the rest of the building: large casement windows, white coving, and high ceilings. The furniture was antique, with a mix of heavy Victorian pieces and lighter Edwardian counterparts. The walls were painted dark cream, and an Aubusson rug covered the hardwood floor.

"Barb Sebring?" he asked.

"Yes," she said, extending her hand. He clasped his around hers and gave it a hearty shake.

"It's nice to finally put a face with the name," he said with a warm smile. His teeth were crooked, but Barb was always suspicious of people whose teeth were a little too perfect. A little too white. A little too straight.

"Come on in and let's see the Polaroids," he said. He held out his arm, indicating she should go first. As she walked into his office, she was aware of the secretary's eyes on her. As she brushed past Mr. van Dusen, Barb got a whiff of heady cologne.

"Sit down, sit down," he said, indicating one of the two chairs parked in front of his desk, an antique partner's desk with a red leather inlay. "Can I offer you something to drink?"

"No thank you, that isn't necessary," she said. She'd just spent twenty minutes in her car eating her lunch. She unclasped her handbag and drew out the three Polaroids she'd taken earlier.

Mr. van Dusen sat behind his desk, and Barb reached across and handed him the three snapshots.

"It must be hard to see the differences week to week as it is such a slow, laborious process," she said with a smile.

Mr. van Dusen studied the three photos. "Yes, it is a painstaking process, but even my untrained eye can see the progression. Amazing really." He looked up at her and smiled.

Barb returned the smile. They talked for a few minutes about his yacht, and Barb wondered about him. There was something about him that was mesmerizing. He certainly did not tick any boxes: he was short, he had a receding hairline, and he was older but despite all this, Barb found herself attracted to him. It was odd that she would find a man so much older than herself appealing, but she couldn't deny the attraction she felt for him. The word she'd use to describe him was "dashing." She could practically picture him in Regency era England, wearing a cravat and a top hat and stepping out of a brougham.

Or maybe she could explain it. Maybe the attraction was because he was so different than either of her first two husbands.

"Barb, tell me, do you send Polaroids to all of Diamond's clients?" he asked. He looked up at her. His eyes were amber in color. Barb stared for a moment.

"No, you're the first," she said. But her boss was considering sending snapshots to the more demanding clients if only to keep them off the phone and out of the boatyard.

"I'm really impressed with you and your initiative."

"Thank you," she said.

"Are you married with children?"

She hesitated. "No to both."

"Interesting," he said.

"I should get going," she said, conscious of the time. She stood, and he escorted her to the door.

"Good luck, Mr. van Dusen," she said.

"Please, Barb, call me Trevor."

As she left, she was aware that the secretary's eyes were on her the entire time.

The next morning, a dozen long-stemmed red roses arrived at the office for Barb from Trevor van Dusen and when Heidi discovered the source of the flowers, she didn't speak to Barb for the rest of the day.

Thus Barb began a whirlwind courtship with Trevor van Dusen. For their first date, he took her on a helicopter ride over the Golden Gate Bridge and San Francisco Bay. For their second date, he took her to the Brown Derby restaurant on North Vine Street in Hollywood. Barb was so nervous she could barely eat her food. John Wayne sat at the table next to them. She couldn't wait to tell her mother.

Three months later at a romantic restaurant in Los Angeles, Trevor leaned across the table, took her hands in his and said, "Barb, I think you're a great gal, and I think we could have a lot of fun together."

She nodded. By now the age difference didn't bother her. What was that song from the 1950s? "Young at Heart." That's what Trevor was. He had more energy than men half his age. He was interesting; everywhere they went, he knew people, or he would wax poetic about the history of the place. Being with him was like being with a good book—you fell right in, and it became a part of you. It was a book she wanted to reread again and again. And after six months, when he asked her to marry him, she didn't have to think twice.

They discussed what they both wanted out of marriage: to enjoy the best that life had to offer and to travel extensively. She was as excited as Trevor about the prospect of traveling the world.

"Where would you like to go for our honeymoon?" he asked. "We can have a quiet little ceremony—or did you want a big wedding?"

She paled. "Oh, gosh no. This is my third marriage. Let's keep it quiet. And as for a honeymoon, I don't really care. Surprise me!"

He laughed. "I will. Barb, you're magnificent."

She sighed and leaned into him, needing to be closer to him and his energy. "I can't wait."

He beamed at her. "We are going to be so happy together!"

Her face hurt from smiling so hard, but she agreed with Trevor; they were going to be happy together. Just the two of them.

1974

"Are you sure?" Junie asked.

It was early spring, and they sat in Junie's dining room in the house on Star Shine Drive, playing cards. Thelma kept score. She sat across from Barb, staring at the cards in her hand, quiet, which was nothing short of miraculous.

Barb was home for a short visit. A Stevie Wonder album played on the record player in the next room.

Junie and Paul had done a lot with the house on Star Shine Drive. It had been a fixer-upper and although it had taken them years to renovate it, it was in great shape now.

"Yes," Barb said firmly.

Her decision to marry Trevor had taken everyone by surprise back home. She didn't know if it was because he was fifty-five years old or because it was her third marriage.

Thelma finally broke her silence, pulling her assessing gaze from the cards in her hand. "It's not a rebound thing, is it?"

Barb squinted. "You mean from Tony?"

"Yes," Thelma said, taking a sip from her mug of instant coffee. "Maybe subconsciously you were looking for someone totally unlike Tony. It sounds as if Trevor has some qualities that Tony did not have: maturity, stability, and . . . he's interested in the finer things in life."

Maybe she *had* been looking for someone who was the opposite of Tony. But just because she'd been married twice before, that didn't mean she'd given up on finding her Mr. Right. It didn't mean she didn't want a happy marriage. She was young, and she didn't want to spend the rest of her life alone.

"If you're sure . . . " Junie said, her voice trailing off, seemingly not convinced.

Barb had expected more support from her friends. "I think it's obvious I'm not going to have children," she said tightly. "So I might as well have some fun. And it is a lot of fun with Trevor. We travel a lot." What she didn't tell them was that Trevor was old-fashioned and treated her like a lady, unlike Tony who, despite all his talk about women's rights and women being equal, had treated her like an object.

Thelma leaned forward in her chair, laid down three aces, and marked the score sheet with her stubby pencil. "As I've told you before, Barb, you've got to do what makes you happy. Don't settle for less."

Thelma had been divorced from Bobby for a few years now and seemed to be doing okay. She seemed happier. But Thelma was an independent woman borne of a tough childhood; they were two different people, she and Barb. Barb admired her friend's resilience and determination, but she knew she was not made of the same sturdy stuff.

"After one miserable marriage, I'm happy to be a single mom raising Donny," Thelma said. But she eyed Junie and added, "I'm glad you've done well, Junie, with your marriage. Paul's a gem. And Barb, you seem over the moon with Trevor and that makes me happy. When I see both of you happy, then I know that I don't have to worry about either one of you."

Barb considered Thelma's statement, a little surprised that Thelma actually worried at all.

The music had stopped playing and Junie jumped up and said, "What album should we listen to next? I've got Elvis Presley's *Aloha from Hawaii* or Elton John's *Goodbye Yellow Brick Road*. Which one?"

"Elvis," Thelma said.

"Elton," Barb replied at the same time.

They looked at each other and laughed.

"Go ahead, play Elton and then we'll listen to Elvis," Thelma said agreeably.

It was good to be back in Hideaway Bay. Barb had come out to the cottage with her mother and her father. Her father had cut back his hours at his practice considerably, getting ready to retire. They'd spent the last year winterizing the cottage so they could spend more time there, extending their summer stays.

Her parents also had reservations about her impending marriage. They felt she was rushing into things. They felt the age difference might be a problem. But once they aired their concerns, they said no more.

"Where are you going for your honeymoon?" Junie asked when she returned to the porch.

"Alaska," Barb said.

"Alaska?" Thelma asked. "Why would you want to go there? It looks cold."

"It also looks very beautiful."

"It sounds nice," Junie said with a laugh.

"I hope so!" Barb said. She couldn't wait for her honeymoon. In the last few months, she and Trevor had been up and down the west coast from as far as Seattle to the Baja California peninsula. Her favorite spot would have to be Monterey, where they had taken out a boat—Trevor's yacht was still not complete—and sailed around the bay. It had been heaven. She loved thinking about all the places they would visit in the future. Trevor spoke of a dream to go to Europe, and Barb was as excited about that as her future husband was.

At the end of her week's stay with her parents, she was sorry to go. She'd miss her parents, her friends, and the beach town. As her mother drove her back to the city to take her to the airport, Barb looked over her shoulder at Hideaway Bay until it disappeared from sight. Turning around, she settled in her seat, looking forward to the life she was determined to make for herself.

Chapter Thirty-One

Isabelle

"I brought the ice cream to you," Joe said as Isabelle stepped out of the lake from her evening swim.

"What's this?" she asked with a nod toward the plaid blanket spread out on the beach. Charlie and Luther lay next to each other on the sand next to a small wicker hamper.

Joe held open her towel for her, and she stepped into it and let him wrap it around her shoulders.

"Look at that sky!" he said, looking up to the heavens.

She followed his gaze. The clear sky resembled purplish-black velvet with shimmering diamonds scattered across it. It was breathtaking.

She got comfortable on the blanket next to Joe, and he pulled out two small tubs of ice cream and handed her a plastic spoon and one of the tubs. She took the lid off; it wasn't melted but it was soft.

"Who watches your kids at night?" she asked.

"I'm not out *every* night," he said. "My parents live on our street, and one of them comes over to sit with the kids for an hour while I walk the dog. Although Casey is already in bed."

She felt better knowing his kids weren't home alone, but she should have known better. He wasn't the irresponsible type.

"I even brought this," he said, pulling out a small telescope.

Isabelle frowned, spooning ice cream into her mouth. "That looks like a kid's telescope."

"That's because it is. I had to pay Aiden five dollars to borrow it."

Isabelle snorted and covered her mouth with her hand. "Downright larcenous."

"That's what I thought, especially since he hasn't used it in about three years," he said. He handed the telescope to her. "Here, take a look."

She set the ice cream down on the blanket, lifted the telescope, and peered through it with one eye. The magnification was very limited. Squinting, she tried to get a better look, moving the telescope around. When she handed it back to Joe, he looked through it.

"It's not very good, is it?" he said.

"Oh, I don't know," she said easily, finishing her ice cream.

He laughed. "No wonder my kids lost interest—they couldn't see anything."

They tossed their empty containers into the wicker basket, then leaned back and stared up at the sky. It was brilliant.

"I wanted to invite you to a Fourth of July party at my house," he said. "I'd like you to meet my kids."

Isabelle froze. "Is that a good idea?"

"Sure, why wouldn't it be?" he asked.

Did she have to spell it out?

"I don't know what my plans are long-term," she started. "I wouldn't want your kids to get the wrong impression."

"We've already been through this. I know you don't know what your plans are. I know that you travel all over the world for work." He used his fingers to list off these facts. "And I also know that we're just hanging out, enjoying each other's company." He paused, leaned back until his head hit the blanket, and yawned. He placed his hands behind his head and stretched out his legs, crossing them at the ankles. "And I'll explain all that to them when I tell them you're coming over on the Fourth of July."

"Can I at least think about it?" she asked.

"Sure, take all the time you need," he said. He rolled over on his side and propped himself up on one elbow. "Now can I kiss you, or do you need some time to think about that too?"

She laughed and shook her head. "I've already thought about it. Go ahead."

Isabelle was glad she'd put sunscreen on the back of her neck, but she wished she had worn a hat like her sisters. Lily and Alice had chosen wide-brimmed summer hats that kept the sun off their faces and necks.

The three of them stood in a strawberry field just outside of town that was part of the Anderson Farm. The white stand with its sloping shelves stood at the corner where the highway met Erie Street. They'd parked their car at the stand and hiked to the strawberry fields with a long cardboard box and some empty straw quart containers. Alice's enthused query, "Why buy them when we can pick them ourselves?" was the reason they were here. Isabelle wasn't sure how her sister had managed to convince her this would be fun. And it might have been fun, except for that blazing afternoon sun. Even though she wore sunglasses, she shielded her eyes against the bright orb up in the deep, cloudless blue sky.

The strawberry plants were profuse with berries, close to the ground and running in even rows. Isabelle couldn't believe the amount of fruit. They gathered them from the runners, tossing them into their quart baskets and laying those in the flat cardboard box. At last count, they'd collected ten quarts.

"What are we going to do with all these strawberries?" Lily asked.

"All kinds of things! I'm going to make a strawberry rhubarb pie tonight," Alice enthused.

"Do you really want to turn on the oven in this heat?" Lily asked, echoing Isabelle's thoughts.

"I suppose I could bake it over at Jack's house," she said. "He's got central air." She stuck her tongue out at her sisters.

"Oh, you little brat," Lily said, laughing.

Isabelle bent over, plucking three strawberries that sat next to one another. One was rotted on one side, so she left it for the birds. The sun continued to beat down on her back. Once they were finished, she was definitely going for a swim in the lake.

"Will there be any pie for us? I mean, I know Jack likes your baked goods," Isabelle asked Alice with a lift of her eyebrow.

"Among other things," Lily muttered.

Grinning, Isabelle slanted her head and regarded Lily: her fine blond hair was tucked neatly beneath her hat, and she was dressed in a tank top with skinny straps and shorts with sandals.

"And what about you and Simon?" Isabelle asked.

"Yeah, what about you and Simon?" Alice parroted.

Lily stared at them. "What about us?"

"You must see the way he looks at you," Isabelle said.

The expression on Lily's face could only be described as guarded. Maybe her sister wasn't ready to share yet. Lily was slowly navigating her way in the world since the tragic death of her husband. Maybe she wasn't there yet, not ready to move on.

"I'd say he has a soft spot for Lily," Alice said.

"I've never noticed," Lily said honestly. She threw a couple of berries into her basket, straightened up, and put her hands on her hips. "And what about you and Joe? What is going on there?"

"Nothing. We're just hanging out and enjoying each other's company," Isabelle said, using Joe's words.

"You see him almost every day," Alice said with a smirk.

So?

Isabelle snatched a strawberry, removed its stem, and popped it into her mouth, the juice exploding as she bit down on it. "He makes me laugh, that's all."

Lily and Alice looked at each other and said in unison, "He makes her laugh!"

"Well, he does!" Isabelle said.

"It's a start," Lily said.

Joe did make her laugh. They were just having fun, passing time together over the summer. Both of them knew it would come to an end and she'd be moving on. She'd said as much way back when she'd first met him.

"He's invited me to a party for the Fourth of July at his house."

"He wants you to meet his kids," Lily said softly.

Isabelle shrugged, trying to adopt an air of indifference. "I suppose so."

"You should go," Alice said.

"Do I want to get entangled in his domestic life?" Isabelle asked. Since he'd asked her the other night, she'd thought of nothing else.

"But aren't you curious about the little Joes and little Josettes?" Alice said. The three of them laughed.

"Go and meet them. If this guy makes you laugh, then meet his kids," Lily said.

"I'll think about it," Isabelle said.

When her sisters realized she would say no more on the subject, they went back to picking strawberries.

"Come on, we're almost at twenty quarts. Let's pick two more and call it a day," Alice announced.

It only took the three of them a few minutes to fill up the last two quarts, and they walked back up to the stand, Isabelle on one dirt row with the long box in her arms and Lily and Alice on the other, strawberry plants between them.

They piled into Lily's SUV and made their way home, where they were greeted at the door by Charlie, whining and wagging his tail.

Alice carried the box of berries inside.

"I thought you were baking a pie at Jack's," Isabelle said.

"I'll do that tomorrow," Alice said. "I'll start the jam this afternoon."

When neither sister said anything, Alice said, "Anyone want to help? We've got to get the Mason jars up from the basement and clean and destem the strawberries—"

"I'll bring up the jars from the basement and run them through the dishwasher for you. But then I want to go for a swim," Isabelle said.

"In broad daylight?" Lily said in mock exaggeration of shock. "Do you have a fever or something?"

"Ha-ha," Isabelle said.

"That would be great if you could bring up the jars, and I'll get started on the strawberries." Alice turned to Lily. "Are you game for making jam?"

"All right, Alice, you've twisted my arm," Lily said. "But first, I'm going to take Charlie for a quick walk."

In the dark, dank basement, Isabelle found boxes of jars, about three dozen in total. She stacked them in her arms and carried them up the basement stairs, taking her time.

When she landed in the kitchen, she set the boxes on the countertop and began to remove the jars and their matching ring lids. They were in pretty good shape, indicating they must have been a recent purchase. After the dishwasher was loaded, she left Alice in the kitchen, sitting at the table with the strawberries before her, destemming them and tossing them in a colander. Gram's big stockpot stood on the stove. Next to the pot was a five-pound bag of sugar and a few boxes of Certo.

Isabelle darted up the stairs and changed into her bathing suit, anxious to get into the lake as her skin felt sticky and sweaty.

The beach was packed with people seeking relief from the relentless heat and humidity. Isabelle found an unclaimed spot on the sand and tossed her stuff in a pile, stripping off her cover-up. Finally, she set her sunglasses on top of the pile and waded into the surf, letting the water splash over her feet. She waded further in, going out until she was chest deep. Gulls circled overhead, crying, and the muted conversations from people on the beach floated out to her. She slid into the cool water, feeling it rush over her body and along her scalp. She glided along, one stroke after another, coming up for air when needed. Within minutes, her body began to relax, languid and fluid with the movement of the water. After a half an hour, she emerged from the lake, feeling cooled off. She picked up her towel, patted her face, and rubbed some of the moisture out of her hair.

She decided against returning home, choosing instead to stretch out on her towel on the sand. She extended her legs in front of her and leaned back on her arms, watching the goings-on around her.

A father bent over his toddler—a girl, judging by the pink swimsuit she was wearing—holding both her chubby hands and walking her along the shore. Every time a wave rolled in and covered her feet, the little girl shrieked with delight, which made Isabelle smile.

Directly to her right, a woman had three children under the age of eight sitting on a blanket, admonishing them not to kick sand on it, which caused Isabelle to chuckle as she remembered that was what Granddad had always told them: Don't kick sand on the blanket. Don't walk across the blanket. The mother had a fancy beach blanket with red, blue, and green stripes. When Isabelle was growing up, her mother and Gram always used an old bedspread. The memory of it made her smile. The woman handed out wrapped sandwiches and a juice box to each of her girls with the instruction that if they finished their sandwiches, they could have a treat.

It was all very charming. Isabelle waited for some sense of longing to overtake her. It did not. Instead, she decided that as cute as that little vignette of the mother and children enjoying the day on the beach was, there was so much more to having children. They did not magically disappear when you left the beach, by her understanding. She was pretty sure they were with you twenty-four seven. They were needy and demanding, and she'd once heard that a mother was expected to sacrifice everything, all her hopes and dreams—and transfer them to her children.

Chapter Thirty-Two

1974

Barb

Barb threw her hand over her mouth and made a dash for the bathroom in their cabin. The sight of the toilet caused her to wretch and heave until her stomach's contents evacuated at a rapid pace.

"Sick again?" Trevor stood behind her in the doorway of the bathroom. Disappointment laced his voice.

Some honeymoon. The Alaskan cruise would have been spectacular if Barb had been able to leave the cabin. She must have picked up a bug prior to their departure.

Thinking she was totally empty, she straightened up and made her way to the sink. She brushed her teeth and refrained from taking a sip of water, as tempting as it was. But she was too afraid she would start retching again. There was a washcloth hanging over the sink, and she rinsed it out with cool water and pressed it against her face. All she wanted to do was take a nap. Day three of their ten-day cruise, and Barb had spent most of it in the bathroom. Trevor was beginning to lose his patience, and this annoyed her; it wasn't as if she was doing this on purpose.

"Go on without me," she encouraged.

"Are you sure?"

Apparently, he was done arguing with her about going off on his own. The first few days, he had indeed argued—"But this is our honeymoon"—as if her stomach cared. He'd dared to suggest she could carry a bag with her. That hadn't sounded like fun. His gaze settled on her for a moment now, and he said, "You're very pale."

"That's because I'm sick," she said, annoyed yet further that she had to point out the obvious.

"All right then, I guess I'll see you later," he said slowly.

"I'm sorry, Trevor," she said.

They were scheduled to disembark to Ketchikan, a town in Alaska. Barb had been excited to see it. But now, all she'd be seeing was the inside of her cabin.

She waved him off. "Go, go. Have fun. You don't want to be stuck inside in the cabin with me all day."

One thing she had learned in their short time together was that Trevor didn't do anything he didn't want to do. It's not that she wasn't happy; she was. She hardly had to cook as Trevor preferred to eat out every night in a restaurant. It was exciting, but sometimes Barb preferred to putz around in her home, cooking and baking while the music played, and reading in the evening. The only time she had to herself was when her husband golfed, which was frequently. She'd quit her job at Diamond Marine as Trevor said there was no need for her to work and she needed to be available to fly off at a moment's notice. She'd been relieved not to have to return to the dumpy trailer and the surly Heidi.

Once Trevor left, she curled up in the fetal position on the bed, wishing the roiling in her stomach would settle down. She'd only brought one book with her on this trip, thinking she wouldn't have time to read, but she'd finished that the previous night.

Exhausted from the non-stop heaving, she began to drift into a half sleep and as she did, she thought of Junie and Thelma and wished she were young again instead of thirty-one and on her third marriage. She hadn't been dozing long when the retching started again, and she pulled herself off the bed, her hair plastered to her forehead, and made a dash for the bathroom.

After a week home, when the vomiting continued, Barb made her way to her doctor, convinced she had picked up some kind of rare bug.

After a thorough exam, the doctor handed her a specimen cup and asked her to provide a urine sample. She used the bathroom off the examination room and provided a sample quickly, leaving it on the counter.

"Sit down, Mrs. van Dusen," the doctor invited, indicating the table she'd just hopped off of a moment ago. "When was your last menstrual period?" His wore a pristine white lab coat over his shirt and tie. His hair was combed back neatly, and a pair of eyeglasses magnified his dark eyes.

"Oh, um . . ." Barb paused, trying to think back. "Gosh, I don't remember. We've been so busy . . ." Had she had a period after they went to Taos? Or was it before?

"I'm going to send your urine sample away for a pregnancy test."

She sat there, stunned. In all the realms of possibility, the idea that she might be pregnant had not presented itself. Why couldn't she remember when she had her last period?

"But in the meantime, I'm going to admit you to the hospital," he said, pushing his glasses up on his nose.

Barb was only half-listening. Since he'd mentioned the word "pregnancy," she'd had a hard time focusing, and her mind drifted. But at the mention of hospital admission, she pulled herself together and repeated, "Hospital? What for?"

"You're dehydrated from all the vomiting," he said.

"Oh," she said. "When will it stop?"

He shrugged. "If it's pregnancy, it might end by the end of the first trimester. Although some women do experience hyperemesis gravidarum, where they vomit all through their pregnancies."

The thought of possibly being pregnant after all this time—all these years—buoyed Barb, and she didn't care if she vomited for nine months straight. It would be worth it. The thought of a baby, her very own, filled her with so much happiness that she could barely contain it.

An ambulance was called to transport her. She didn't see what all the fuss was about; she could have driven over to the hospital. But the elderly doctor insisted she was too delicate to drive herself.

Her excitement over the prospect of a baby was tempered by the thought of Trevor. When they married, he'd made it clear that he didn't want any more children. So different from Jim, who'd wanted a big family just like she had. After having been married twice and never conceiving, she had sadly concluded that she might be one of those women who couldn't have children, and so she'd never thought it would be an issue inside her marriage to Trevor.

But now what would happen? She loved Trevor, she was sure she did, but she'd also learned that he was never going to get a father-of-the-year award. He barely saw his children and when he did, he kept the visits short, gave them a wad of cash and sent them on their way. Barb had suggested maybe he spend more time with them instead of throwing more money at them. He'd scoffed and said they'd prefer the cash.

Barb had no sooner been admitted to the hospital than Trevor arrived at her bedside. He brought a big bouquet of roses and laid them on the table next to the bed. When she'd called him at the office, she'd asked him to bring in a few items from home. He set the small bag down between the hospital bed and the table.

He leaned over and kissed her on the forehead. "How are you feeling, darling?"

"I'm all right. I don't see what the big deal is," she said, feeling as if she were taking a bed from people who were truly sick.

He glanced at the bottle of intravenous fluids that hung on a pole, the line ending at Barb's arm. "I don't think the doctor would have put you in here if he didn't think it was necessary."

"Pull up a chair," Barb said. She had originally been sent to a ward of six women but then was transferred to a private room. When she questioned this, she was told her husband had called the hospital and made the arrangements. Honestly, she would rather have stayed in the ward with the other women if only for the company.

Trevor pulled up the chair, placed it next to her bed, sat down, and crossed his legs. "Now, what did the doctor say?"

"That I'm dehydrated."

"From what?"

"From all the vomiting," she answered, omitting the possible reason for it.

"Then you're in the right place. Rest up and get well," he said, smiling warmly at her. "We'll be off to our next destination before you know it."

He spoke about the progress with the yacht and how it was almost completed. He talked about work. Then he segued into how she needed to rest up and get better so they could get on with their lives. Barb appreciated the fact that he was solicitous and was trying to take her mind off of feeling so terrible, but it was hard to concentrate when she was faced with the possibility of pregnancy.

In six months' time, she might be getting ready to deliver a baby. A wave of excitement washed over her. But she wouldn't tell Trevor yet, not until it was confirmed. She was sure once he got used to the idea, he'd be as over the moon as she.

Trevor smiled. "I'm glad to see you're as excited as I am about Europe."

She didn't have the heart to correct him. Half interested, she listened to him drone on about the sights they'd see in London, Paris, and Rome. As he spoke about a tentative itinerary, she wondered what color she'd paint the nursery and whether she was having a girl or a boy. She really didn't care either way.

As her husband's enthusiasm over a possible trip to Europe increased, so did Barb's as she speculated over the possibility of being pregnant, convincing herself she was.

"What?" Trevor asked.

"I'm pregnant," Barb repeated. Her stomach did a somersault, awaiting his reaction.

It was a rare night where they'd stayed in for dinner. Trevor had wanted to go out; there was a new Chinese restaurant somewhere he wanted to try. But Barb insisted, saying they needed to discuss something.

Trevor had gone ashen beneath his perpetual tan, his mouth hanging slightly open. It was not the reaction she had anticipated from him. Despite knowing that he hadn't wanted children, she'd been hopeful, optimistic that once he knew she was carrying their child, he'd be delighted.

While she was in the hospital, they'd done another test and confirmed that she indeed was pregnant. Barb cried tears of joy, but kept her news to herself, not telling anyone. It was only right she told her husband first, and the hospital wasn't the place she wanted to share this news, even if she was in a private room.

When Trevor finally found his voice, he said, "But you can't have children."

"That's what I thought. I mean, I was married twice before you and I never got pregnant," she reminded him.

"You lied."

Barb bristled. "I didn't lie, Trevor. Please be careful what you accuse me of." Her voice was tight.

"But I don't want any more children," he said.

She smiled and reached out for his hand. He did not clasp hers. She placed her hand over his. "I know, darling, this isn't what you had planned. But we're having a baby, something *we* created together, and I can't tell you how happy this makes me."

Quietly, he said, "At least one of us is happy."

"Oh, please don't be upset." She'd grown to love the man and she didn't want him to be unhappy, but there was nothing she could do about this.

"But what about our trip to Europe next year?" he asked, his face aghast at the possibility that they might not be able to go.

"I don't think I'll be able to go to Europe, not when I'm nine months pregnant." She laughed, trying to opt for a cheery countenance.

He didn't respond.

"I understand you're upset. You've been blindsided, we both have, but we're going to be happy," she said firmly. "We'll still be able to travel."

He regarded her with a sour expression. "How will we be able to do that with an infant? A toddler? A child?"

"Granted, it presents some challenges, but I'm game if you are," she said. She laughed again but it was shaky.

"Again, Barb, I don't want a child. Not another one," he said with finality.

"What should I do? Send it back?" she asked with a quirk of her lips.

He regarded her for a moment and said quietly, "No, but you can get rid of it."

CHAPTER THIRTY-THREE

Isabelle

"The orange one with the wooden beaded necklace is the best choice in my opinion," Alice offered.

"I suppose you're right," Isabelle said, slipping the green maxi dress up over her head and tossing it onto the upholstered chair in the corner of her room. She picked up the orange summer dress off the top of the cedar chest and pulled it back on.

Isabelle had said yes to the Fourth of July barbecue at Joe's house and then had regretted it. But Lily and Alice talked her out of backing out, with Alice saying, "Just go. It's only hot dogs and hamburgers. Meet his kids. It's no big deal."

But was it not a big deal? Isabelle was filled with trepidation and must have changed her outfit three times as Alice lay on her bed and gave feedback.

"I have no idea what to say to kids," she fretted. "I don't know what to talk to them about."

"They're kids, they're not expecting you to discourse on anything big," Alice said helpfully. "Just be yourself and act interested in them."

Isabelle stood in front of the cheval mirror and straightened her dress. "Are you sure this dress is okay?"

"It's perfect."

"You don't think I should wear something in red, white, and blue?"

Alice grimaced and shook her head. "No, it will look like you're trying too hard."

Isabelle grabbed a leopard-print scrunchy and pulled her hair back into a loose ponytail. "How do I act interested in them?" In her life and her travels, children were not part of her circle.

She dusted some bronzer over her face, applied a little mascara, and dabbed some lipstick onto her lips. When she finished, she spun around to face Alice.

"Well?"

"Beautiful, you look beautiful," Alice said with a generous smile.

Before Isabelle left the house, Alice handed her a canvas bag.

"What's this?" Isabelle asked, peering inside.

"I made some desserts for you to bring."

"I'm bringing a bottle of wine," Isabelle said, lifting it up off the counter.

Alice rolled her eyes. "Are his kids going to be interested in wine? No, they're not. There's brownies and chocolate chip cookies. Start off on the right foot."

"It's only a barbecue, no big deal, remember?" Isabelle protested.

Alice glanced at the clock and shooed her out of the kitchen. "Come on, Izzy, stop dragging your heels, you're going to be late."

Isabelle carried the tote in one hand and the bottle of wine in the other and made her way to the front door. "What are you and Lily doing tonight?"

"Simon and Jack are coming over, and we're going to sit on the front porch with mixed drinks and hot appetizers and watch the fireworks going off on the beach."

Isabelle hesitated, filled with doubt about her own plans. "Maybe I'll stay home with you guys."

"Nope, you'll be a fifth wheel," Alice said firmly, giving her a gentle push. "Off you go."

Isabelle looked at her. "You're harsh and cruel, Alice Monroe."

"If it's for your own good, I have to be."

Isabelle exited the house and Alice stood in the doorway, quite possibly to make sure Isabelle didn't do a runner. As she was laden with wine and the bag of goodies, she decided to drive. Alice had said she could take her car.

The day had been sunny, and there'd been a small parade earlier along Main Street. Red, white, and blue bunting hung over the shopfronts in town. Earlier, she and Alice had walked up to Main Street, carrying lawn chairs, and they had found a vacant spot in front of Lime's Five-and-Dime and parked themselves to watch the parade.

Since the previous day, the atmosphere had been punctuated with premature fireworks going off that increased in volume and intensity as the day wore on. Isabelle had always loved the Fourth of July.

Joe lived on Moonbeam Drive, which ran off Erie Street. Isabelle slowed as she approached number 829. The house was situated at the corner of Moonbeam and Crescent, and both streets were packed with cars. His house was a Dutch colonial revival painted in white with dark green shutters on the windows. An American flag hung from the porch, and flower beds with trimmed green shrubs ran along the front of the house. A white vinyl fence closed off the backyard and when Isabelle got out of her car, she heard splashing, music, and children's voices.

Why had she thought it was only going to be Joe, his kids, and her? As she walked up the asphalt driveway, she realized he had a houseful of guests. By the time she landed on the front porch and rang the bell, and before a greater unease set in, she wondered if a larger crowd might actually work in her favor. She could disappear among the guests, and then it might not be so awkward with his children. They probably wouldn't even notice she was there.

Within minutes, a teenaged boy appeared at the door. His brown hair was longish and almost covered his eyes. He wore a black T-shirt and jeans. Isabelle guessed him to be Kyle, Joe's oldest.

"Hi," Isabelle said with a little wave that felt foolish. She dropped her arm to her side.

"Hi. Are you Dad's friend?" he asked.

"Yes, I'm—" but before she could finish the sentence, the boy headed back down the hall toward the kitchen, leaving Isabelle standing outside.

"Dad! Door!"

As the seconds ticked by, Isabelle's courage diminished, and she contemplated stepping off the porch and heading home, but then Joe finally appeared.

"Isabelle! I'm so happy you could make it," he said, holding the screen door open for her to step inside.

The house, though spacious, was close in the way houses were when they didn't have air conditioning and depended on the lake breeze to dispel the humidity. It was done up in muted earth tones, and Isabelle wondered if his late wife had decorated it.

"Come on back. I'd like you to meet everyone."

She followed him back to the kitchen. It was another spacious room, with dark cherry cabinets, pebbled granite countertops, and stainless steel appliances. The chairs had been taken away from the table, and food was laid out in various bowls and disposable aluminum trays. She was glad she'd brought more than a bottle of wine and gave a silent prayer of thanks to Alice.

She held up the bag and the bottle of wine. "I've brought brownies and chocolate chip cookies."

"Oh, nice," he said, raising his eyebrows. He took the canvas bag from her, pulled out the containers, and set them on the table.

Through the kitchen window, she spied a rectangular in-ground pool. Kids of various ages stood in line for the diving board. Some yelled "cannonball!" as they jumped into the pool, but some dove in and swam over to the shallow end. An older man with short white hair stood at the side, monitoring them.

"Nice form, Casey," he called out and clapped.

This made Isabelle smile.

"That's my dad," Joe said. "He's the unofficial lifeguard."

"It's an important job," she said.

He leaned over, grabbed her hand, and gave it a squeeze, kissing her cheek and whispering, "I'm glad you're here."

Isabelle blushed.

"And is this your special friend?"

Isabelle turned to find an elderly woman with a red-lipsticked smile.

"Mom, please, don't embarrass Isabelle," Joe pleaded halfheartedly.

"Oh, stop it," his mother said with a laugh. She stepped toward Isabelle, extending her hand.

"I'm Joe's mom, Ethel Koch," she said.

"Isabelle Monroe," Isabelle said.

The older woman was stylish, with her white hair cut into a sleek bob and wearing gold jewelry around her neck and on her fingers and wrists. She wore a black top with white capris. "Are you from around here?" she asked.

Isabelle nodded. "I grew up in Hideaway Bay. I'm living over on Star Shine Drive."

"Nice area," Ethel said.

Isabelle had not meant for it to sound like she was bragging. She felt compelled to add, "My sisters and I inherited our grandmother's house."

Ethel tilted her head slightly and asked, "Who was your grandmother?"

"Junie Reynolds," Isabelle replied.

An expression of recognition blossomed on Ethel's face. "Oh my goodness, I didn't know you were Junie's granddaughter. Why didn't you say so?"

"She just did," Joe interjected.

Ethel smirked and said to her son, "Okay, smarty, thanks."

Isabelle laughed.

Ethel took Isabelle's hands in hers and shook them up and down as she pronounced each word of her sentence: "Your grandmother was a lovely, genuine woman. She is missed!"

"Thank you, we think so too," Isabelle said, smiling at the workout her arms were getting.

They were interrupted by a preteen boy sailing through the kitchen. His hair was blond, his eyes blue and overall, his looks were sunny.

"Grandma, can I have a fudgesicle?" he asked.

"No, you'll spoil your dinner," Joe said.

Ethel waved him away. "Of course you can. It's the Fourth of July." She rested her hand on the boy's shoulder, possibly to prevent him from running off. "Have you met your father's friend, Isabelle Monroe? Isabelle, this is Aiden. He's eleven."

The boy smiled, revealing teeth covered in braces, and lifted up his hand in a greeting. "Hi."

"Nice to meet you, Aiden."

He nodded at Isabelle and then returned his attention to his grandmother.

Aiden's beseeching smile was rewarded with an adoring look from Joe's mother. "Go on, then, get yourself a fudgesicle."

"Thanks, Grandma," he said and took off.

Ethel shook her head. "That kid, always smiling, always in a good mood."

"Come on, Isabelle," Joe said. "I'll take you outside. What would you like to drink? I've got pop or wine, or would you like a mixed drink?"

"A glass of wine is fine. Red if you have it."

"I do," he said, picking up a bottle off the kitchen counter and taking a wine glass out of the cupboard. He poured half a glass and handed it to Isabelle.

"Thanks," she said, taking a small sip.

"We'll talk to you later, Mom," Joe said, steering Isabelle out the back of the house and introducing her to some of the neighbors.

When Isabelle took a seat at a table, a small blond-haired girl came running up to her, and immediately Isabelle recognized the girl to be Casey as she was the female version of her older brother Aiden.

As soon as Casey landed in front of Isabelle, her mouth opened in a wide, gap-toothed smile. Her hair hung in wet hanks around her face, and her blue eyes were bright.

"Are you going to be my new mommy?"

Caught off guard, Isabelle stumbled, "Er . . . what?"

Joe picked up his daughter, whose legs started kicking, and said, "Isabelle is my friend."

"Aiden said she's going to be our new mom," Casey said excitedly.

"Remember what I've told you about believing everything your brother says?"

The little girl, whose smile never disappeared, nodded her head. Joe set her down and she ran off.

"And that was my youngest, Casey."

Isabelle laughed. "She certainly says what's on her mind."

"Unfortunately, sometimes, yes."

Isabelle mingled with some of the neighbors, introducing herself. Joe's kids seemed to keep clear of her, and she drank more wine. Joe's house was busy; there was activity everywhere. Although Luther got around as fast as his little legs could take him, she saw no evidence of two cats. They were probably hiding, and she couldn't say she blamed them.

The evening went well and after the fireworks show was over, Joe walked her to her car. He leaned in and kissed her. Pulling away, he brushed a strand of hair off her forehead.

"There now," he teased. "That wasn't so bad, was it?"

"No, it wasn't," she said truthfully.

They spoke a few more minutes, and then Casey appeared at the front door. "Daddy, are you going to read me a story?"

"Be right in!"

"I'll let you go," Isabelle said. She watched him go inside. At the door, he turned and waved to her, smiling.

He's a great guy.

So why was she filled with doubt?

Chapter Thirty-Four

1975

Barb

Barb's heart pounded as she cradled the infant in her arms. Stunned was the word. She couldn't believe that she had a child. It was as if all the Christmases were wrapped up into one. But once she got over her disbelief, her dominant feeling was one of profound euphoria. She'd never felt anything like it.

Suzanne Ellen van Dusen. *But I'm going to call her Sue Ann.*

Barb kissed the top of the baby's head, reveling in the newborn smell. *If only they could bottle this up and sell it.* She cradled her daughter against her breast, watching with delight as the baby latched on. She was in a ward with six beds, but only three of them were occupied. The two other mothers had received flowers, bouquets of roses from their husbands.

Barb looked over her own floral arrangements. Junie and Thelma had sent a green houseplant in a ceramic vase that read "diaper delivery." Her parents had sent her a big, beautiful bouquet of pink flowers: roses, carnations, dahlias, and one hydrangea. But conspicuously absent were any flowers from Trevor. He had not been in to see the baby yet, and Barb didn't think he was coming.

He'd been ambivalent during the entire pregnancy. There had never been one inquiry as to how she was feeling. Whenever she tried to tell him what was going on with the pregnancy, he appeared disinterested or brushed it off.

She leaned over and kissed Sue Ann again. "Don't worry, you have a mother who loves you more than anyone or anything."

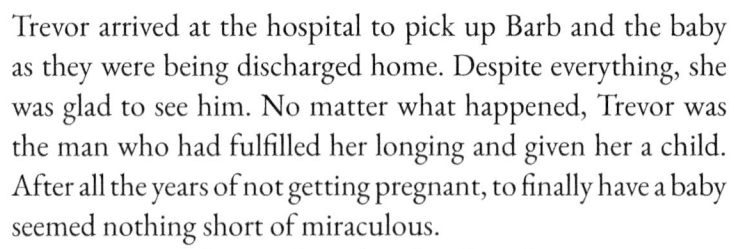

Trevor arrived at the hospital to pick up Barb and the baby as they were being discharged home. Despite everything, she was glad to see him. No matter what happened, Trevor was the man who had fulfilled her longing and given her a child. After all the years of not getting pregnant, to finally have a baby seemed nothing short of miraculous.

Trevor stood there with his hands at his side.

Cradling little Sue Ann closer, Barb leaned over and kissed him on the cheek. "Thanks for picking us up."

"I'm not such a complete monster that I'd make you take a taxi to the house," he said.

"How is Mother?" Barb's mother had arrived late last night and would be staying for a few weeks to give her a hand.

"Settled and anxious to see you and . . ." His voice tapered off as he nodded to the newborn.

Barb stepped closer and with her forefinger, pushed the blanket back so Trevor could see his daughter's face.

He contemplated her for a moment, then removed his gaze from the baby and said, "Are you ready?"

"I've named her Suzanne Ellen. We'll call her Sue Ann." Barb beamed. She tried not to read too much into the fact that he was in the same room with them. Her heart ached that things were so wrong between them.

"That's fine," he said. He glanced at his wristwatch. "We should probably go." He picked up her suitcase and stood in the doorway. "I'll bring the car around to the lobby."

A nurse wheeled Barb down to the lobby in a wheelchair. She held her baby close.

On the ride home, Trevor said, "Your mother had a good idea. Said we might want to consider hiring help for the baby, like a nanny."

"Oh, I don't know about that," Barb said, watching the familiar landmarks pass by en route to the home they shared. After all these years trying to have a baby, she wasn't about to hand her off to someone else to take care of. Barb relished the role of mother. Besides, there'd be no more children, not with Trevor.

He turned sharply and stared at her. "Why not? I want my wife back. When I married you, you were a lot of fun, and we wanted to do things and go and see different places."

"You can hardly fault a mother for wanting to stay home with her child," she said.

"But we can afford help."

She sighed. Trevor pulled in to the long driveway of their Frank Lloyd Wright–inspired home. There were palm trees out front, and the landscaping consisted of low-maintenance plants and shrubs.

"Can we discuss this another time?" she asked, suddenly feeling weary.

The baby began to mewl in her arms.

Trevor looked over at the two of them and frowned. "Don't you have a pacifier?"

"No. She doesn't need one. I'm breastfeeding."

Trevor lowered his eyebrows, and his bottom lip protruded.

As soon as he pulled the car up the drive, the front door burst open and Mrs. Walsh appeared, neatly coiffed, wearing her pearls and sporting a big smile on her face.

"Mom," Barb said, her voice breaking.

Her mother leaned into the car and patted the side of Barb's face and kissed her cheek. "Welcome home, Barbara."

Barb was filled with gratitude for her mother's presence.

"Let me take my new granddaughter." Mrs. Walsh cooed at the baby, "Who's Grandma's best girl?" Barb thought it was funny how her mother had morphed into her role as grandmother, as if she'd been born for it. Gone was the woman who wore gloves when she drove, and the etiquette book she lived and died by was thrown out the window. When Mark had children, she became someone Barb didn't recognize: a doting, hands-on grandparent.

Barb stepped out of the car as Trevor removed her suitcase from the trunk and carried it into the house.

Mrs. Walsh looked up from the baby, beaming. "She is beautiful." She looked around to make sure Trevor was out of sight. "She looks like you when you were born!"

"Thanks, Mom," Barb said. It was nice to have someone make a fuss over her baby.

"Come on, let's get the two of you inside and get you settled. I've set up the nursery to make it easier for you, everything within reach."

"Thank you," Barb said, stepping up to the front door. She didn't care how her mother had arranged the nursery; she was grateful that she was there.

"That's what I'm here for, to help," her mother said.

"How's Father?"

"He's well. Anxious to hear all about his new granddaughter. I told him I'd take plenty of photos."

Barb smiled, happy that there was someone who wanted to see her baby.

Two days before Mrs. Walsh left to return home, she sat with Barb in the nursery as Barb nursed Sue Ann.

"Wouldn't it be easier to use formula?" Mrs. Walsh asked.

"It probably would, but I prefer to breastfeed," Barb said.

"All right, just making a suggestion," Mrs. Walsh said.

Barb did not want to fight with her mother. Tears filled her eyes. "Oh, Mother, I appreciate everything you've done since you arrived." Her mother had been managing the household, which allowed Barb to give her undivided attention to her baby.

Mrs. Walsh smiled, pleased. When Barb was finished breastfeeding, she handed the baby to her mother, who cradled her in her arms and cooed at her. After a moment, she looked up and asked, "Is everything all right between you and Trevor?"

Barb felt herself pale. "Yes, why do you ask?"

"I don't know. It seems there's some tension between the two of you," her mother said.

"Oh." Was it that obvious?

Her mother watched her, studying her reaction.

"And he doesn't seem that impressed with Sue Ann," Mrs. Walsh went on, astonishment underlying her tone. "He's not one of those men who only wants sons, is he?"

Barb shook her head. "Oh no, not at all. He didn't care one way or the other." That certainly was the truth.

Her mother waited.

Was it hormones? Barb didn't know, but there was a sudden rush of emotion that came from deep within. She pressed the side of her hand to her mouth, trying to stifle the upswell, but was unsuccessful. The tears burst forth.

Mrs. Walsh became alarmed. Still holding the baby with her left arm, she leaned forward and reached out with her right hand. "Barbara, what is it?"

Barb lifted her head and reached for a tissue from the box on the table next to her chair, blowing her nose heartily. Once the crying stopped, she said, "Trevor didn't want any more children. He made that very clear when we got married."

"But you're a young woman, and you've always dreamed of having a family."

Barb drew in a ragged breath and exhaled loudly. "Um . . ." she stammered. "When we married, he was under the impression I couldn't have children."

"Because you had no children with Jim or Tony," her mother guessed.

"Right."

"But once the baby arrived, how could he not fall in love with her?" Mrs. Walsh said.

Barb shook her head again. "I thought once I had the baby he would change."

Her mother appeared thoughtful and said, "You know, I thought it was odd that none of his children from his first marriage came by to see their new sister."

"He's not close to them."

"Barb, before this, I liked Trevor. I thought he was a little old for you, but he seemed like a nice man. I liked him much better than Tony, although I can understand your marrying Tony."

Sue Ann whimpered, and Mrs. Walsh immediately turned her attention to the baby, cooing at her until she settled down. "But since I've been here, I've realized Trevor's a very selfish, self-absorbed man."

Usually, Barb would rush to defend her husband, but she was weary, and her mother's assessment was accurate.

"I don't know what to do, Mother," she admitted.

"There isn't much you can do, unless it's so bad you can't tolerate it, and then you get a divorce."

Barb's eyes widened. Her mother was old-fashioned; to hear her throw around the suggestion of divorce meant that either her views had been liberalized or that to an observer, Barb's marriage was much worse than she thought.

"Maybe over time, he'll get used to Sue Ann and warm up to her," her mother speculated. "Let's hope so."

Barb doubted it. So far since the baby had been home, Trevor didn't seem all that interested.

"Barb, you're in a bind. My belief is that the marriage has to come first, always. However in this case, I would advise you if you're to remain in this marriage to put Sue Ann first. Trevor looks out for himself. Let him continue to do so. You concentrate on the baby."

When Barb didn't say anything, her mother continued. "You've survived tragedy and a divorce, and you'll survive again, whatever comes your way. You have to; you have a child depending on you."

Barb felt better after talking to her mother.

"In the meantime, why don't you come home for the summer? Junie and Thelma would love to see you and the baby. And with Thelma's upcoming nuptials in July, it would be a good time to visit."

There was nothing more Barb wanted than to go home for the summer. But would her marriage fall apart if she swanned off to western New York for three months? The thought of spending the summer at the cottage with her parents and Junie and Thelma sounded like heaven. And she'd be lying if she said she wouldn't like to put some distance between her and Trevor.

"Bring your baby home to where she'll be wanted and loved."

Barb broke down crying again.

Chapter Thirty-Five

Isabelle

The rain fell relentlessly for three days at the end of July. Isabelle had seen Joe and his kids almost every day. They'd planned to have a cookout and sit around the fire pit, but the rain prevented that. Currently they were seated around the kitchen table, playing the family version of Trivial Pursuit. Empty pizza boxes and Styrofoam containers that had once held chicken wings littered the counter.

While they played, Luther slept at their feet, growling, his legs going as if he were running.

"Must be some dream," Isabelle said with a laugh.

"He'll be exhausted by the time he wakes up," Joe said.

When they finished the game, Kyle leaned back in his chair, satisfied. He and Isabelle had been teamed up together against Joe, Aiden, and Casey, though Casey seemed more interested in the Barbie dolls she'd parked on the table. Isabelle and Kyle had won, but barely.

Joe instructed Casey to head off to the bathroom to brush her teeth and get ready for bed. Aiden disappeared and settled in the family room and turned on the television. Kyle made no move to leave. Joe stood and began clearing off the counters.

"Your dad tells me you like natural disasters," Isabelle said.

He nodded, his hair hanging over his eyes.

"I took a course in college called Natural Disasters," she told him.

He looked up at her. It was the first time he'd made eye contact. He was the spitting image of his father but instead of Joe's easy manner and lightheartedness, the boy's eyes were heavy with anguish.

"They have a course like that in college?"

Isabelle nodded. "They sure do. We spent the whole semester talking about hurricanes, tsunamis, and volcanoes."

"That sounds awesome."

"It was," she said truthfully.

"I'd love to take a course in college like that," he said.

"What degree are you planning on?" she asked.

He shrugged and the shutters came down, making him appear remote once again as he folded his arms tightly across his chest. "I don't know."

"I'll let you in on a little secret. Sometimes, when you start college, you don't know what you want to major in. And that's all right. And sometimes, you might change your mind again when you're thirty or forty, and that's all right too."

He seemed to process this and looked up at her again under the canopy of his bangs.

She didn't know why, but this kid tugged at her heartstrings. She wanted so badly to engage with him.

The fluffy white cat named Minerva jumped up on Isabelle, startling her. A small chuckle escaped from Kyle's lips. The cat made herself comfortable in Isabelle's lap, and she stroked its back. Minerva closed her eyes and purred. They had another cat named Gus, but Isabelle had yet to meet him. Apparently, he was shy.

"Have you ever heard of Krakatoa?" she asked.

Kyle's head snapped up. "Yeah. I saw a documentary on it once. Seventy percent of the island was destroyed by a volcano."

"That's right. I was there," she said, and hurriedly added for clarification, "of course not when the volcano exploded but about ten"—she glanced up at the ceiling, trying to remember dates—"or eleven years ago."

"You've been to Krakatoa?" he asked, with a hint of awe in his voice.

She nodded.

"Why'd you go there?"

"Well, I'd heard about it, and I happened to be in Jakarta researching an article and decided I'd take a side trip to Krakatoa. I've always found that interesting."

"Did you like it?" he asked, his eyes glued on her.

"I did. I liked it so much I took a ton of pictures and wrote several articles about it for my travel blog."

He seemed to digest this, possibly less closed off than he was previously, though it was hard to tell.

"Would you like to see the photos I took sometime?" she said. She had a 35mm camera with all the accessories as she liked to take her own photos for her articles. All photos were stored online. They would be easy to access.

Though his eyes briefly sparked with life, he only nodded and did not verbally commit.

Joe finished cleaning up and wiped his hands on a towel, standing near the table. "I can walk you home," he said.

"Not necessary," she said.

"I don't mind."

She tilted her head and smiled. "I know you don't. But it's not far. I don't want to take you away from your kids."

She said goodnight to Kyle and Aiden. Casey had already gone to bed. She promised Kyle she'd show him the photos the next time she saw him.

Joe walked through to the garage from the kitchen with Isabelle following him. She expected to see all sorts of power tools and garden and automotive equipment, but the space was occupied by a large, partially constructed backyard glider. The interior of the garage smelled like sawdust, turpentine, and wood stain. The large garage door was open, spilling fluorescent light out onto the driveway.

Isabelle ran her hand along the surface of one side of the glider, loving the smooth feel beneath her fingertips. "Did you make this?" she asked. She could barely keep the awe out of her voice.

"I did," he said. He stood there with his hands in his pockets.

The double bars of fluorescent lighting hummed overhead.

"It's beautiful," she said truthfully. Along the back of the seat was carved a scrollwork of roses and thorns. This was not the product of some flat-pack assembly but of an obvious laborious process.

"Thank you."

She looked at him, impressed. "Do you make a lot of furniture?"

"My goal was to make a new piece every year but I'm busy with the kids, so it's more like every two to three."

"What else have you made?" she asked.

He scratched the back of his head and appeared thoughtful. "I made a cedar chest for my niece when she got engaged. A liquor cabinet for my parents. I made the kids' cradles when they were born."

"That's marvelous."

"It's a nice hobby. I find it relaxing, and it helps me to think and sort out my problems."

Isabelle nodded. It was how she felt about swimming. "What about the kids? Have any of them shown an interest in woodworking?"

"I've taught them all how to use a planer and how to hand sand things, but most of all it was a way to connect with them, especially after Tracy died," he said.

She nodded. He really was a great guy, a wonderful father. Those kids were lucky to have him holding it all together.

She stepped outside with Joe and was pleased to see the rain had stopped. They stood at the end of the driveway under the spotlight of the streetlamp. She looked back at the glider sitting in the middle of the garage.

"That went well," he said, referring to the evening with the kids.

She agreed. "Your kids are great, Joe. I can't believe how different their personalities are from each other." She grinned at him. "And whew, no talk tonight from Casey wondering if I'm about to become her mommy."

Joe smiled and wrapped his big, strong arms around her, pulling her into his embrace. He laid his lips on hers and kissed her with warmth and insistence. She melted into his touch, her body relaxing.

When they parted, Isabelle spotted Casey in one of the upstairs windows. She waved and smiled at Isabelle.

Laughing, Isabelle cleared her throat and took a step back. "Um, I think we have an audience."

Joe looked up and called, "Go to bed." Casey waved some more, laughing. He sighed. "You can't have five minutes to yourself around here." He didn't sound put out, more like he was stating facts.

"Maybe I should say goodnight," Isabelle said, amused.

"Hey, we should talk about what we want to do for Labor Day," he said, shifting his weight to one leg. His left knee bothered him from time to time, an old football injury from when he played in high school.

"Well, it's a little early yet for that," she said. It wasn't even August. September was so far away.

"I was thinking the five of us could go camping," he said. "It's a long weekend. The kids would love it."

Isabelle stiffened. "We'll talk about it later."

"Not crazy about camping?" he asked softly.

"I like camping," she said, her voice trailing off.

He leaned into her, nudged her shoulder with his, and grinned. "There'll be s'mores."

She laughed but said nothing.

"You seem less than enthusiastic about a weekend of camping with me and my kids," he said, adding with a grin, "I get it though, sometimes I feel that way myself."

She couldn't help but smile. She felt she could be honest. "Joe, as I've said, I still don't know what my plans are long-term. I'd hate to commit and then have to back out because I'm no longer here." She looked away from him toward the house. "I would hate to disappoint anyone." She spotted Casey still standing in the window. "You better go in. I'll talk to you tomorrow."

"Okay, goodnight, Isabelle. No pressure, just think about it. If you're here in September, and you want to join us, you're more than welcome," he said. Placing his hand on her shoulder, he leaned in and gave her a quick kiss on the lips.

She folded her arms across her chest and walked quickly home. The night air was damp from all the rainfall.

Joe Koch was making plans for the future with her, and she didn't know how she felt about that. It did scare her a little bit, but in no way did she feel pressured by him. If she did, she would have put an end to it.

CHAPTER THIRTY-SIX

1980

Barb

"Isn't Daddy going to live with us?"

Considering the bewildered frown on her five-year-old, Barb cleared her throat and shook her head. "No, honey, he's not. Sometimes people don't get along and they can't live together." She left out the part about him carrying on with his secretary, Miranda. Barb supposed Trevor's getting involved with his middle-aged secretary guaranteed that there'd be no more children in his future.

Their marriage had never quite recovered after the birth of Sue Ann. Truth be told, Barb had been too wrapped up in her daughter to give either time or energy to her marriage—a choice she did not regret at all.

"Can I get a dog?" was Sue Ann's next concern, which about summed up the influence her father had in her life.

At Trevor's directive, there'd been no pets allowed.

"We could get a kitty, if you'd like," Barb said with a smile and an arch of her eyebrow.

Excited, Sue Ann jumped up and down and clapped her hands. Effusive with her affection, the little girl threw her arms around Barb's neck and laughed. Barb squeezed her daughter, closing her eyes and reveling in the hug.

When her daughter pulled away, she brushed her blond bangs away from her forehead with her small fingers. "Can I call Grandma and tell her we're moving and getting a kitten?"

Barb laughed. "Yes, go ahead."

She had already informed her parents of her impending divorce. Her mother had not been surprised, and reiterated that she'd like Barb and Sue Ann to come back to Buffalo, an idea Barb was giving serious consideration.

She watched with amusement as Sue Ann climbed up on the stool, picked up the receiver of the harvest gold rotary phone, and dialed the long-distance phone number from memory. She stepped down and twirled the corkscrew telephone cord around her hand as she'd seen her mother do hundreds of times before.

"Hi, Agnes. It's me, Sue Ann. Is Grandma there?" She bent her knee and put one hand on her hip, looking like a little lady. "I'm good. Agnes, I'm getting a kitten." Sue Ann listened and grimaced. "They poop in a box?" A moment later, she said, "Oh, hi, Grandma. Agnes said cats poop in a box, is that true?" Her face was a study in concentration as she listened to her grandmother on the other end of the line, three thousand miles away.

Barb and Trevor would go their separate ways. Her plan was to go home to Hideaway Bay for the summer, spending the whole season there with Junie and Thelma. It was going to be great for Sue Ann. And when they returned, she'd look for a new place for them to live, Sue Ann would start kindergarten, and she'd get her daughter a kitten.

Chapter Thirty-Seven

Isabelle

"The Arctic Circle? What's up there?" Lily asked Isabelle.

The two of them had just returned from blueberry picking. They'd picked twelve pounds of berries. Alice, who was out with Jack, had left instructions for them to rinse them off and load them into freezer bags. She planned on making jam, pancakes, and pies throughout the winter.

"An article to be written about a research vessel up there," Isabelle answered. An editor at a magazine she wrote for regularly had contacted her, asking if she had any interest in doing a story on a Canadian research vessel doing important work on the declining permafrost.

She'd already started packing her bag. There was a flight leaving from Buffalo in two days that would take her to New York, then to London, and then to Oslo, where she would hitch a ride with the research vessel.

"How long will you be gone?" Lily asked, pulling a pile of freezer bags from the box as Isabelle rinsed off some of the blueberries in a colander in the big white ceramic sink in the kitchen.

"About three weeks," Isabelle replied.

"Are you coming back afterward?"

Isabelle turned off the tap and looked at her sister. "Why wouldn't I?"

Lily put her hands up. "Just asking. Usually, you go from one assignment onto the next, so I didn't know what your plans were after the three weeks."

"No, I'm coming back," Isabelle said. She turned the cold water back on, setting it at a gentle stream, not wanting to crush the berries. She stared out the window at the backyard, thinking she'd tackle the landscaping there next year. The shed at the edge of the property had been renovated for Lily to have a workspace to create her beach glass crafts, but the area around it could use some sprucing up.

"I'm sure you're anxious to get traveling again," Lily said. She turned the kettle on. "Did you want some coffee? I'm going to make tea."

"No thanks, too late. I'll be up all night," Isabelle said. She shook the colander vigorously to empty it of any extra water. "I am looking forward to traveling again." She was also curious to see how she would feel being away from Hideaway Bay for three weeks.

She'd been there two months, and she'd settled in so much that she felt as if she'd been there forever. "I should be back by late August."

"We'll be here," Lily said, pulling down a teacup from the cupboard and putting a tea bag into it.

Lily held open the freezer bag while Isabelle poured in the blueberries. When it was full, Lily pushed the air out of the bag, sealed it, and tossed it into the freezer. Isabelle set about rinsing the next round of blueberries.

"I think it's nice how the three of us have grown closer," Lily said as the kettle began to whistle.

"Lots of wasted time," Isabelle said with a sigh, thinking of the decades they were apart. If only their mother and grandparents could see them now.

"I know, but maybe we just weren't ready to be close," Lily said, pouring boiling water into her teacup.

"Are you happy here in Hideaway Bay?" Isabelle asked.

Lily nodded. "I am. So is Alice."

Isabelle smirked. "I know Alice is. She wears her heart on her sleeve."

"She does. Always has. Always will."

The next batch was ready to be placed in the freezer bags, and they repeated the same steps. When finished, Isabelle poured more berries into the colander for rinsing.

"What about you, Izzy? Could you ever be happy here?"

She stared out the window over the kitchen sink. "Funny, when I was eighteen, I couldn't wait to leave but honestly, I've been content here for the last two months."

"Any chance you might stay permanently?" Lily asked with a lift of her eyebrow. She blew on the surface of her steaming tea before taking a tentative sip.

Isabelle shrugged. "Not sure yet. I'll see what happens when I go away."

Lily frowned. "What do you mean?"

"I want to see at the end of the three weeks if I want to come back or go on to the next destination," Isabelle explained.

"So, there is a possibility you might not come back."

"No, I'd come home, but then I'd go off again. I'm just feeling my way around things." It had been a long time since she'd referred to Hideaway Bay as home. She smiled.

"For what it's worth, I hope you stay here permanently with us," Lily said with a warm smile. "And I know Alice feels the same way."

Isabelle returned the smile. "Thanks."

"Heading over to Joe's," Isabelle called out as she dashed out the door the following afternoon.

"Okay, bye," Alice called from the kitchen, where she was busy making blueberry scones.

Isabelle could have borrowed Alice's or Lily's car, but she thought the walk might be nice. The sun was bright in a deep-blue, cloudless sky and although the temperature was high, the humidity wasn't. After she saw Joe, she thought she might go for a swim. It would be just the thing before she left.

She strolled up Joe's driveway, watching with fascination as a goldfinch flew by, rising and falling in the air. As she neared the front door, she heard numerous giggles, shouts, and shrieks.

Her hands were clammy. She worried that Joe might not want her to go away. There was always the fear that he might try to clip her wings. Just because he was tied to Hideaway Bay didn't mean she was. *Stop it. Give him a chance.*

The shrieking and hollering grew louder as a gaggle of girls—about seven or eight in total— ran through the front yard, led by Casey. All of them wore glittering tiaras. Bringing up the rear was Joe, who chased the screaming girls.

Isabelle's hands flew to her mouth.

Joe Koch was dressed as a clown. Full gear. She took it all in, her mouth hanging open. His face was covered in white greasepaint with drawn-on, exaggerated red lips and dark eyebrows. He had on big brown pants with patches on them and a red, blue, and yellow striped shirt. But it was the big red clown shoes that had her clamping her lips to suppress the laughter.

He pulled up abruptly in front of the porch, sweat dripping down his white-painted face.

"Isabelle! I didn't know you were coming over," he said.

"Nice shoes," she said.

Joe shook his head. "A week ago, Casey informs me that more than anything, she wants a clown at her birthday party. But all the clowns were booked up, so I ordered a kit. I figured how hard could it be?"

Isabelle grinned from ear to ear. He was just too adorable.

"What brings you around?" he asked.

"I wanted to talk to you, but I can see you're busy," she said as the girls ran by again, this time going in the opposite direction, but still shrieking and shouting.

"Just a little bit," he said with a laugh. He pulled his clown handkerchief out of his pocket and mopped his forehead. "Are you in a hurry?"

"No, why?"

"I could use a little help," he said.

"Sure, what can I do?"

"I bought temporary tattoos, and they need to be applied to the girls' arms. Plus, I need to get the ice cream cake out of the freezer or we won't be able to cut it."

"I'd love to help out," Isabelle said truthfully. She could tell him about her writing assignment and her upcoming trip later, after the party was over.

As they walked through the backyard, she asked, "What are the chances of me getting a tiara?"

He laughed. "If you play your cards right, I could be talked into making you one."

"You made those?" Isabelle was both astounded and impressed.

"Yeah, but don't let that get around. I wouldn't be able to hold my head up around the boys in my class. Oh, and there's another condition, if you want a tiara."

"And that is?" she asked, enjoying the playful clown.

"You have to help clean up all the glitter," he said and rolled his eyes dramatically. "You have no idea how that stuff just gets everywhere. And I mean everywhere. I even saw some in the freezer when I checked on the cake."

Walking ahead of him, Isabelle smiled broadly, happy to be there. With him.

Chapter Thirty-Eight

1991

Barb

It was good to be back at the cottage in Hideaway Bay. Barb sat on the top step of her parents' porch. The flower beds down below were lined with orange marigolds. Another bed running along the side of the house, dividing the two properties, held her mother's pet project: roses. If there was so much as a gentle breeze, the heady fragrance would drift over to them on the porch. In the evenings, her mother could be seen tending them, deadheading the old blooms and removing Japanese beetles and putting them in a jar. What she did with the jar's contents later on, Barb had no idea. Her grandmother used to put them into a jar of turpentine.

"Here comes Sue Ann, look," her mother said behind her on the porch.

The three of them turned their attention to Sue Ann, just coming from Main Street. Beside her were Junie's granddaughters Isabelle and Lily, who were eight and six. Nancy had just had another baby over the weekend, a little girl named Alice, and Barb had sent Sue Ann down to pick up the older girls and keep them busy for a while to give Nancy a rest.

"She's a natural with children," Dr. Walsh remarked.

Each one of them held an ice cream cone. Lily stopped every so often and licked her cone, and then ran to catch up with Sue Ann and Isabelle. They were heading toward the gazebo in the town square.

Sue Ann turned her head in their direction and gave a hearty wave. Then she bent down to the girls and pointed to Barb and Dr. and Mrs. Walsh, and the two girls waved excitedly.

Behind Barb, her father chuckled.

"That Sue Ann is a good girl," Mrs. Walsh said with approval.

"She sure is," Dr. Walsh said.

Even though she was biased, Barb had to agree. Sue Ann never gave her a moment's trouble. She was, truly, a good girl. Barb often thought it was compensation for her three marriages.

They'd arrived in Buffalo three weeks ago after Sue Ann finished her sophomore year of high school. They spent a week in the city and then drove out to open up the cottage for the summer. The weather had been great so far: hot, sunny, and no rain. The lawn was beginning to show signs of a drought by its stiff brown and gold blades. Every evening, Sue Ann dragged the sprinkler out and doused it with water, but it didn't seem to be enough.

When she wasn't babysitting Junie's granddaughters, Sue Ann was out on the beach, working on her tan. She'd become friendly with some of the girls, and two boys had called to the house in the last two weeks to see if she was home. So it began. The pull of the world. As much as Barb wanted to keep her to herself, she knew she had to let her daughter live her life. There'd been talk of college, and Sue Ann had said she'd like to go away, which made her grandmother very happy.

"Would anyone like some lemonade?" Mrs. Walsh asked.

"That sounds great. But let me get it, Mother. Stay seated," Barb said. She stood from the porch and frowned. Her right leg felt like dead weight. This was happening with more and more frequency over the last few months. She couldn't figure it out.

When she started up the steps, she tripped and stumbled, putting her hands forward on the porch floor to break her fall. Her parents jumped up and rushed to her.

"I'm all right," she said, not wanting to cause them worry. "I just tripped."

"You need to be more careful, Barbara," her mother said. "Are you hurt?"

Barb shook her head and brushed off her knees. The one knee had a scrape on it, but it was nothing serious. She straightened, her face red, and said, "Let me get the lemonade."

Her father regarded her with an expression of consternation. "Barb, that's the fourth or fifth time you've tripped or fallen since you've been home."

She laughed it off. "I'm getting clumsy in my old age."

"How long has this been going on?" he asked.

She shrugged, brushing her hair out of her eyes. "I don't know. It's been almost a year now. It's my right leg. It started with weakness."

"Have you seen your doctor?" he queried.

"Oh yes. He did a complete work-up, but nothing was found to be amiss."

"Thank God for that," her mother said.

"Has it gotten worse in the last year or stayed the same?"

Barb thought a moment. "The tripping and the clumsiness are new within the last few months."

"Really? Anything else?"

She shook her head. "Only that. Sometimes I feel as if it might be easier to just lift the leg and then put it down. It doesn't do what I want it to do."

"Hmm, that's interesting."

"I'm fine, Dad. I'll get the lemonade," Barb said, stepping into the cool house. They didn't have air conditioning, but the giant oak out back and the chestnut tree on the side shaded the house and kept it cool.

"Bring out a plate of lemon coolers," Mrs. Walsh called after her.

"Okay, Mother."

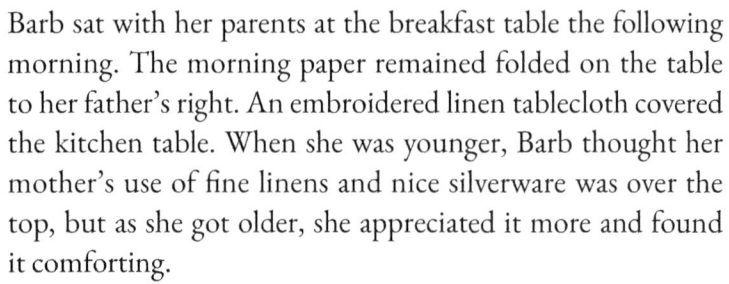

Barb sat with her parents at the breakfast table the following morning. The morning paper remained folded on the table to her father's right. An embroidered linen tablecloth covered the kitchen table. When she was younger, Barb thought her mother's use of fine linens and nice silverware was over the top, but as she got older, she appreciated it more and found it comforting.

She asked her mother to pass the salt and pepper, and she sprinkled a little on her poached egg. They all looked up as

Sue Ann breezed through the kitchen in a bathing suit and flip-flops, a beach bag slung over her shoulder.

"I'm going to the beach. Going to meet some friends up there," she said. She leaned over her mother's shoulder and grabbed two pieces of bacon off the serving plate.

"Why don't you eat some breakfast before you go?" her grandmother said.

"This is fine. See you all later!" Sue Ann said.

"Don't forget the sunscreen," Barb called after her.

The screen door slammed behind Sue Ann.

"She probably won't be back until dinnertime, I suppose," Mrs. Walsh said with a sigh.

"She's young, let her have her time," Dr. Walsh said, stirring a teaspoon of sugar into his coffee.

"Why don't we all go up to the Pink Parlor tonight after dinner? The four of us," Barb said.

"That sounds like a good idea," her mother replied.

Dr. Walsh had been unusually quiet. He took a sip of his coffee, set the cup down, and pushed his metal-framed glasses up on his nose.

"Barb, I've made an appointment for you with one of my colleagues," he said.

Both Barb and her mother swung their gazes to him.

"Why?" Barb asked.

He cleared his throat. "I think it's probably nothing, but the symptoms you described to me should be investigated further. We'll leave early and drive up to the city first thing in the morning."

"Is it necessary?" Mrs. Walsh asked.

"I'd like to have it checked out," he said.

"What could it possibly be? I'm a little clumsy, that's all," Barb said.

"Like I said, it's probably nothing, but I'd still like it checked out."

It was what he wasn't saying that scared Barb. She didn't know if he was being purposefully evasive to avoid causing them worry or if he actually didn't know.

"What time would you like to leave?" Barb asked, tamping down her rising anxiety.

"I can go with you," her mother said.

"No, Evelyn, stay here. I don't know how long we're going to be," Dr. Walsh said. "Besides, we don't want Sue Ann to worry."

"Is Grandpa worried about this?" Sue Ann asked her mother.

They sat in the gazebo in the green directly across from the Walsh cottage. Barb had suggested a walk on the beach, but it quickly became evident that that wasn't going to happen. Her leg was weak and felt heavy, and at times it practically dragged. She couldn't begin to hazard a guess as to what was wrong with it. Probably a pinched nerve or something.

The sun shone from the west and would soon begin its slide toward the horizon. It had been a good summer as evidenced by Sue Ann's golden tan. Barb kept her eyes on a sailboat gliding across the lake, its form sleek, its white sail pristine against the deep-blue sky.

She smiled, lifting her hand to shield her eyes from the late-afternoon sun as it had just dipped below the roofline of the gazebo. "You know Grandpa, he always errs on the side of caution."

There was a deep burrow between Sue Ann's eyebrows, disfiguring her otherwise unblemished skin. "Maybe I should go with you." Her tone was serious.

"No way," Barb said. "You're sixteen years old. I don't want you hanging around a hospital all day with me."

Sue Ann looked at her mother, her expression soft and innocent. "I don't mind, Mom. You'd do it for me."

"That's because I'm your mother."

"So?"

"No, Sue Ann, it would make me happier if you stayed in Hideaway Bay and hung out with your friends," Barb told her.

Sue Ann was not convinced. "But I'd rather be with you."

"I won't be long, honey," Barb said. Tired, she patted her daughter's knee. Their cottage across the street was quiet. Her mother was probably getting the dinner ready. Barb stood, trying to bear weight on her affected leg. "We should head back and see if Grandma needs any help."

Sue Ann jumped up and, noting Barb's hesitation as she tried to get her leg to work, said, "Here, Mom, take my arm."

Barb looped her arm through her daughter's and carefully stepped down from the gazebo with Sue Ann's help.

Changing the subject, she asked, "How come I haven't seen Bryce around anymore?" Bryce Jensen was a young man who lived locally and who would be going off to college in another state at the end of the summer. He'd taken Sue Ann out a couple of times.

Sue Ann scrunched up her nose. "He's not my type."

"Why?" Barb had thought he was a nice young man.

"Because all he talks about is how wonderful he is and all the wonderful things he's going to do," Sue Ann huffed. "He never asks me what my dreams are."

Barb gave her daughter a reassuring smile. "He's young and may be a little self-absorbed."

Sue Ann did an exaggerated eye roll. "A little?"

Slowly, they made their way back to the cottage.

"I got the feeling that I was not only to be impressed with him, but I think he expected me to be grateful that he decided to take me out," Sue Ann complained.

"Yes, maybe it's best to cut him loose."

The two of them walked, arm in arm, talking about everything and nothing, headed back to the cottage on the other side of the green.

Barb and her father ended up staying at the house on Coolidge Avenue for the week as the neurologist ordered all sorts of tests: bloodwork, urinalysis, electromyogram, nerve conduction study, and an MRI.

Initially, Barb hadn't been worried, but the longer they stayed in the city and the more tests that were ordered, the more Barb filled with anxiety. At night, her father went into the den and spoke in hushed tones to her mother and her brother, Mark, who was a doctor who lived and practiced out of town.

They had one final meeting with the neurologist at his office at the hospital before they headed back to Hideaway Bay.

Dr. Walsh shook hands with the specialist, and they exchanged a few pleasantries before the doctor adopted an air of gravity and indicated the two leather chairs in front of his desk, inviting them to sit.

Barb sat next to her father and braced herself. She had no idea what kind of news the neurologist would give her. Her fear was that it would be cancer, and she knew that would be a grim hand to be dealt.

The neurologist, Ned Richardson, tapped his pen against Barb's chart.

"Sometimes there are no tests to accurately confirm a diagnosis. We operate on the patient's medical history, presenting symptoms, and by ordering tests to rule out other diseases."

Barb wished he would dismiss with the preamble and get on with it. Her stomach felt queasy, as if she were standing at the edge of a cliff looking below at a deep divide.

"From my own assessment, I've come to the conclusion that it's amyotrophic lateral sclerosis."

Her father sagged in his seat and went ashen.

"That's a mouthful." Barb laughed nervously, trying to lighten up the situation. She couldn't be sick. Other than a weak leg, she felt fine. She didn't even know what this was. Whatever the prescribed treatment was, she'd do it.

Her father was staggered, which really worried her.

"Ned, are you sure?" he asked.

Dr. Richardson looked sympathetically at her father. "I am. But if you'd like to get a second opinion—"

"Can someone tell me what I have?" Barb said, raising her voice to be heard.

Her father turned toward her, his eyes darkened by anguish. "Dad?"

Dr. Richardson spoke up. "Amyotrophic lateral sclerosis. Also known as Lou Gehrig's disease."

She sank in her chair, stunned. She'd seen the black-and-white movie *The Pride of the Yankees* years ago with her mother, when she was younger. She vaguely remembered it, only knowing it had not ended well.

The doctor droned on about how there was no cure and how the only thing that could be done was to manage her symptoms, which would get worse. In a few short minutes, she watched her father age in front of her eyes.

Dr. Walsh turned to her. "That's what we'll do, Barbara. We'll go to New York City and get a second opinion."

"Okay, Dad," she said quietly, distracted by the awful verdict.

The diagnosis didn't seem real to her. She felt as if she were having an out-of-body experience, as if all this had to do with someone else. She was only forty-eight years old— how could this be possible? Her mind spun in different directions, and all roads led to Sue Ann. She was still in high school with her whole life ahead of her: college, marriage, children. And Barb would be robbed of the joy of experiencing those things with the person she loved most in the world? Plus, there were so many things she needed to tell her. How was that fair? The thought of her only child being left alone in the world made her want to lash out and cry in pain.

She'd leave it in her father's hands. After all, he was a doctor and he'd know what to do. Her father would help her.

They stood up to leave, and Dr. Richardson shook their hands. "Let me know who you'll be consulting for that second opinion, and I'll forward your test results."

"Thank you," Dr. Walsh said blankly.

Barb and her father walked in silence toward the bank of elevators. She was more worried about her father than herself.

"Dad, it'll be okay," she said, attempting to reassure him. "We'll go to New York City and see someone else. It'll be fine." She hoped she sounded more convincing than she felt. She was scared, of course, but right now the news was just on the surface, like pond scum, and hadn't settled in yet.

The bank of elevators was at the end of the hall, and it seemed as if they were taking forever to get there. Her father didn't say a word. Perspiration lined his forehead.

Barb stopped and turned, laying a hand on his arm. "Dad, what's the matter?"

He fell away from her grasp and landed on the floor, leaving Barb to stare after him, mouth open, unable to fathom what was going on. Hurriedly, she knelt down next to him, but in her heart, she knew he was gone.

CHAPTER THIRTY-NINE

Isabelle

"Hideaway Bay? Is that right?" the taxi driver at the airport asked, looking at her in his rearview mirror.

"Yes, that's right," Isabelle said as she settled into the back seat of the cab. She buckled her seat belt and yawned.

"That's a long drive, might as well get comfortable," he advised.

She nodded and turned her head to look out the window. Jet lag from four flights settled in around her and she fought the urge to doze off.

"Are you visiting the area?"

She shook her head. "No, Hideaway Bay is my home."

It felt good to say that. To finally admit that.

The Arctic Circle had been amazing as she knew it would be. But while she was up there freezing, she often thought of the little town on Lake Erie and longed for home. The memories of the last two months in her hometown had kept her warm.

Strawberry picking with her sisters in the hot sun. Preparing the flower beds, and the improvement in the landscaping that she'd worked on all summer. The new and delicious feeling of being a homeowner for the first time in her life. The evening swims in the lake and how they relaxed her. Joe waiting on the beach with Charlie and Luther. Spending time with Joe and his kids.

For as long as she could remember, she'd always looked forward to the journey, to the next assignment and the ensuing adventure. She'd always loved traveling. It was in her blood.

Except for this time. This time, she couldn't wait to return home. She was anxious to see her sisters and her house and Joe and his kids. The sense of connection to her sisters and Joe was a new sensation for Isabelle, and she enjoyed it. At forty, this was her new adventure: staying put in Hideaway Bay and setting down roots.

The last time she'd seen Joe, he'd been dressed as a clown. At the end of the party, after all the guests had left and Casey had fallen asleep on the couch, the two of them sat out back in front of the pool, the water crystal clear and the color of turquoise. He'd removed his red clown wig, his hair plastered to his head, and had kicked off the ridiculous shoes. She'd told him she was going away for three weeks to do research for an article. His reaction had been unexpected. He'd simply asked her about the article she was going to write, what angle she was going to take. He had lots of questions about the journey and the research vessel. It had been nice to talk to someone about her work. When she stood up to leave, he pulled her close and kissed her, leaving greasepaint on her face. He whispered, "I'll see you when you get back."

It was not lost on her how she and her sisters had all left Hideaway Bay just like their father, but unlike their father, they all returned and stayed. Although they'd been flung all over the place, the cords and connections had remained and eventually pulled them back home.

All these thoughts floated through Isabelle's mind as her eyelids drooped with exhaustion. Ten minutes from Hideaway Bay, something caught her eye. As they passed a car dealership, a red convertible sat out on the grassy verge with a "for sale" sign attached to the windshield.

Isabelle's eyes popped open, and she leaned forward and said to the driver, "I'm sorry, could you turn back and take me to that car dealer we just passed?"

Chapter Forty

1994

Barb

It was a beautiful morning. "Soft" was the word Barb would use to describe it. The leaves on the trees shivered slightly in the morning breeze and the sunlight was pale, giving everything outside an ethereal look.

The first of June. She would love to see the whole summer, but her intuition told her that her days were winding down. There wasn't much left of her body that was usable. But her mind, that was a whole other thing. As much as she didn't want to leave Sue Ann, she'd made peace with it.

Sue Ann had turned on the stereo and removed the album from its sleeve. The soundtrack of *South Pacific*. Barb knew compact discs were all the rage these days, but she still preferred the static-y sound of a record album playing on a turntable.

How she had loved that movie all those years ago, and how those songs brought back memories from when things were a little simpler, a little easier. A little gentler.

She watched from her wheelchair as her daughter stripped the hospital bed of its sheets, threw them aside for the wash, and made up the bed with freshly-laundered linens. This was something Sue Ann did every other day. In the beginning when Barb still spoke clearly, she'd protested, saying it was too much work, but Thelma—who'd been present— had laid her hand on her arm and said quietly, "It's a cheap luxury, let her do it."

A personal aide came five days a week to give Barb a bed bath and use the mechanical lift to get her out of the bed and into the wheelchair.

The thing that hurt her the most was that her nineteen-year-old daughter left college in her first year to come home and take care of her. *Hopefully, I'll be gone before the start of the fall semester so Sue Ann can get on with her life.*

"You should be a nurse," Barb said. Since she'd lost the ability to swallow, her speech had also become garbled. For the most part, Sue Ann, Mrs. Walsh, Junie, and Thelma were able to understand what she was trying to say. She didn't talk a lot anymore, trying to save her energy.

Sue Ann laughed. "Do you think so, Mom?"

Barb nodded.

"I never thought about it. I don't think I'd like it," Sue Ann said with a grimace. "It's one thing to take care of someone you love but a completely different thing to take care of a stranger."

You're so kind and caring you'd be able to take care of them too.

Sue Ann fluffed the pillows. "There, all done." She blew her bangs out of her face.

Mrs. Walsh appeared in the front room. She bent over and kissed Barb on the forehead and murmured, "Good morning." In the last few years, she had aged considerably. She no longer dyed her hair, and it had turned snow white. But she still wore it up in a neat chignon.

She picked up the towel that lay across Barb's shoulder and wiped away drool from Barb's mouth.

"Good morning, Grandma," Sue Ann said.

Mrs. Walsh smiled at her granddaughter. "What did you want for breakfast, Sue Ann?"

By now, Sue Ann knew better than to say "cereal" as her grandmother found a sense of purpose in cooking breakfast, shopping, and running things.

"A poached egg if it's not too much trouble," she said.

"Not at all. I was thinking of having one myself." Mrs. Walsh retreated to the kitchen, and the sounds of water running and pots coming out filled the air.

That sounded good to Barb, and she imagined buttery toast and the soft-boiled egg with its runny yolk with a little bit of salt and pepper. When she'd lost her ability to swallow, she'd had a feeding tube inserted, and now received all her nourishment through that. But she would have loved to sit down to a meal.

She wished she could shift her weight on the wheelchair. She had a sore on her bum, and it was tender.

Sue Ann lifted up the pile of laundry from the floor, breathless at this point, and pushed an errant strand of hair away from her face.

"Too much," Barb said, her voice garbled.

Sue Ann waved her away. "Nah. We're fine."

Barb looked around the cottage. She missed her father. Everywhere she looked, there were memories. Tons of them.

"It's still a little cool out," Sue Ann said. "I think they said it was only going to seventy today. If we sit outside, we might need our sweaters."

Barb wanted to laugh. Her daughter sounded like a little mother.

"Junie won't be here until dinnertime, but Thelma will be here after lunch," Sue Ann announced.

Dave Monroe had disappeared weeks ago, and things over at Nancy's house were in an uproar. Junie and Paul were trying to help out as much as possible with the three girls.

Sue Ann parked the wheelchair on the other side of the room, next to the sofa but in front of the television.

"Do you want me to turn the TV on?"

Barb shook her head. "Music."

"Okay, Mom, I'll leave the music on."

Sue Ann sat in the corner of the sofa, tucking her legs up beneath her. She pulled a women's magazine off the coffee table and began to leaf through it.

This was what it meant to love someone. Or one of the many things. They were able to sit there together in companionable silence, no demands, just being, as music played in the background.

From her position, Barb could see out the big picture window, across the green and beyond that, the lake. Town workers were busy giving the gazebo a fresh coat of white paint. The day before, they'd cleaned up all the flower beds, removing debris and edging around them. In a month, red, white, and blue bunting would be hung from the rails of the gazebo in preparation for the Fourth of July. Barb wondered if she'd be here to see another summer holiday. Tears stung her eyes. She chastised herself, not wanting to get maudlin. Sometimes the fight was real.

The problem wasn't having a terminal illness—she'd accepted that—and it wasn't even the dying. It was leaving behind the people she loved: Sue Ann, her mother, Junie, and Thelma. Sue Ann would get married and have children, and Barb would not be around to see it. That was a pain that would never go away. The thought that there might be grandchildren in the future. But Barb had no future.

"Sue Ann."

Her daughter turned to her. "Yes, Mom?"

Barb regarded her daughter for a moment. Here she was, not even twenty years old, and she should be out having the time of her life and meeting people and being with her friends. Instead, she was here taking care of her mother without complaint.

"Don't be sad too long," Barb said. There was so much she wanted to say to her. That she would grieve, of course she would, after her mother was gone, but that Barb didn't want her wallowing in it. Sue Ann was young; she wanted her to move on with her life. Frustration mounted within her at the lack of a usable, understandable voice.

"Mom?"

"After I'm gone," Barb managed to get out. Tears pooled in her eyes.

"Oh, Mom!" Sue Ann said, her chin quivering. She sprang from her position on the sofa and gently wrapped her arms around Barb's neck, kissing her on her forehead. "Don't worry about me." Sue Ann's voice shook.

"I do worry about you," Barb managed to get out.

"I don't want to live without you," Sue Ann wailed.

Barb buried her face in her daughter's neck, breathing in the clean smell of her: laundry detergent and some light perfume. It was a pity Trevor never wanted anything to do with her.

Barb wasn't even sure if he was still alive. But that had been his choice and as far as Barb was concerned, his huge loss.

They settled down and Barb spent the rest of the morning listening to music and watching the activities out the front window.

Thelma arrived after lunch. Barb's friends had been wonderful. Jumped right in to help. Thelma was there every afternoon, and Junie brought dinner and stayed in the evening to help Sue Ann get her mother to bed. The first few times, Sue Ann hovered, anxious, afraid to let her mother out of her sight. But Barb encouraged her to leave, telling her she'd be fine. Finally, it took Thelma pushing her out the door to give her a break.

Thelma was still recovering from Stanley's death. She looked thinner and hollow-eyed. There was no bite to her bark or bounce to her step. And sometimes when you spoke to Thelma, she was not present. She had a faraway look in her eyes as if she were someplace else. And Barb supposed she was.

"Sue Ann," she managed to get out.

"Sue Ann? What about her?" Thelma asked.

"Worried."

"Don't worry about Sue Ann, we'll always be here for her," Thelma said.

There was some relief in that. Barb wanted Sue Ann to head back to college, away from Hideaway Bay. There was a big, wide world out there and she wanted her daughter to see it. But there would always be Hideaway Bay.

Thelma assisted Sue Ann in getting her mother from the wheelchair to the bed using the mechanical lift. Barb tended to doze in the afternoon, and the bed was more comfortable than the wheelchair.

"What are we reading today?" Thelma asked, getting comfortable on the sofa. She picked up a novel from the coffee table, put on her reading glasses, looked at the cover, and grinned. "Oh my, she'll get a draft with her dress hanging off like that."

Mrs. Walsh popped her head around the corner of the kitchen.

"Thelma, would you like some coffee?" she asked.

"Do you have instant?"

"We do."

"One cup. Two sugars. Splash of milk," Thelma instructed.

Barb regarded her friend. She knew she missed her husband. It must have been wonderful to have a love like that. Thelma often lamented the fact that it took them so long to get together, but Barb thought her lucky that she had the time she had with him.

Thelma opened the paperback to the bookmarked page. "Now, where are we?"

Barb closed her eyes.

"Right here. Let's see what happens to Trinny and Morgan. How was he described? Oh, yes, that's right, 'He was a big, strapping lad.'" Thelma laughed. "How could I forget that?"

She began to read aloud: "Her emerald satin gown slipped off, exposing a bare shoulder of silky ivory skin. Morgan devoured her with his hot, heavy gaze. In two strides, he was at her side, pulling her into his arms. His lips hungrily met hers, and his hands began to roam over her body, landing on her heaving bosoms..." Thelma shook her head. "Don't do, it, Trinny! Don't be seduced by that big, strapping lad!"

Barb smiled to herself. She loved when her friends read to her and for different reasons. Thelma provided humorous running commentary, and Junie's voice was so soft and melodic that by the time she was finished, Barb always felt she'd just had a facial, she was that relaxed.

Her attention drifted back to Thelma.

"'When I take you tonight, you'll be mine,' he growled," Thelma continued. "Where's he taking her? Hope someplace nice. At least get a steak out of it, Trinny."

Barb chortled, which led to a choking episode. Thelma bounced up and was at her side in a flash. Tears rolled out of the corners of her eyes, and she felt her face get hot. She continued to cough.

Thelma, with the strength of a dockworker, leaned Barb forward and patted her on the back. Relief eventually came, and the coughing subsided. Thelma repositioned Barb and asked if she was comfortable. Once Barb nodded, Thelma settled back on the sofa and picked up where she had left off.

The coughing jag left Barb wilted and as soon as she closed her eyes, she began to drift, Thelma's voice in the background.

"Trinny stood before him, letting her underslip fall to the ground and pool around her feet. His gaze raked over her naked body . . ." she read. "Not me. I would never stand in front of any man buck naked like that. Except for Stanley, of course."

Thelma's voice seemed to be getting farther and farther away. Barb smiled as her mind wandered in and out. She began to think of Sue Ann.

All her life, Barb had been looking for "the one." Her soul mate. Her other half. And she supposed after three marriages, one tragically cut short and two of which failed miserably, she could say with confidence that she had failed in that remit.

But as she watched Sue Ann over the past year, taking care of her with only love and kindness and never a complaint, it made Barb think back to the beginning, when Sue Ann was born. When the nurse brought the infant to her, all swaddled in the universal white hospital receiving blanket with the red and blue stripe, the newborn's tiny head in a cap and her cheeks puffy, Barb had been overcome with a sense of euphoria. She could still recall that instant love, how immaculate and deep it had been. And many times since, Barb would only have to look at her daughter and her heart would fill so full of love it was ready to burst. Not for anything Sue Ann had done or said, but simply by her existence. If that wasn't true love, then Barb didn't know what was.

She had found the love of her life, and it was Sue Ann.

Chapter Forty-One

1958

Barb, Junie, and Thelma

"Come on, I'll teach you how to swim," Barb said to Thelma.

It was a perfect summer's day in the middle of August. There wasn't a cloud in the sky, and the sand was a golden color. The lake was as warm as bathwater. Barb, Junie, and Thelma stood up to their hips in the water.

It was Thelma's first time in Hideaway Bay. Junie had come out several times before, but Thelma had never been able to. She'd finally made it out this weekend.

"We both will," Junie said.

When Junie had come down the first time, Mrs. Walsh had paid Kathy Brennan, a local girl, to teach Junie. Kathy had said Junie had a natural ability for it.

Thelma looked skeptical and snorted. "How can you teach me how to swim?"

"Did someone teach you how to swing a bat, or were you born knowing how to do it?" Barb retorted, but there was no sting in her words.

"Jimmy Blake taught me back in the third grade," Thelma replied.

"Exactly. And now you're one of the best female ball players in the city," Barb said.

Thelma glowed. They all knew it was true; Barb wasn't buttering her up.

"Okay, hotshot, how are you going to teach me how to swim?" Thelma demanded with her hands on her hips.

"You're going to lie flat on your belly on the water. Junie and I will hold you up. Start kicking with your feet and paddling with your hands," Barb said. She demonstrated to Thelma how to use her hands in the water. Thelma scowled. "Come on."

With some grunting and sweating, they got a hold of Thelma and held her beneath her torso. Barb instructed her to start kicking, which she did energetically and with force, splashing water in their faces. "Keep your legs straight, Thelma."

"I am!"

"Now use your hands like paddles like I showed you."

"And hurry up, you're heavy," Junie complained.

Over her shoulder Thelma said, "What did you think, I was going to start swimming off to Canada?"

Barb and Junie giggled and lost their grip on Thelma, who immediately sank, spluttering as she took in a mouthful of water. She sprang up, a thick wad of wet red hair hanging down in front of her eyes. She swiped it away. Barb and Junie got another fit of giggles.

"Thanks a lot, you two!" Thelma said, spitting water out of her mouth.

"Come on, let's get out and dry off and then we can get ice cream," Barb said, heading toward the shore with her friends following in her wake.

They ran toward their beach towels, kicking sand behind them and laughing and giggling. They collapsed on their towels, Barb in the middle with Junie and Thelma on either side of her.

All three of them turned over onto their bellies because the sun was too bright on their eyes, and Barb was the only one who had a pair of sunglasses.

"Do you know I've never been to the beach before?" Thelma said.

"Me neither until I came out with Barb," Junie chimed in. "My mother hates sand."

Barb looked from one friend to another and asked, "What do you think?"

"It's all right," Thelma said with a nod of approval. "I like it."

That might sound stingy to some but knowing Thelma like she did, Barb considered it high praise.

"Wouldn't it be wonderful if we could live out here all year round? The three of us?" Junie said.

"Do they have a baseball team?" Thelma asked. "Then I'm in."

"They do." Though Barb didn't tell her that they weren't very good.

"I would love to live out here," Junie said again.

"Maybe someday, we'll all live out here," Barb said, hopeful that they'd always stay together, that they'd always be friends.

"Come on, let's get some ice cream," Thelma said, jumping up from her beach towel. "I could go for some chocolate ice cream on a waffle cone."

Junie bounced up, following her, "Lemon sherbet for me."

They grabbed their beach towels, slung them over their shoulders, and ran along the beach toward the boardwalk, kicking sand everywhere. As the sun beat down on them, the three of them laughed.

Barb wished it could always be like this.

CHAPTER FORTY-TWO

Isabelle

Isabelle pulled off the highway and sailed over the railroad tracks in her just-purchased 1968 cherry red Chevy Impala convertible and headed toward Star Shine Drive. The sun was shining and the top was down. Up ahead, the lake looked dark, with orange glints on its surface from the late-afternoon sun in the western sky above the lake.

The air was warm and comfortable, not muggy. Typical for August. Although Alice had informed her that it had rained most of the days she was gone. She hadn't missed that. But at present, it was a lovely evening in Hideaway Bay. The golden orange sun slid behind trees dense with dark green leaves.

As she drove down Erie Street, she spotted a walker on her right side. It was a teenage boy wearing a black T-shirt and a baseball cap, walking along, hitting the road with a long stick, his head down. As she drew closer, she realized it was Kyle, Joe's oldest child. She slowed the car and pulled up next to him. First, his eyes widened at the sight of the vintage car, then when he recognized her behind the wheel, he appeared wary. He stopped but did not step closer.

"Hi, Kyle," she said, the car idling. "Do you want a lift home?"

He looked west toward the lake and then east toward the railroad tracks. "Nah. I'm good."

But Isabelle wouldn't take no for an answer. "Come on, get in. I'll get you home. Why walk when you can drive?"

He looked down, hitting the stick against the loose gravel at the side of the road. What was it about this kid that broke her heart? She threw the car into park and leaned over to the passenger door, releasing it and pushing it open.

Again, Kyle looked up and down the street before ambling over to the car and slowly getting in. He slouched in the seat, looking at his hands in his lap.

"How've you been?" she asked. She looked over her shoulder before pulling back out onto the road.

He shrugged. After a moment, he said, "Nice car."

"Thanks. I got it to kick around in for the rest of the summer. I'm glad you like it."

He didn't say much, and Isabelle drove slowly to his house.

"Does Dad know you're back?" he finally asked.

"Not yet," she said. She'd sent Joe an email letting him know that she'd be back soon.

"Are you here to stay?"

She nodded. "Yes, I am."

She pulled up in front of his house. Looking at it made her smile. From the backyard came the sounds of splashing water.

"Is it okay if I tell him?" Kyle asked, his hand on the door handle.

"Sure," she said.

"Thanks for the ride." He got out and stood on the sidewalk, watching as she started to drive away. With one hand in his pocket, he gave her a small wave, and there was a slight upturn to the corner of his mouth. As Isabelle drove down the street, she glanced in the rearview mirror and saw him running into the house.

She cut through town center, smiling as she passed all the shops with their colorful awnings, thinking she'd made the right decision to return. She crossed over Erie Street and headed onto Star Shine Drive. She drove slowly, happy with her decision to purchase the convertible.

As she neared Gram's house, she slowed down, staring at the place. The flowers out front were full and vibrant. Before leaving, she'd instructed her sisters to water in the evening or early morning. Along the porch overhang were multiple windchimes that Alice had hung. From time to time, she'd purchase a new one. No beach towels hung over the porch railing, but they would again, soon, as Isabelle resumed swimming.

There was still a lot of work to be done on the house. It needed a new roof, there was one shutter that was in dire need of repair, and of course the whole thing needed to be painted, freshened up. Now that it was home, she wanted to take care of it. And she knew her sisters felt the same way. She'd realized one thing these last few months that surprised her: she liked being a homeowner.

It seemed as if her sisters were right where she'd left them: sitting on the porch with Charlie at their feet. Slowly, she pulled into the driveway, sticking her hand up into the air and waving.

It was Alice who jumped up first. "It's Isabelle!"

Lily threw her hands to her mouth, staring at her older sister in disbelief, following Alice off the porch. Charlie stood and when he spotted Isabelle, his tail wagged furiously.

Isabelle stepped out of the car, slamming the door behind her. She pushed her sunglasses to the top of her head. She met her sisters halfway, her arms outstretched. Alice slid into her embrace.

"Why didn't you tell us you were coming home?" Lily asked. She was next to hug Isabelle. "We weren't expecting you for another two days."

When they pulled apart, Isabelle said, her voice shaky, "I wanted to surprise you."

"Consider us surprised!"

"And what's this?" Lily asked, looking at the car. She ran her hand along the smooth red finish.

"I thought it might be fun for us to drive around in during the summer months," Isabelle explained.

"I like that idea."

Alice covered her mouth with her hands as tears filled her eyes. "I'm so happy I could die."

"Oh, don't do that," Lily said with a laugh.

"This must mean you're staying permanently, right?" Alice asked, her expression hopeful.

"Yes," Isabelle said. "I'm home for good."

They hugged each other tightly and when they pulled apart, all three of them had tears in their eyes.

Isabelle glanced at the car and then back at her sisters. "Want to go for a spin?"

"Yes!"

"Let me put Charlie in the house," Lily said.

"Nah, just put Clumsy in the back seat," Isabelle said. She opened the driver's side door, pushed the front seat forward, and waved for Charlie to get into the back. The dog jumped in and stood on the back seat, looking out over the trunk.

"I'll get in the back with the dog," Lily said.

"Come on, we can all fit up front," Isabelle said. "Alice, you sit in the middle."

Alice slid across the bench seat and announced, "This is so much fun. Oh gosh, look at the radio. Does it work?"

"It sure does."

Lily climbed in, turned around, and told Charlie to sit down, which he did, right behind Lily on the passenger side.

Isabelle closed her door, started the car, and checked for traffic on the street. Once it was clear, she slowly reversed out of the driveway.

"Watch those kids there," Lily said.

"I see them." After the three kids passed on their bikes, Isabelle backed out into the street. "Let's take a slow drive down Main Street."

The sun was an orange fireball heading toward the horizon, the sky awash in pink and lavender. With the three of them crammed into the front seat and Charlie behind them, Isabelle drove slowly around town. They cruised along Main Street, Isabelle careful of all the pedestrians. Alice found a radio station that played oldies and they sang along to all the old songs, remembering how their mother and Gram always had music playing in the house.

When they passed Simon and Jack standing outside the Hideaway Bay Olive Oil company, Isabelle honked the horn and the three sisters hooted and hollered. Both men turned in their direction and waved, big grins breaking out on their faces.

They giggled as they drove on. They passed Thelma's house. She sat on her porch and put up her hand as they passed by.

"Hi, Thelma," they called out in unison.

Their last stop before they headed home was their old home, the one their parents started their marriage in. The house where they were raised. It was on one of the back streets off Erie and had no view of the lake.

Isabelle pulled up in front of the house and parked the car along the curb. She leaned back as Lily put her elbow on the car door and leaned on it. In front of the house were twin maple trees that Granddad had planted when they were young. They were taller than Isabelle remembered them and dense with leaves.

The house was a two-story cottage with a small porch. The overhanging roof of the porch sagged in the middle, and one of the gutters lay on the front lawn. After their mother had died, they'd sold the house, each taking their share and going to start their lives somewhere else.

"There were some happy times here," Lily said, breaking the silence.

"It wasn't all sad or bad, was it?" Alice asked.

"No, of course not," Isabelle said.

"I think like most families, we had our share of bad times, but the good times far outweighed the bad," Lily said softly.

"Maybe that's what my problem is," Isabelle said. "I need to concentrate more on the good times." She wasn't sure yet how she felt about their father now that she had met him, but she did feel different. Neither better nor worse. Once she settled in, she'd examine it more closely. Maybe it was time to move on. She was ready.

"Mom did a great job by herself," Alice said.

"And we were lucky to have Gram and Granddad," Isabelle added.

"We sure were," Lily said.

After a few thoughtful minutes, Isabelle pulled away from the curb. She couldn't help but feel lucky.

"Hot Fun in the Summertime" by Sly and the Family Stone played on the radio. Lily leaned over, cranked up the volume, and the three of them sang along at the top of their lungs, laughing.

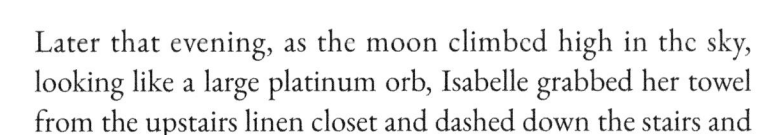

Later that evening, as the moon climbed high in the sky, looking like a large platinum orb, Isabelle grabbed her towel from the upstairs linen closet and dashed down the stairs and out to the porch, where Lily sat alone with Charlie. Alice had gone out with the Colonel.

Charlie was sound asleep at Lily's feet, snoring loudly.

"Are you sure you don't want to take Charlie?" Lily asked.

"Nah, he's sleeping. Leave him be."

"Enjoy your swim."

"I will. Won't be much longer. I suspect the night air will be getting cooler."

Isabelle waved a quick goodbye and headed across to the lake. As soon as she crossed the street and cut across the short swathe of grass, she removed her sandals and trudged through the cool sand. The streetlights behind her cast shadows on the beach and the moonlight shimmered across the lake, making it look inky.

A young couple walked arm in arm on the beach. They waved to Isabelle, and she waved in return. Out in the distance she could see the lights of the various sailboats and speedboats gently bobbing up and down on the surface of the lake.

Slowly, she entered the water, noting the difference in the temperature from when she was last here. It would be a short swim.

She didn't go out far, just up to her waist, walking forward, pushing her hands out in front of her so the water sluiced through her fingers. She'd miss her evening swims. She came to a standstill and tilted her head back and looked up at the night. It was beautiful. Stars twinkled across the vast expanse of sky.

Isabelle sighed, happy. She didn't stay long in the water and by the time she turned around and headed back toward the shore, she was shivering. Now that she'd returned, she'd look into joining the local pool so she could swim through the winter.

Her heart leapt as she made her way out of the water. Joe stood at the shore, holding her towel. A smile formed on her lips as her heart filled to bursting.

When she reached the beach, Joe opened up the towel and stretched it out. He was grinning. She walked into it, and he wrapped it around her shoulders. He rested his hands on her shoulders and whispered, "I'm glad you're back."

She didn't have to ask how he knew; Kyle had probably told him.

Joe said, "I was going to ask you if you wanted to go for ice cream, but your teeth are chattering."

"Water's cold," she said, pulling the towel closer around her.

"Then how about a coffee?"

She didn't care if she'd be up all night; she'd drink a pot just to be with him.

"Sounds good. We can go back to my house. I'll put a pot on," she said. Still keeping the heavy towel wrapped around her, she bent and picked up her wrap and sandals.

"Where's Luther?"

"I left him home tonight. What about Charlie?"

"Same."

"I'm happy to see you," he said. He took her hand in his and gave it a gentle squeeze.

"Me too." Isabelle placed her hand on the side of his face and kissed him. She'd thought about doing this a lot while she was away.

"Am I allowed to read anything into your return? Dare I be hopeful?" he asked, his gaze not leaving her face.

"Joe, I need to go slow with this. With us."

He nodded. "That's fine."

With that sorted, they crossed the street to the house on Star Shine Drive. The porch was empty. Lily must have gone in.

"Is there room for one more on your camping trip over Labor Day weekend?" Isabelle asked without looking at him.

Beside her, Joe burst out laughing. "There sure is." He wrapped an arm around her toweled shoulder and pulled her closer, planting a kiss on her forehead.

"Come on then, let's put on the coffee," Isabelle said with a smile.

"Sounds good to me."

***

Sign up for my newsletter at www.michelebrouder.com to stay up to date about new releases and receive bonus exclusives including the Hideaway Bay novella that tells Sue Ann's story.

ALSO BY MICHELE BROUDER

Hideaway Bay Series

Coming Home to Hideaway Bay

Meet Me at Sunrise

Moonlight and Promises

When We Were Young

Escape to Ireland Series

A Match Made in Ireland

Her Fake Irish Husband

Her Irish Inheritance

A Match for the Matchmaker

Home, Sweet Irish Home

An Irish Christmas

Happy Holidays Series

A Whyte Christmas

This Christmas

A Wish for Christmas

One Kiss for Christmas

A Wedding for Christmas

Printed in Great Britain
by Amazon